MINTY ALLEY

About the Author

C. L. R. James was born in Trinidad in 1901 and was one of the prominent figures in the West Indian diaspora. He was a writer, socialist and pioneering voice in literature. He wrote extensively on Caribbean history, Marxist theory, literary criticism, Western civilization, African politics, cricket and popular culture. His works include *World Revolution*, *The Black Jacobins*, *Beyond a Boundary* and his only novel, *Minty Alley*. He died in 1989.

MINTY ALLEY

C. L. R. James

With a new introduction by
Bernardine Evaristo

PENGUIN BOOKS

PENGUIN BOOKS

UK | USA | Canada | Ireland | Australia
India | New Zealand | South Africa

Penguin Books is part of the Penguin Random House group of companies
whose addresses can be found at global.penguinrandomhouse.com.

First published by Secker & Warburg 1936
Published by New Beacon Books Ltd. 1971
First published with a new introduction by Penguin Books 2021

001

Text copyright © C. L. R. James, 1936, 1971
Introduction copyright © Bernardine Evaristo, 2021

The moral right of the copyright holders has been asserted

Set in 11.6/15pt Fournier MT Std
Typeset by Jouve (UK), Milton Keynes
Printed and bound in Great Britain by Clays Ltd, Elcograf S.p.A.

The authorized representative in the EEA is Penguin Random House Ireland,
Morrison Chambers, 32 Nassau Street, Dublin D02 YH68

A CIP catalogue record for this book is available from the British Library

ISBN: 978-0-241-48266-7

In association with New Beacon Books

www.greenpenguin.co.uk

To my mother

Introduction

Black Britain: Writing Back is a new series I've curated with my publisher, Hamish Hamilton, at Penguin Random House. Our ambition is to correct historic bias in British publishing and bring a wealth of lost writing back into circulation. While many of us continue to lobby for the publishing industry to become more inclusive and representative of our society, this project looks back to the past in order to resurrect texts that will help reconfigure black British literary history.

The books included in the series are my personal choices, determined by my literary values and how I perceive the cultural context and significance of the books. The series is not to be regarded as an attempt to be definitive or to create a canon. Canons are by their very nature hierarchical and have traditionally been constructed by the prevailing white orthodoxies of academia. Black British writers rarely appear on these reading lists, are rarely taught to new generations of readers and unless they become commercial successes, their legacy very quickly disappears.

My aim is to present a body of work illustrating a variety of preoccupations and genres that offer important and diverse black British perspectives. Good books withstand the test of time, even if they are of their time. I am very excited to introduce these books to new readers who will discover their riches.

In 1986 I went to see a production of *The Black Jacobins* (1967), a play about Toussaint L'Ouverture and the Haitian Revolution by C. L. R. James, at the Riverside Studios in London. He was, at this stage, considered the elder statesman of black intellectuals and writers. Sadly, I never met him, but I knew that this impressive man was now frail, elderly and living in a flat above the offices of the radical *Race Today* collective at 165 Railton Road in Brixton. Its members included his nephew Darcus Howe, a familiar cultural figure on British television in the 1980s, and the dub poet Linton Kwesi Johnson.

A previous incarnation of the play, entitled *Toussaint L'Ouverture: The Story of the Only Successful Slave Revolt in History*, had been staged at the Westminster Theatre in 1936, starring the famous African American film star, theatre actor, baritone and left-wing political activist Paul Robeson.

Born in Trinidad in 1901, Cyril Lionel Robert James attended Queen's Royal College, the country's top school, where he became a keen cricketer and athlete. With aspirations to become a novelist, he had already published three short stories, *La Divina Pastora* (*British Saturday Review*, 1927), as well as *Triumph* and *Turner's Prosperity* (both in *Trinidad* magazine, 1929), when he migrated to Britain in 1932, settling in Lancashire with his friend the great Trinidadian cricketer Learie Constantine, who was his mentor and sponsor. He eventually took up the post of cricket correspondent for the *Guardian* (a national newspaper based in

Manchester then called the *Manchester Guardian*), which was an incredible achievement for a black man in Britain at that time. James became very involved in the Marxist left, anti-imperialism and especially Pan-Africanism, emerging as a powerful advocate for West Indian independence. He also helped found the International African Friends of Ethiopia when that country was attacked by the Italian dictator Mussolini. He moved in English literary circles and met the aristocratic writer and literary doyenne Edith Sitwell, in Bloomsbury, with whom he debated poetic form. His influential pamphlet, *The Life of Captain Ciprani*, was excerpted and published as *The Case for West Indian Self-Government* (1933) by Virginia and Leonard Woolf's Hogarth Press. He was a Trotskyist for many years, visiting Trotsky at his home in Mexico where they discussed 'the Negro question', and where he also met Frida Kahlo and Diego Rivera.

James lived in the States from 1938 to 1953, finally rejecting Trotskyism in 1951. He was imprisoned on Ellis Island in 1953 for overstaying his visa, afterwards leaving the country before he was expelled. He voluntarily moved back to Britain in 1953 and returned to Trinidad for the new West Indian Federation celebrations in 1958, where he edited the People's National Movement pro-Independence newspaper, the *Nation*. In Britain, he lived in Hampstead and Willesden, and eventually in Brixton, where he died in 1989. A blue plaque was erected outside the Brixton house in 2004.

One of James's most celebrated books was *The Black Jacobins* (1938), the history of the Haitian Revolution which abolished slavery, and the inspiration for the two plays. He'd wanted to write a social history that showed black empowerment and Africans with agency in their own lives and futures, as opposed to being victims of oppression. His other highly celebrated work was *Beyond a Boundary* (1963), a book about cricket but which mixed memoir, sports commentary and social history with a focus on class. In 2005, it was ranked by the *Observer* as the third best book on sport ever written. He also published a book about Kwame Nkrumah, the first post-independence leader of Ghana, whom he had known as a student. *Nkrumah and the Ghana Revolution* (1977) was published by Allison & Busby, co-founded by Margaret Busby, Britain's first black publisher.

James only ever wrote one novel, *Minty Alley* (1936), although as the first novel by a black Caribbean writer to be published in England it was an historic achievement. One can imagine how hard it was for him to publish a book about black Caribbean people all those years ago. He wasn't part of the wave of Windrush-era writers such as Wilson Harris, George Lamming, Edgar Mittelholzer, V. S. Naipaul, Andrew Salkey and Samuel Selvon, who benefited from being part of the larger movement of Caribbean migration to Britain. James had been a lone pilot in the 1930s.

Minty Alley, a social-realist novel, never made its mark when it was first published and while it was republished by New Beacon Books in 1971, it is still not widely discussed or acknowledged, even though it definitely deserves to be. The only black British book to have received a degree of sustained interest from the twentieth century to today is Samuel Selvon's immigrant caper *The Lonely Londoners* (1956), about black Caribbean men newly arrived in London. Selvon and his generation are indebted to James for breaking new ground with the way in which he validated ordinary, working-class Caribbean experiences and his groundbreaking use of the vernacular.

Minty Alley was written in 1928 and set in Port of Spain, the capital of Trinidad. It centres on Haynes, a twenty-year-old middle-class black man who can no longer afford to stay in the house his deceased mother purchased and has had to downsize to a rented room in lodgings at No. 2 Minty Alley, a rundown 'barrack-yard'. There, he gets to know the people living in the property and we experience them through him. Haynes is a reclusive, friendless, essentially spineless figure who has led an uneventful life. First his mother looked after him and planned his future; then the family servant, Ella. However, through staying at No. 2, his hitherto empty life soon fills up with the whirlwind of dramas, conflicts, subterfuge, entanglements, rages and desires that storm around him while he remains the still centre of the house – quiet and observant, a listener rather than a speaker; in fact, so unassuming that the other characters are magnified and intensified in comparison. Light-hearted, comic, occasionally sobering, always engrossing, the novel is a lovely and captivating read. It feels like eavesdropping on history, a sensation at once intimate and distant. Class features strongly, with the protagonist, in effect, slumming it with the lower classes but being deeply enriched and enlivened by the experience. The author pays attention to skin tone, describing the colouring and race of the characters, and through this he creates a microcosm of the pigmentocratic Caribbean long before racism and colourism began to be widely deconstructed and contextualized for debate. It's a colonial novel rather than a post-colonial one, written thirty-three years before Trinidad gained its independence in 1962, but the British imperial power structures that governed this country are not the focus of the novel. This is a story about a Caribbean community in relationship with itself; about life on an island before the mass movement of people to either the United States or the United Kingdom. They are not foreigners in a hostile environment struggling to be accepted, although many of them have the ambition to migrate, but right now they are among their own and leading ordinary lives within a complicated web of entertaining relationships. I would argue that it laid the foundations for Naipaul's most celebrated novel, *A House for Mr Biswas* (1961). For the contemporary reader, we are allowed a peek into a society of nearly one hundred years ago, which shows us that while the circumstances are different, our essential passions, preoccupations and ambitions remain the same.

Chapter One

Haynes concluded his calculations and decided that he could not continue to live in the whole house. He would occupy two rooms and let the rest as soon as he could; but leave the house, that he would not do.

He would tell Ella. As soon as he called, she came. He never had to call Ella twice. Wherever she was, whatever she was doing, she seemed to have one ear open in case Haynes called. Her fat black face shone with perspiration and good nature.

'Sit down, Ella. I want to have a long talk with you.'

'That's all right, sir. What is it, sir?'

'Sit down, Ella.'

'It's all right, sir. The dinner is cookin', sir, and I have to go at once.'

The influence of his dead mother still dominated the house. She was a perfect mistress, but never would she have asked Ella to sit down. And Ella remained standing.

'I have worked it all out carefully, Ella, and shall live in half the house and let the other half. I shall take my mother's bedroom and the study. I shall have a door cut to connect them. I don't want to move. And with the rent from the house and the rooms in George Street and with my salary, I can just manage. That settles it.'

'You think you will manage, sir?'

'We'll have to manage.'

She made no reply, but she turned her head sideways and looked at him questioningly. He knew what that meant.

'Look here, Ella. We can get eight dollars a month for the rest of the house.'

'I doubt it, sir. If you let the whole house you can get sixteen dollars or even sixteen-fifty. But if you let half, even if you get seven it means you payin' nine-fifty for these two rooms, sir. And then you have to pay a servant. It's a lot of expense, sir.'

'But—'

'You see, sir. I have been thinking it over, sir, and as I told you the other day, the best thing for you is to go and board and lodge with a family.'

'And do what with you?'

'I will go and get other work, sir.'

'No, no, no. You are going to stay with me.' He looked at her apprehensively. 'You don't want to leave me, Ella?'

'No sir. I don't want to leave you.'

'Well, what were you saying?'

'If you don't want to board and lodge and you want me to go on seeing after things, sir, get a room, sir, a large room. It will cost you about four or five dollars. All I will want is a place to cook. You can take in your own things from here, sir. We can sell the piano and the furniture and use the money to repair the kitchen and the fence and help to pay some of the mortgage. I was talking to the man from Price & Co., sir. They will auction the things, sir, and take on the repairs and give you the balance. You can leave that to me, sir. They wouldn't cheat me, sir.'

'God, I wish I were rid of all this bother.' He put his elbows on the table and rested his face on his hands.

'Don't let it trouble you, sir. You need a change, sir. You should move from this place.'

'But where shall I go? The month will end in four days. If I don't move it means another long month here.'

'I thought that perhaps you would want to move and I've been looking, sir. There is a room vacant in a house in Charles Street, Mr. Newstead, the solicitor and his wife.'

'I know them. They come to the shop. I don't want to go and live near those people, Ella.'

'There is another one, sir. It's not nice, sir. I pass up and down there every day, and I saw the notice. It's in Minty Alley, the second street from here. They are ordinary people, sir. Not your class of people.'

'Who are they?'

'A Mrs. Rouse, sir. She makes cakes for sale, and she lives with a man who helps her. She has a very large kitchen where I could cook. But I don't think you'll like the place, sir.'

'How much is it?'

'Very cheap, sir. Two dollars and fifty cents.'

'Well, let's take it then, Ella.'

'You had better go and see it first, sir.'

'If I am to move I had better move quickly.'

'Go and see it, sir.'

'I'll go and see it.'

'All right, sir. And meanwhile, I'll look for another place. Tell me when you want your dinner, sir.'

Haynes tore up his calculations and threw them in the wastepaper-basket. The short tropical twilight had departed and it was already dark.

Ella came back in.

'You want the light on, sir?'

'No, thank you, Ella.'

'You want your dinner, sir?'

'No, Ella, not yet. I am not hungry.'

She did not go.

'Perhaps you want to stay here, sir?'

'No, Ella, no. It isn't that. You go on. I'll call you in a few minutes.'

Yes, Ella was right. He wanted a change. It was better that he should move. Most of his childhood and his youth had been passed here, untroubled about anything except his own adolescent dreams. He had spent seven years at the secondary school, a shy, solitary boy, doing his lessons, playing games but making few friends, no friends – no, not one. (There was Boyce, but Boyce was not a friend.) He had grown up under the shelter of his mother, to whom he was everything and who was everything to him. Ever since he had known himself, he had known and accepted her plans for his future.

'You are black, my boy. I want you to be independent, and in

4

these little islands for a black man to be independent means that he must have money or a profession. I know how your father suffered, and you are so much like him that I tremble for you.'

In the West Indies, to get a profession meant going to England or America, and his mother had decided she would send him to England. She was a headmistress and in her spare time taught unwearyingly. First she had bought the house on a stiff mortgage. Haynes was to work in the island for a year or two and then, when the mortgage had been paid off, she would send him abroad and keep him there. Medicine it was to be. 'Law wouldn't suit you, my child. You are your father's son.' She got a job for him in the only book shop in the town, and Haynes worked in the day and came home and read the books in the evenings. For all the change it made, he might have been still at school. And then, suddenly, his mother had fallen ill, and after months of wearisome illness which had cost hundreds of dollars, she had died. Ella, the servant, who had been with them about a year before she fell ill, took charge of the house, and had continued as housekeeper for the helpless Haynes. Relations he had none that mattered. He shrank from his mother's middle-aged friends. From sheer inertia he had continued living in the house. But he knew, long before Ella hinted it to him, that a change had to be made.

Yes, he would leave and go and live somewhere else, save some money and do something. It was time. He was twenty. Twenty – and his life still a blank page.

It would be best to take the cheap room. If he lost his job, what would he do? He wasn't trained for anything. The book business, such as it was in that small island, he knew inside out. But if he should displease old Carritt all his knowledge would go for nothing and he would have to begin again elsewhere. The mortgage swallowed up a good portion of his small salary. There would be rent from the house, and there was the rent from two or three rooms in the slum quarter. But there were rates and constant repairs and the rent was irregular. Ella was right. It would be better to live cheaply, for a time at least. As long as Ella was there he would not suffer any inconvenience. And at the back of his mind unformulated, but nevertheless a steadily growing influence, was the desire to make a break with all his monotonous past life, school, home and the drowsy book shop. His mother was no more than a memory, a tender memory, but nevertheless only a memory. His life was empty. He did not think these things out clearly, but he knew them as people are aware of things without putting them into words. The sea of life was beating at the walls which enclosed him. Nervously and full of self-distrust, he had been fighting against taking the plunge, but he would have to sometime. Better now. He looked round at the pleasant furniture, the mahogany sideboard with its spotless china and the silver pieces. He could barely see them, but he had lived with them so long that they were stamped on his mind. The silver he would keep, but the rest would go. Ella was right. He must move. He had promised his mother to keep the house and he would keep it at whatever cost. He would marry some day and bring his bride home. But till that time, anywhere except staying there.

He rose and turned on the lights.

'Bring my dinner, Ella,' he said, and when she brought in the first dish he smiled at her.

'Where did you say that room was, Ella?'

'Two streets from here, sir. No. 2, Minty Alley. It's a very short alley.'

'Well, we'll go there.'

'But you haven't seen the place, sir. I don't think you'll like it. There are a lot of people there, sir. Ordinary people.'

'So much the better. I am sure I will like it. 2, Minty Alley. It sounds good. I shall go down and look at the room tomorrow.'

Chapter Two

Minty Alley was not two hundred yards away and the house was one on which his glance must often have rested. But it was only now when he approached it as a prospective lodging-house that he took particular notice of it. No. 2 stood at a corner, far in from the street. He walked down the yard, mounted a few steps, knocked and waited. The yard was quite clean; so was the front of the house, though badly in need of a coat of paint. Through the open jalousies he could see a neat little drawing-room, centre-table, bentwood chairs, antimacassars, what-nots and china ornaments. Among the pictures was one of Christ with a bleeding heart.

Haynes knocked again, and then he heard a voice, a woman's voice.

'Maisie! Somebody knocking. Go and see who it is. Don't keep the person waiting.'

But nobody came.

The same voice spoke again, more sharply.

'But, girl, you didn't hear me? The bigger you grow, the lazier you getting. Go at once.'

There was the sound of bare feet in the room behind the drawing-room. The blind opened, a good-looking young face, presumably Maisie's, appeared and asked sourly:

'Anybody there?'

'Yes,' said Haynes, 'I want to see Mrs. Rouse, the owner of this house, about a room she has to let.'

'Wait, please,' said the young woman and turned back inside. 'Tante, it's somebody come to see about the room.'

'Who is it?'

'I don't know.'

'Jesus give me patience with this child!'

There were rapid footsteps and a slight scuffle. A short, stout woman came quickly to the door, opened it, and said:

'Come in, Mr. Haynes. We know you. We see you passing up and down.'

'Yes,' said Haynes, 'and you are Mrs. Rouse, I expect. My servant told me you had a room here to let and I have come to have a look at it.'

'Yes, sir . . . You must excuse my appearance. I make cakes for sale, you know, and I am busy in the kitchen with them.'

She had no need to apologize for her appearance. She was a woman somewhere in the forties, fat, yet with a firmness and shapeliness of figure which prevented her from looking gross. Her face was a smooth light-brown with a fine aquiline nose and well-cut firm lips. The strain of white ancestry responsible for the nose was not recent, for her hair was coarse and essentially negroid. Her apron was dirty, but the dress below was clean.

'Will you follow me, sir?' She made a slight bow and turned

9

and led the way, carrying herself erect with a mature grace and dignity which Haynes thought assumed for the occasion but which he learnt to know later were natural to her.

In the dining-room they met Maisie – the same girl whose face had peeped through the blind, only now her hair was smoother. Though not as light in colour as the aunt, she also was smooth-skinned and brown. Haynes looked at her, but saw her smiling at him and turned his eyes away.

'You want the key, Tante?' she said.

'I don't wish anything,' said Mrs. Rouse, and descended four or five steps into the yard.

The house was built in a simple style, square and containing five rooms, drawing-room and dining-room on one side and three bedrooms on the other. But at some time after it had been built, two rooms had been added to the original structure on the side opposite the kitchen, which was a separate building about ten feet away.

'This room is tenanted already, sir,' said Mrs. Rouse, pointing to the first, 'and this is yours.'

The room was small, but clean, with two large windows. Haynes knew that he would take it, had, indeed, decided to do so from the time Ella had mentioned the place, but he did not say so at once. He stole a glance at the kitchen and saw a number of people.

'No one will disturb you here, you know, Mr. Haynes. You'll be quite private,' said Mrs. Rouse. 'Any – er – friend of yours you want to come and see you at any time, you will be able to have them.'

Haynes felt the blood in his face, but that decided him.

'You think it will suit you, sir?'

'Yes, madam. I think it will . . . And the price is two dollars and fifty cents?'

'Yes. Two dollars fifty.'

'Well, I'll pay you now and come on the first.'

'Thank you. But if you want to move in now you can, you know, Mr. Haynes. That will be all right.'

That would suit Haynes very well. He would move at once.

'You are a bachelor, Mr. Haynes?'

'Yes.'

'Well, if you like we can board you, you know. All your meals, clothes, washing, you can get everything done here.'

She smiled at him hopefully.

'Thank you very much, Mrs. Rouse. But Ella, my servant, is in charge of everything. She washes the clothes, cooks all my meals and so on. I could not think of carrying on without Ella, she has been with me so long and understands me so well.'

'I only thought as you were giving up house you wouldn't keep a servant. That's why I asked.'

'But if I do make a change, of course, I'll board with you,' said Haynes.

'Thank you,' said Mrs. Rouse, smiling happily.

At the front door she paused.

'I hope you'll be comfortable with us, sir,' she said.

'I am sure I will be, madam,' replied Haynes. He stood for a second uncertainly, and then, quite spontaneously, offered her his hand. She took it with a little start of surprise, and looked at him so kindly and with such a gratified smile that he could see he had made a good impression on his future landlady.

Chapter Three

Early next morning began the transfer of Haynes's belongings. Ella remained at No. 9 to despatch and he went to No. 2 to receive.

He was down pretty early, about seven o'clock, but Mrs. Rouse and her household were already quite busy. Yesterday, while he was in the room making arrangements with her, he had been aware of people in the kitchen, but had no opportunity of noting more than that the majority were women. But now as he sat in his room facing the kitchen, idling, while Ella was packing things on the cart (and, no doubt, having stiff arguments with the man as to how much exactly constituted a load), as he sat there he could make a more detailed observation of his surroundings and his future neighbours.

The surroundings were nothing the eye would dwell on without reason. The yard was reddish dirt and bits of stone, but much more dirt than stone, so that on rainy days it would be a mass of slippery mud, treacherous to shoe and slipper, and needing care even from naked feet. Opposite his room was the kitchen, long, low and concrete-floored, with two doors that opened on to the yard and two windows that looked into the alley. As is usual in the tropics, all windows and doors were wide open and he could see straight into it. Joined to the kitchen was the bathroom, and in front of the bathroom but to one side was a pipe with a sink. For the rest there was nothing else to see but the encircling hedge and the upper portions of the neighbouring buildings. A dull enough prospect. But if the surroundings were drab, the inhabitants were busy.

First there was Mrs. Rouse, who gave him a fine good morning, but had no time for anything else. She concentrated on the contents of two or three pots on the fire, but at intervals turned to a table, where, unfortunately, he could not see what she was doing. She called frequently to one Aucher, a tall, heavily-built, quiet-looking youth of about twenty — dressed in a patched and dirty pair of blue trousers and an old jacket without shirt or merino. He seemed rather dirty to be making cakes. He put large sheets of tin covered with cakes into the stove and took them out for Mrs. Rouse to see if they were baked enough, meanwhile regulating the heat by attending to the wick, usually at the dictation of Mrs. Rouse, who from her frequent admonitions and exhortations to those around her was clearly the officer commanding. In the kitchen was another black man with curly hair, wearing socks and slippers, black trousers and a white jacket. He was kneading flour and never once did he turn his head. He had a good deep voice.

At first the yard was empty, but after a time a long, bony black girl came out of the kitchen and went to the sink, where she washed dishes; and not long after, a little boy, nearly white, came from inside the house. He played about in the yard with two marbles, stopping to take an interest in the contents of the first cartload which Ella sent down, only the first, because Mrs. Rouse, happening to see him, told him not to be fast, and to go inside and take his book. The boy, who at once obeyed orders, was about eight years old, unhealthy-looking but cute. It was his colour, however, which rather startled Haynes. He wondered at the presence of so fair a skin among all those dark people. Brownish though Mrs. Rouse might be it was inconceivable that she should be a party to any form of miscegenation which would produce offspring with hair so straight and complexion so fair.

He had not taken his book for ten minutes when Mrs. Rouse called to him by name, Sonny, and sent him to the front to see if Philomen and Maisie were coming. He came back and said 'No.' Mrs. Rouse said that she could not understand what was keeping them back, and added that it was the last day she would let Maisie go.

When Haynes went up for lunch, Ella came down. Haynes ate quickly and went back to release her. As soon as she had left, Mrs. Rouse came to the door of the room, followed by the black man.

'Mr. Haynes, this is Mr. Benoit, your landlord.'

The man came in, and she went back into the kitchen.

'I am Benoit,' he said and shook hands.

He was rather a big man with a slight paunch. His very black face was undistinguished-looking, neither handsome nor ugly. The very dark skin and curly hair showed traces of Indian blood. The only thing one might have noticed was a rather cruel mouth below the sparse moustache. He might have been anything between thirty-five and fifty, perhaps somewhere in the forties. Benoit was very much at his ease at once, and, as he told Haynes not long afterwards, he knew from Mrs. Rouse's description that Haynes was not one of those chaps who was stuck up.

'You do a lot of reading, I see,' he said, looking at the books.

'Do you like books?' said Haynes.

'No time for that, man. Since I leave school I ain't open a book.'

While he spoke he was eating ground-nuts which he took from his pocket and shelled expertly. He chewed with short quick bites.

'Have a few,' he said suddenly.

'Thank you,' said Haynes and took two.

'Nuts is good things for men to eat,' he observed. 'You had lunch already?'

'Otherwise I couldn't eat these,' Haynes said. 'They would ruin my appetite.'

'You different to me. I not going to eat till near two, but I will eat four cents nuts and roast corn, I'll suck orange, eat fig, mango, anything, the whole morning; and that wouldn't prevent me eating my regular.'

He laughed, shelled two nuts at once, blew the thin skin away, threw the kernels into his mouth and walked over to the window to look at something or someone in the street.

'Ella is coming,' he said. 'You have a nice, fat cook, man. The first day she come here to ask about the room I like her, though I didn't know who she was. Mrs. Rouse tell me you say she does everything for you, and you wouldn't let her go.' He laughed again. 'Anyway, guard your property. I am a man girls like, you know. If she fall in my garden I wouldn't have to lock the gate to keep her in.'

He laughed so heartily that Haynes was compelled to summon a sickly smile and ignore the shocking insinuation.

'Well, I'll see you later, Haynes,' said Benoit, shaking hands again. 'If you want any help in moving anything just call me.'

Chapter Four

On the Saturday evening Haynes, his back to the yard, sat by the window smoking. The first exhilaration of newness had already worn off, and he contemplated his immediate future with a lack of enthusiasm almost amounting to gloom. The room was small and irksome after the luxury of five rooms in the other house; particularly one of the book-shelves was four inches too short to fit in with the other against the only available side. It stuck out at an offensive angle. From the open doors of the kitchen came an unwavering smell of baking and cooking. One door was directly opposite the door of his room, and so many people were up and down and taking a glance at him that he often had to keep his own door closed, a grave hardship in a tropical climate. And there were more people to come yet. In the room next to his was a Miss Atwell, who was in defensive confinement. She was kept by a Mr. Cross, who had not turned up for weeks, and Miss Atwell consequently owed. She owed rent, she owed for other things, and was in fear of seizure. So she preferred to stay inside, keeping door and window tightly closed, running a serious risk of suffocation in the terrible heat. He had been taken by Maisie's face the first day, but whenever he looked at her she was looking at him and smiling, which discouraged him. Also she had a cold and spat voluptuously. Philomen, the Indian servant, who lived in the house, was fat and brown and pleasant-looking. Her masses of straight black hair banded down by a white cloth gave her a picturesque effect. She exuded good nature and smiled amicably, so that Haynes felt as much at ease with her as with Mrs. Rouse. But on the whole he wished he had not decided so precipitously.

Ella interrupted his reflections.

'Good night, sir.'

'Good night, Ella.'

But she did not go.

Haynes swung his chair round.

'What is wrong, Ella?'

'Nothing, sir. Good night, sir.'

Well, it wasn't Ella's fault. She had acted for the best.

In the kitchen the lights were bright. Everything had been washed and cleaned and put away, for tomorrow there would be no cakes to make. Supper would soon be ready. Sometimes the family ate in the dining-room, but more often they snatched their meals in the kitchen. Tonight, however, a large white cloth had been spread on the kitchen table. Wilhelmina was washing dishes at the sink. Philomen was out, probably buying the groceries for the Sunday cooking. Benoit was nowhere to be seen. John, the cake-seller, and Aucher were sitting on a little bench which faced the room, Aucher replying in monosyllables to John's casual remarks.

Aucher was as taciturn as he looked and inspired a vague

respect. John was quite unremarkable except for a prevailing simplicity of disposition and a fondness for cast-off garments.

Suddenly Maisie rushed round the house calling:

'Sonny! Sonny! Look, your mother come.'

Mrs. Rouse came to the kitchen door. Sonny, who was in the kitchen waiting for his supper, dashed out, held hands with Maisie, and the two of them ran round the house to the front.

'Our lodger has come, Mr. Haynes,' said Mrs. Rouse.

'Everybody seems very glad.'

'Yes,' said Mrs. Rouse. 'We all like her. She is a nurse, you know, so that if you get sick you have somebody on the spot to attend to you.'

'I hope I don't get ill,' said Haynes, for want of something to say rather than with any intention of mischief.

'Oh, Mr. Haynes! I didn't mean that. Nothing like that must happen to you while you are here,' she said.

The dining-room door opened and a short, thin, fair woman in a nurse's uniform came down the steps, her son holding on to one hand. Behind came Maisie with two or three parcels in her arms. The nurse went to the kitchen door, held Mrs. Rouse's face in her hands and kissed her twice.

'So you are back, nurse?'

'Yes, Ma Rouse. And how you all pass the time? Everybody well?'

'Everybody. Come in.'

Maisie had entered the kitchen by the other door and was opening the parcels at a table while John and Wilhelmina and even the solemn-faced Aucher crowded round her.

'Come to the light, Sonny. Let me see you well.' It was the nurse's voice. 'How is mother's child? Come and kiss me again, child.

'How did he behave, Ma Rouse?'

'He behaved well, nurse,' said Mrs. Rouse.

'Good. There's a kiss for that. Come and see what I have brought for you.'

'But Maisie! What do you mean? Opening everything the nurse bring like that!'

Maisie danced gaily outside.

'The nurse bring rum and wine and cherry brandy and cake. And garters for me and stockings for Mrs. Rouse and cloth to make a suit for Sonny; and a tie for Mr. Benoit . . . And when she opened her purse to pay the taxi-man was only notes. Big times!'

This she said partly to John and Aucher, who had followed her outside, and partly to nobody in particular.

'I ain't going home until I get two drinks o' that rum,' said John.

'I ain't goin' till the bottle finish,' said Aucher. 'Wait till Mr. Benoit come.'

'The boss mustn't drink. It not good for 'im,' said John.

'Tell 'im that you,' said Aucher. 'If is the doctor 'e wouldn't listen to, is you 'e goin' to hear?'

The two of them sat down on the little bench and the others began to eat inside. Philomen came in, on her arm a heavy basket.

'Eh, nurse? You come, then. O Lord!' and she started to laugh.

'How are you, nurse? You lookin' well,' she laughed again.

'But how is Miss A.?' said the nurse during a pause. There was a burst of rippling laughter from Maisie.

'Behave yourself, girl,' said Mrs. Rouse, and there was some whispering. Nurse called out.

'Good evening, Miss A.'

The door did not open, but a voice from inside replied, 'How are you, nurse? I am glad you is back. I myself is not too well.'

There was some more talking, voices lowered. Haynes felt sure this was about him. The voices rose again. Aucher was sent for ice and there was drinking. He and John went inside and had a drink each. There were jokes about the amount John poured out.

'You think is beer?' said Maisie.

And again there was a general laughing.

The two men came back and sat on the bench. Mrs. Rouse called Wilhelmina to put out some supper for them, while she and the nurse sat talking. Philomen moved in and out, joining in the conversation and calling out bits of news to the nurse whenever she happened to remember them.

'Eh, but nurse, you know we have a new cook? Mr. Haynes cook. Her name is Ella.' This from the sink.

'Eh, but nurse, you know my mother came down last week and brought some eggs? I remember you to her. She ask me for you too.' This from the yard.

'But, nurse, you mean you couldn't get away even once? We all was so longin' to see you.' This from the dining-room.

Mrs. Rouse rebuked her, but without severity. Philomen only laughed louder. Maisie and Sonny kept running backwards and forwards from the kitchen to the front, begging for prunes and cakes. Maisie had to be reprimanded once for interfering with the cherry brandy.

Gradually the household settled down. They all went in and closed the back door, after a perfect chorus of good nights.

Haynes was bored and yet when they left missed them. For want of something better to do he went to bed, but slept fitfully, and at five o'clock was awake. Tired from lack of sleep he lay in a drowsy condition, annoyed with himself and a determination to move from No. 2 steadily taking shape in his mind.

He would have to stay a month at least. Leaving so quickly would undoubtedly upset Mrs. Rouse, who was very nice. He would leave it to Ella. Ella knew how he felt. She would find new lodgings and he would leave this blasted place with its eternal smell of cakes. He heard voices in the yard. In the stillness of the early morning, they were very clear. One voice was deep. Benoit's, but talking in a low tone. Through the thin wood of which the house was built sounds from outside came through distinctly. Haynes's eyes, looking idly at his toes, were caught by a wide crack of light between two of the boards. It had been pasted over with paper, but the paper had burst or been punctured long ago. He threw the pillow to the bottom of the bed, put his elbows on it and peeped through.

Benoit stood by the kitchen door and Wilhelmina, the servant girl, stood washing at the sink.

'Come here,' said Benoit.

'Wait till I wash my face. This cold morning you so hot!'

'Me, I am always hot,' said Benoit.

Wilhelmina wiped her hands on her dress and came up to Benoit.

'Well! What you want?'

21

'What I want?' He held her and placed her against the kitchen door. Then he leant himself against her.

'This is what I want,' he kissed her savagely. 'And this,' he kissed her again. 'And this, too, and this.'

She pulled herself away.

'You are hurting me,' she said.

He made to hold her again.

'No,' she objected, and shook her head, 'you said you was comin' last night and you didn't come. This is the second time.'

They went into the kitchen.

Haynes fell back on his bed, his eyes hurting him from the strain. He was suddenly no longer sleepy. Instead, he was very much alive. In fact, he behaved quite idiotically. He balanced himself on the small of his back and kicked his feet up in the air.

To read of these things in books was one thing, to hear and see them was another. And Haynes, though passionately interested in women and always reading about them, had never since he was grown up kissed or been kissed by a woman who was not related to him. He had at sixteen, after much cogitation, but without preliminary, put his arm round a girl's waist and been soundly slapped. Since then he had never repeated the experiment, and often experienced difficulty in looking young women fully in the face. And here now he had been pitch-forked into the heart of the eternal triangle.

He lay on his stomach and peered through the crack again. He had heard the nurse's high-pitched, rather refined voice:

'Go quickly and don't stay, Wilhelmina. The Madam and Maisie gone to early Mass and nobody is here.'

Haynes continued to peep, saw nothing, lay down again for five minutes and then, hearing nothing, thought he might as well have another peep. His eyes almost fell through the crease.

Just inside the kitchen door he could see the nurse, her arms raised, probably round Benoit's neck, for his left arm was around her waist and his black fingers stood out against the base of her neck into which they pressed. The two remained almost unmoving for about a minute. Then they broke apart.

Benoit came outside, but the nurse did not come at once.

'Quickly, nurse,' he said, bending his head towards the kitchen. 'Mass will be over soon.'

The nurse came out with a hairpin in her mouth and shaking her long fair hair which had fallen loose. She and Benoit went towards the house.

Haynes could stay in bed no longer. He began to walk up and down the room. He began to dress intending, vaguely, to go for a walk. But he didn't go for any walk. Instead he opened his door and sat waiting to see the household set about its daily tasks. The stage, he felt, was set for a terrific human drama.

Ella came, made tea, and when Haynes had eaten and lighted a cigarette she closed the door.

'I asked a friend of mine to look for another place, sir. I see you don't like it here.'

'Ella, don't worry,' said Haynes. 'I like here well enough. I was a little tired yesterday, that was all.'

'You want to stay, sir?'

'Yes, we'll see how things turn out. Can't come one month and leave the next.'

'It wouldn't be any trouble for me to get another place, sir.'

'Don't you worry, Ella,' said Haynes. 'We'll have to make the best of this for the time being. Don't you worry.' He smiled benignly. 'I'll stay and I think I shall get to like it very well.'

Chapter Five

The nurse dominated the house. When she was not there the others talked about her. For a time, but not for long, she fascinated even Ella, who never let Haynes go long without telling him all she knew or thought. For seventy-two hours after her return the nurse slept almost continuously, only getting up to eat and to talk a little. She usually worked for the white people who could afford one nurse for the day and another for the night. But the nurse was greedy (Ella's phrase) and always worked day and night. She could do this for weeks. When she came home she slept for two or three days and then emerged as fit as when she left. She did no work in the kitchen, but she took charge of the house. She had it scrubbed and cobwebbed. She shifted the pictures, she sat on the top step while Maisie, for hours, and Philomen, Aucher and Wilhelmina, at odd times, cleaned and varnished the furniture. She bought new curtains. She made Benoit and Aucher clip the hedge. Supper was more often eaten in the dining-room than in the kitchen, but even when they ate in the kitchen there was always a cloth spread. One day she bought a large fish when the hawker came into the yard, and made a fish soup; it was an occasion. She mixed multi-coloured cocktails. She made jokes all through the day, particularly at supper, which was punctured with choruses of laughter. Philomen often had to beg her to stop. Sometimes Mrs. Rouse protested against these jokes, but feebly, she herself was laughing so much. Some of the best Ella, who was not squeamish, refused to repeat to Haynes.

On a very hot day she would have a bath at midday, just before lunch, and after lunch with her hair drying on her shoulders she sat in the yard under the mango tree on one chair, with her feet on another, smoking cigars and drinking tumblers of brandy and soda from which she gave Maisie sips. She grew very red in the face and a little more talkative, but that was all. Once she knocked at Miss Atwell's room, insisted on going in and had a talk with that invisible person. On Philomen's birthday the postman brought two cards, one from her lover and one from No. 2, Minty Alley. The nurse had sent it. Everyone was happy that morning. Philomen was almost as pleased over the one as over the other. But though the eager Haynes looked with all his might he could see nothing in the behaviour of Benoit or of the nurse to confirm what he had seen through the crack in the wall. Benoit usually went to town after lunch, returning in time for supper to check Philomen's accounts. On rare occasions he stayed and drank brandy and soda with the nurse, but very openly. He called her nurse. She called him Mr. B. Mrs. Rouse also called Benoit Mr. B. She and Mrs. Rouse were affectionate, often tender, with each other. After work they sat talking in the kitchen. When Benoit was at home the three of them talked. Haynes sat in his room on edge expecting at any minute to hear the murmur of voices burst into dramatic explosion. But nothing ever happened. Round about eleven he would hear them get ready to go in. They would come out leisurely and Mrs. Rouse would close and lock the kitchen door. They would go up the dining-room steps together and the dining-room door would close behind them. Mrs. Rouse did not know, obviously. So tranquil was everything that Haynes at times felt that he had not seen what he had seen, but had dreamt it. He was almost persuaded to speak to Ella. If she knew anything, she would tell. But Haynes for once preferred to say nothing to her and kept his secret.

The nurse rather ignored Haynes. They gave each other the time of day and that was all, until one morning, Sonny, her son, was the cause of sudden and violent contact.

The nurse idolized Sonny. She paid two dollars a month for him at an exclusive private school, she dressed him expensively, she gave him frequent pocket change. The school was not near and she paid someone not far from it to give Sonny a good hot lunch. On mornings before he set out and on afternoons when he returned she embraced him and kissed him in an almost sensual manner, with a string of mammy's darlings, sonny boys, honeys and the like. Once, Haynes caught Benoit looking rather savagely at the nurse indulging in one of these rhapsodies over her son. It was the only time he ever saw anything indicating the special relationship between the two.

One morning the nurse went away early. Haynes remained at home that day, nursing an injured foot. A case of books had fallen on his shin and bruised him severely. He had struggled on with his work, but his limp was so obvious that old Carritt had told him to go home and stay there until he was better. Haynes went gladly, his first holiday for two years. He could sit in an armchair and read as in the good old days, and not feel any twinge of nervousness about his job. After all, Carritt himself had said to go home and not come back until he could walk properly. And he could not only read but could always turn from his books and watch No. 2 at work and at play.

After morning tea, Maisie and Sonny played together under the window. It was a game with marbles and the loser of each set had to pay a forfeit. Haynes lost track of their talk until Maisie's voice drew his attention.

'But, Ma Rouse, this little boy Sonny getting very fresh. He win and you know what he ask for?'

'What?' said Benoit.

'He asked me for a kiss.'

'You little whelp,' said Benoit. 'You looking for a wife already?'

He unloosed his belt from round his waist and gave Sonny two or three whacking blows. Sonny screamed.

'Don't beat the woman's child, McCarthy,' said Mrs. Rouse.

Sonny ran to the far end of the yard yelling.

'You have no right to beat me,' he stammered, 'you are not my father.'

'None of your cheek out there or you'll get some more,' said Benoit, but Mrs. Rouse intervened.

As soon as the nurse came in for lunch Benoit met her with the tale.

'And when I give him one with the belt, he tell me I am not his father.'

'I see,' said the nurse. 'Young man, come here. So Mr. Benoit is not your father. You know where your father is? You ever saw him? So you looking for woman already? Into the bedroom, take off all your clothes and prepare yourself.'

'What is she going to do?' whispered Haynes to Ella.

'I hear she does beat him terrible, sir. All morning Mrs. Rouse begging the man not to tell the nurse.'

The nurse had her bath, lunch, a cigarette on the bench with her hair on her shoulders. Then she went in and soon came the sound of blows and Sonny's screams, with the nurse telling him, 'Hush, I say. You wouldn't? Well, go on. We'll see who will stop first.'

But Sonny either could not or would not hush. He got away from her and ran into the yard, then into the kitchen. The nurse followed him and, desperate, he ran up the steps into Haynes's room.

'Mr. Haynes, Mr. Haynes, save me.'

He dropped on his knees, his hands resting on the floor, his face turned upwards in supplication. He was stark naked and his whole body heaved. All over his skin the cane had raised red weals of flesh, one almost continuous from the left shoulder across the chest almost down to the navel.

Haynes sickened at the sight.

'Come, get up, don't kneel down.'

He helped the weeping, quivering boy to his feet and sat on the bed holding his hand expecting the nurse to come. But the nurse did not come. Outside was very still and he understood that they were waiting to see what he would do. He waited a little longer. Nothing. He could not wait for ever, so he went to the door.

The nurse sat composedly on the little bench, Mrs. Rouse stood at one door of the kitchen, apprehension and uncertainty on her gravely handsome face. Maisie was next to her, grinning. At the other door was Philomen. Benoit and Wilhelmina he could glimpse behind her, Benoit apparently keeping himself in the background. All looked at Haynes and Haynes looked at the nurse. Ordinarily pale, she was a little red in the face, but otherwise showed no passion. She held the cane across her knees, a hand gripping each end. So unperturbed and ready she was, she frightened him.

'Nurse,' he began falteringly.

'Don't waste your breath, Mr. Haynes,' she said gently but without a smile. 'I am not going to let him off one. I am sitting here waiting. And the longer he stays the worse for him.'

Her tone and her manner, so controlled and so falsely cool, froze Haynes. Sonny in the corner of the room could not see her, but he felt the menace of the woman and he started to wail again.

'O God, nurse, spare him,' said Philomen, and the apron went to her eyes.

Mrs. Rouse spoke to Haynes.

'Mr. Haynes, i's no use. I know the nurse better than you. The best you can do is to bring Sonny out. Sonny, come on to your mother. I's your mother. You must obey. And you have no right in Mr. Haynes room.'

But Sonny began to cry in quick short jerks which made Haynes fear that he would go into hysterics.

'Let him come, Mr. Haynes,' continued Mrs. Rouse. 'I's better for him. Maisie, inside, you wretch. Wilhelmina, go on with your work. Philomen, child, go on to town with your basket.'

The group broke up. Mrs. Rouse disappeared in the kitchen. Benoit could not be seen. It was left for Haynes to do something, if something was to be done.

'Come along, Sonny,' he said. 'I'll go with you, come on.'

But Sonny threw himself on the floor again. He was almost foaming now. If Haynes could have taken the blows for him he would have done so. (Never had Haynes's mother even hinted at the possibility of his being beaten.)

'Come,' he said, bending down and trying to raise the boy. 'Come.'

'You will hurt your foot, Mr. Haynes,' said the nurse, 'and it's no use your bringing him. He has to come to me by himself. And he knows it.'

'Mammy, Mammy, I beg your pardon, I beg your pardon. Mr. Haynes, beg Mammy's pardon for me.'

'Mammy! Mammy! Beg pardon!' sneered the nurse, and she showed her teeth in a smile for the first time. She shook the cane playfully at him.

'Doggie! Doggie! Look bone,' she said.

Mrs. Rouse came resolutely out.

'Nurse,' she said, 'he's your child to do as you like with. But don't tell him that doggie, doggie, look bone. I can't bear to hear you say that thing.'

'It isn't what I tell him, Ma Rouse, it is what I am going to do to him. Doggie! Doggie! Coming for bone? Longer doggie stay, sweeter the bone.'

Mrs. Rouse came to Haynes's door.

'I am sorry for all this, Mr. Haynes, but you see how it is? And the longer he stop the worse for him. Come on, Sonny. Perhaps your mother will spare you if you come at once. Come on, you remember the last time.'

At last, Sonny, with a despairing look at Haynes, walked slowly down the steps. His naked little body, all white with red weals, grovelling on its hands and knees, crawled inch by inch towards his mother. She sat watching him come, each hand still gripping an end of the cane, as still and as cold as a marble statue.

'Doggie coming at last, eh? Bone sweet. Come on, doggie.'

'Go on, Sonny,' said Mrs. Rouse. 'I's your mother, go on.'

'Spare him, nurse,' said Haynes.

The nurse did not answer. She had her eyes fixed on the boy.

When he stood within a foot of her, she spoke to him.

'So you reach. Oh, you want to go again?'

'No, Mammy, no, Mammy.'

'Oh, I see, I thought you wanted to go off again. You can go if you want to, you know. You staying or you going, tell me.'

'I am staying, Mammy.'

She rose above him and he went flat down in the dust before her. She cut him across the shoulders and cut him again and again, and as he rolled screaming in the dirt she pointed to the door.

'Go to the bedroom,' she said, and anxious for even that short respite he ran inside.

She followed him.

Haynes locked his door, and overwhelmed with shame tried in vain to shut out the thud of the cane on the little body, the yells and screams, and the 'Hush, I tell you, hush' of his mother. He felt that he should have done something, that he should do something.

At each blow he winced as if it had fallen on his own flesh. As he moved across the room he struck his damaged foot a sharp blow on the edge of the chair and a stab of pain struck him. Throwing himself on his bed he buried his face in the pillow and cried.

The screams were getting less but the blows were still falling. Good God, was she going to kill the child?

'Hush, I tell you, hush. I will lick you until you hush.' And Sonny hushed at last.

Haynes called Ella.

'Get a room at once, Ella,' he said. 'I am going to leave here as soon as my foot is better.'

He would not stay a moment longer than was necessary in the same house with that woman. He dreaded the thought of seeing her again. Had his foot not been damaged (and also for Mrs. Rouse's sake) he would have left at once. He should have saved Sonny. But what right had he to interfere? There were no laws about child-beating on the island. He thought of the long weal to the navel and shivered. Never did he want to see her again, never. He thought of his own peaceful childhood and limpid life in his mother's house and wished that he could go back to it and never leave it again.

Chapter Six

But that very evening the nurse paid him a visit. As soon as it was dark she came. She knocked, waited a little, said it was the nurse, walked in, drew a chair to Haynes's bedside and sat down.

'Mr. Haynes, I waited until Ella was gone, because Ella seems to believe that you are her property. Sonny send to say good night and to apologize for his behaviour today. I suppose that you think me a cruel mother. But Sonny is my only child and all my hopes are on him. I'll give him anything he wants and that a child should have, but he will obey me until he is a man for himself.'

'Yes,' murmured Haynes.

'I have come to see that foot of yours. Let me feel your pulse. I believe you have some fever.' She took a case from her pocket, opened it and drew out a thermometer.

'Put this in your mouth. A simple bruise shouldn't give so much trouble. If it were only a bruise it should have healed long ago. Yes. You have a temperature. Let me see the foot. Humph! Getting better? It's festering below. This needs attention. It's a good thing I came. Excuse me a minute.'

She returned with a small basin, bottles and cotton wool, and took charge of Haynes as if he were Sonny. He watched her. It was the first time that he had ever been so close to her.

She was very thin, thinner even than she appeared at a distance. She was to all appearances white, but the tell-tale finger-nails showed the coloured blood. She was somewhere in the thirties, in the late thirties, battered by life, but certainly of superior style and breeding to the others in the house. Not that Mrs. Rouse, for instance, was in any way vulgar. Not at all. But from the nurse's deportment and speech, Haynes felt instinctively that she had been reared in surroundings different to her present position. Or perhaps her nurse's training had helped to give a refined quality to her voice and manner. He noted again the extreme fairness of her complexion and her long, silky, almost golden, hair. If she had had money she would have been able to take her place with the white aristocracy, ninety-nine per cent. of whom had more coloured blood than she had. Benoit didn't seem the type of man to attract her. He was very black, with no compensation of money, profession or personal charm to atone for the social and economic disadvantages of his black skin. He was a man as good as married: eighteen years he and Mrs. Rouse had lived together.

Life had left its mark upon her, in her weather-beaten body and hard style as much as in the fact that she, a professional woman with so fair a skin, lived openly and without shame in the house of these lowly black folk. And she was not only Benoit's mistress. She was on the best of terms with the woman who was Benoit's wife – as good as his wife. And now she had come into Haynes's room, and taken charge of him, and having washed and bound his foot, gave him quinine, lowered his lamp and told him that it was time to go to bed. So that what with his illness and the excitement of the afternoon, Haynes merely did as he was told, and when she left lay in bed feeling curiously flattered.

It was only long after she had gone that Haynes recalled with a guilty start that the loathing which he had felt for her over the beating of Sonny had almost entirely disappeared.

After that the nurse came twice a day, morning and afternoon, to attend to Haynes. She talked easily, told him a lot about herself and extracted twice as much from him. She told Haynes that she was not a fully-certified nurse and still had her final examination to take. Her constant failure she attributed to the personal spite of an examining doctor at the hospital. She told him as easily as good morning that she had been engaged to be married to a doctor, who had seduced her and then deserted her. (But Ella said no: she had been wild from early, and Sonny was not her first-born.) Ella, in fact, displayed an open hostility to the nurse's coming into the room at all, and it increased when the nurse began to bring in food for Haynes to eat. Haynes was feverish and had no appetite. And the nurse made egg-nogs and Mrs. Rouse boiled soups and baked custards and the nurse brought them in and insisted that Haynes should have them, and stood up over him and made him eat and drink, while Ella stood in the corner and scowled.

'I cannot understand, sir, how that foot can't get better. That nurse, sir, she is a dangerous woman. It's not good to have anything to do with that kind of person, sir.'

Haynes ate the custard one evening, and next morning Ella

told him that she had got a room. He could move at once if he wanted.

But Haynes told her that the nurse was so kind, and Mrs. Rouse also, that he didn't very well see how he could clear out, even before his foot was better. It wouldn't look well.

'Kind, sir. That isn't kindness. They are both of them up to something.'

He was not altogether surprised, therefore, when the nurse wrote him a note one morning asking him to lend her two dollars till later in the day. A postscript to the note asked him to 'destroy as soon as he had read contents of same.'

Haynes sent the two dollars and destroyed the note.

That night she brought the two dollars back. She gave it to him in an envelope with thanks and a little apology for having had to ask.

'Why I asked you to tear up the note was because Ella has a habit of going into your drawer when you are not here, taking out your private letters and reading them. And as you can understand, I didn't want everybody to know that I had asked you that favour.'

He was further enlightened the next morning. Ella had got to know of the little transaction.

'The nurse borrow money from you and pay you back. But be careful, sir. Next time she comin' for more, sir, and this time she ain't goin' to pay you back. You don't know the tricks of these people, sir.'

The next time she came the nurse, after a little general conversation, suddenly broke out with:

'You know, Mr. Haynes, since you have come here all of us like you very much.'

She washed the wound with dioxygen, delicately but firmly, holding down the leg with one hand. Haynes had some little experience of medical attendance and she was very good at her work – firm and yet not inconsiderate. She threw the piece of cotton into the yellow mixture in the bowl and paused, looking him in the face.

'You can see that.'

He gave a foolish smile.

Perhaps it was because he was not in full health, but he had to pull himself together.

'And we see, too, that you like us. Mrs. Rouse and I were talking it over and we were wondering if you would care to board with us.'

But Haynes was not quite so weak as all that.

'It's very nice of you both, nurse, and I am sure it would be a suitable arrangement, but that would mean giving up Ella, and she has been with me too long for me to do that. I am afraid—'

'No, Ella will be all right. A doctor at the hospital last week asked me for a cook and if I recommend Ella she will get the job. And Mrs. Rouse like Ella a lot. She could sack Wilhelmina and give Ella her job.'

'Ella wouldn't accept any such offer.'

'She is a good girl,' the nurse went on, 'but she is wasteful, Mr. Haynes. You keep no check on her and—'

'You must not say things against Ella's honesty, nurse, and she is not wasteful.' The nurse never flinched.

'I know she is honest, Mr. Haynes. Oh! I know that. And that she will do anything for you. We know that, too; we were talking about it only last night and how lucky you were to have her. But, as I said, you needn't lose her. And it would come much cheaper to you.'

Haynes shook his head.

'And then you will be helping us, too,' the nurse continued smoothly. 'Mrs. Rouse is a great cook, can make nice pastries, etc. And to tell you the truth things are not too good with her, and the little boarding will come in very handy to us. Where I am now I owe her some money and I am looking everywhere for somebody to lend me fifteen dollars.'

This was a home shot. Haynes had intended to give an outright no to the boarding scheme, but shaken by the fifteen dollars hint, he temporized by saying he would think the matter over.

Late that night he was reading when he heard a knock at his door.

'Who is it?'

'Miss Atwell,' replied a whisper.

'Come in,' said Haynes.

Miss Atwell was small, and looked very small, though wrapped in an extensive old kimono. She was nearing fifty, her face sharp and lined, but her eyes keen and alert. This was his first sight of her, but Haynes could see that she was one of those who did not wait for tomorrow but went to meet it.

'And how is the foot, sir?'

'Coming round at last.'

A withering disgust showed in her vivacious and mobile features.

'Mr. Haynes,' she whispered, 'I don't want to say anything unsociable, but if you' foot had less attention, it would 'ave been better by now. I don't believe in all this oxygen and washin'. A little boric powder. That's all, sir. A little boric powder. But what I wants to let you know is this. And I hopes you will take no offence where none is intended. And I know that you is a gentleman and this will go no further. But them people,' she pointed towards the Rouse household, 'them people is a set of thieves and liars. They wants to put you against Ella. I hasn't been listenin' to all that the nurse been tellin' you about Ella. But don't believe a word they say. They wants to get you to board and then rob you. Have nothing to do with them. They does nothing but sit and conspire how to get you into their clutches. When she is talkin' to you in here, be careful. She is talkin' very unsuspectin', but all the time she is crosspickin' you to find out you' business. They see you look soft, Mr. Haynes, and they wants to jostle you, but they can't fool me. Have nothing to do with them, Mr. Haynes. I is Ella's friend and your friend. Good night, Mr. Haynes.'

Before Haynes could say a word she had retired as suddenly as she had come.

Chapter Seven

Haynes decided that he would give a very prompt and definite no to any further attempts of the nurse and Mrs. Rouse to substitute themselves for Ella – if any such plan was in progress. But the nurse's attack never came to a head. The next afternoon she received a sudden call and left to take up duty. She came hurriedly in very late one night, saying that she had to take her examination the following day. But she left the examination room to go back to her patient, sending to say that she had done well, expected to pass this time, and would be home on Friday afternoon. Haynes, meanwhile, had got better and gone out to work. But he spent most of his leisure time at home resting his foot. As soon as he finished work on Friday he returned to No. 2, to be met by Ella with the news that the nurse and Mr. Benoit were carrying on and Ma Rouse had found out and the nurse was coming home that afternoon, and Ma Rouse was waiting for her to come to put her out. She was going to be put out that very day. Ella and Miss Atwell and Maisie had packed the nurse's clothes and had dressed Sonny. When the nurse came she would get her walking ticket.

'Listen, sir, listen. They are plannin' a 'laborate ceremony.'

'Very well, Ella. Go outside and close my door, please.' Ella being dismissed Haynes removed his pillow from the top of his bed to the bottom, fixed his elbows on it and glued his eyes to his peephole, which he had enlarged and arranged (and camouflaged) so as to command a wide and comprehensive view of the whole yard. The others went about their work as usual, but Mrs. Rouse, with red eyes, which she wiped every few seconds, sat on the little bench. Miss Atwell, in a clean print dress and her hair combed in some tight little plaits which sharpened her face more than ever, for two or three minutes sat next to her, then walked up and down the yard talking and gesticulating.

'Now, Ma Rouse, do as I tell you. Don't lose you' temper. When you lose you' temper, you lose you' head; and when you lose you' head, you lose all. Tell her all that you have to tell her. It's you' privilege to do so. But don't lose you' temper. Show her that you is as good a lady as she is.'

'Don't be afraid for me, Miss Atwell,' said Mrs. Rouse. 'I am as good a lady as the nurse any day. And I would scorn to do what she has done.'

'Handsome is as handsome do,' said Miss Atwell. 'Ma Rouse, when you discovered—'

Maisie came running through the space between the house and the kitchen.

'Miss A., Miss A., the bailiff and Mr. Brown coming down Victoria Street.'

'Jesus in Heaven. Thank you, child,' said Miss Atwell, and almost as she spoke her door slammed.

'Everybody to work,' said Mrs. Rouse. 'Maisie, you go inside. Miss A.,' she called in a low voice, 'don't be afraid, I will fix everything.'

But minutes passed and the bailiff did not come. Nobody came. Wilhelmina was sent to investigate, and returned to say that she had been up the road and down the road, but had seen no one and had met no one who had seen the bailiff. Mrs. Rouse herself looked down the alley and spoke to a neighbour. No one had seen the bailiff. Maisie, examined and questioned, stoutly maintained that she had seen the two of them coming down the road. But nobody believed her. Mrs. Rouse threatened her with a licking, and Miss Atwell had just opened her door a second time when Philomen cried:

'Look! The nurse.'

For days after, the scene was discussed from every angle and aspect.

When Philomen said, 'Look, the nurse,' everybody fell back as if by instinct and left a clear path for her to advance to Mrs. Rouse. She came forward, unsuspecting, to embrace and kiss Mrs. Rouse as usual.

'Ma Rouse, I am back,' she said.

Mrs. Rouse stood erect and waiting, and made no move towards her. Even then, the nurse suspected nothing; only when Miss Atwell said, 'Keep you' temper, Ma Rouse,' she looked up at her with a puzzled expression. Then she looked at Mrs. Rouse and realized that something was wrong and what it was. She stopped dead. Her pale face went a blotched yellow. She took one swift glance around her and her eyes came to rest on Mrs. Rouse's face and stayed there, never flinching.

'We have come to the parting of the ways, nurse,' said Mrs. Rouse with consummate dignity. 'You will not sleep in my house tonight. You coming to kiss me the kiss of Judas. I have received many of them from you. But no more, nurse, no more. I forgave you once, but not again.'

The nurse had recovered her self-command – if she had ever lost it for more than a second.

'I don't know what you are talking about,' she said. 'If there is anything wrong choose a proper time and place and we can discuss it.'

'I don't want to hear anything from you. It's no use your denying it. I want no argument, no discussion. Your clothes are all packed in your basket and in parcels. Your son has been washed and dressed. Take him with you when you go. The little pieces of furniture that belong to you you can have any time that you want. But you must leave my house this minute. I don't want any words with you, but you have been carrying on clandestine meetings with my husband, clandestine meetings—'

'He is not your husband,' said the nurse.

From some unseen spot Maisie laughed, slightly shrill but very musical, with the detached appreciation of a disinterested spectator. The nurse's lips trembled in a smile and Mrs. Rouse's temper snapped. She sprang at her enemy.

'By God, woman. You think you are going to stand before me and tell me what you like, you—' The sentence ended in a stream of confused obscenity, Miss Atwell and Philomen rushing to hold back Mrs. Rouse.

The nurse tripped lightly up the steps and came back at once with Sonny and her parcels.

'Keep you' temper, Ma Rouse, keep you' temper,' Miss Atwell counselled and held Mrs. Rouse by the arm.

'Madam, let her go in peace,' said Philomen, and held her by the other arm.

The nurse walked away. But just as she was about to turn into the passage between the house and the hedge she stopped, and looking round at everyone, she said:

'Goodbye, everybody.'

'Go, you snake,' said Mrs. Rouse. 'Go back to the prostitution I took you from.'

The nurse turned back once more and spoke in the same cool and gentle voice she had spoken to Sonny the day she sat waiting for him with the cane across her knees.

'I am going, Ma Rouse, but don't be afraid. Mr. Benoit is coming with me, too.' And then as if suddenly inspired she smiled the same cold little smile and said, 'Doggie! Doggie! Look bone.'

Chapter Eight

That night No. 2 was a curious mixture of brooding quiet enlivened by flashes of excitement. All the talking and discussion and reconstruction came afterwards. What everyone was really waiting for was the appearance of Benoit. As far as they knew he had no inkling at all of all that had happened, having gone away as usual after lunch. Ella said that Mrs. Rouse had learnt what was going on since the day before but had kept her own counsel. It seemed, too, that she had discovered a similar situation some months before, but had pardoned the couple. But this turned out to be some kissing alone, and both the nurse and Benoit swore that there was nothing else in it. Ella enlightened Haynes about Benoit.

'That man, sir! He have a devil. From the time I come here, the man is after me.'

'What!' said Haynes.

He had thought that the nurse, Wilhelmina and Mrs. Rouse represented the limit of Benoit's activity.

'Yes, sir, I had to tell 'im I didn't play so rough. Good night, sir.'

'Good night, Ella.'

'Now that woman gone, sir, there will be peace in the place. Good night, sir.'

'Good night, Ella.'

'Been a busy day, sir. And you were having fever only the other day. Better have a quiet evening, sir.'

'I think I shall, Ella. Thank you.'

But except for Mrs. Rouse, who had gone to her bedroom, every separate member of the household paid him a visit that night.

Philomen came first, with swollen eyes.

'Mr. Haynes, lend me some matches, please.' But she did not go.

'How is Mrs. Rouse?' asked Haynes.

'She had to take to her bed, Mr. Haynes. Her head is bursting and her heart is full. What will happen when Mr. Benoit come I don't know. Mr. Haynes, the nurse behaved too badly to madam. Whenever she out on duty she meeting Mr. Benoit, and the madam been so kind to the nurse. Excuse me, Mr. Haynes. I have to go and boil some tea for the madam. Nothing buy yet in the grocery, the things not washed up, everything in a mess.'

The next was Miss Atwell.

'Mr. Haynes,' she said. 'You must excuse me, Mr. Haynes. A tragedy have taken place. In all my days I never see such a brass face as that nurse. After they do so much for her that is the way she turn round and not only take the man away, but actually give cheeks on the bargain. But she will come to a bad end. Everybody is glad she gone. It puts an end to all her tricks and trapezin' with you and Ella. The house will be at peace now. Good night, Mr. Haynes. I am goin' for a walk on the seawall. I needs a little ozone, Mr. Haynes, to freshen up the lungs.'

Not ten minutes afterwards Haynes heard a knock below the window on the other side of the house.

'Mr. Haynes.'

Before he could move, Maisie's head and shoulders appeared above the sill. Haynes was almost as startled as on the night of Miss Atwell's first appearance.

'Anybody here?' she whispered.

'No.'

'Give me a hand,' she said, and Haynes helped her into the room.

'Close the door, Mr. Haynes.'

Haynes closed the door.

'You had better lock it.'

Haynes locked it.

'If anybody comes don't open.'

Haynes nodded.

'Mr. Haynes, you look frightened. But you are all right. It's me who is in the stew.'

'No, I am not frightened. Why should I be frightened? But what stew are you in?'

'They inside swearing vengeance on me. All of them saying that it is when I laugh, at least Miss Atwell keep on saying so, that it is when I laugh I spoil the whole business. And Miss Atwell vex already because I say the bailiff was coming.'

'But was the bailiff coming?'

'No,' laughed Maisie, 'no bailiff was coming, but how can they know whether the bailiff was coming or not? But there's more in this than you know, Mr. Haynes, plenty more. The nurse gone and the nurse is not coming back. That is what is killing me. If she would only take me— This house is going to be a prison cell.'

She was speaking in a low tone and the last few words had been addressed as much to herself as to Haynes. Suddenly she held her head up.

'Mr. Haynes, I hope you don't mind my being here. I want to see what will happen when Benoit comes.'

'No, not at all,' said Haynes.

And he didn't. He was seeing for the first time what an extremely pretty girl Maisie really was and what a fine figure she had. She sat thinking her own thoughts and Haynes watched her. Never before had he seen her so grave.

'Mr. Haynes, I feel to run away from the place. Only the nurse used to bother with me here. Mrs. Rouse thinks of one thing and that is Benoit. I only had a good time when the nurse was here. The nurse used to stick up for me. They used to pay five shillings a month for me at a private school. I was bright at school, Mr. Haynes, but Mr. Benoit say that it is only a waste of money. He say what women want to get on in the world they haven't to learn in school, they born with it. But the nurse stick out for me to go. And after they take me away she say that if I too big to go to school I big enough to go out. And whenever they counting out money to spend at Christmas and Carnival and Easter, the nurse always put in a dress for me and a pair of shoes and so on. And little dances and bazaars, if wasn't for the nurse I would never go. Mrs. Rouse only used to be thinking of Benoit, Benoit, Benoit all the time. Anywhere to go, Mr. Benoit is to go. Any circus and so on come here, Mr. Benoit going. If they have money or ain't have money, he have

49

to get some to go, and plenty money too. And Mrs. Rouse will break her neck to get it for him. Then she press clothes and buy shirt for him and he gone. She behind: "See for both of us," that is what she always telling him. Then when he go and come back, she sit down to hear what he say. She in the kitchen like a slave and he like a prince. And look what he do her. Serve her damn well right.

'Mr. Haynes, before the nurse come to live here nobody used to come here. Only a lot of old people. I used to go and stand by the gate. As soon as Mrs. Rouse finish in the kitchen she calling me in. I must come in and stay in. If Benoit there they talking. If Benoit out, she sitting down nodding in the chair waiting until he come. I's only the nurse used to bring a little brightness into the house and now she gone.' Maisie lifted her head and looked at Haynes. 'I tell you, Mr. Haynes, what I wish is that Mrs. Rouse had gone and the nurse stopped.' She dropped her head on her arm again and said slowly, 'It's all that Benoit's fault. That man! He would carry his freshness to the Virgin Mary.'

There were footsteps in the yard. Maisie raised her head and listened as a dog does.

'Benoit,' she signalled with her lips to Haynes.

The footsteps, Benoit's footsteps, came to Haynes's door.

'Haynes,' said Benoit, 'you there?'

Haynes was about to answer, but Maisie put her finger before her lips and went to the window.

She swung herself over, but before her head disappeared she gave Haynes a nod and a smile as if to say 'go ahead.'

'Yes,' answered Haynes, and opened the door.

Chapter Nine

Benoit wore a white suit, and a spotted shirt and collar to match. He was, as usual whenever he went out, smoothly shaven, but when he took off his hat his hair was disordered. One of the buttons of his shirt was unfastened, his eyes were bloodshot and his lips were pouted in the centre and drawn at the corners.

'Have a cigarette?' said Haynes.

He took one and lit it and drew deeply two or three times while Haynes watched him and waited.

'Where is—?' He pointed with his thumb to Miss Atwell's room.

'Gone out,' Haynes replied.

He pulled deeply at the cigarette, offering no word of conversation.

'Having a little read?' he said at last.

'Amusing myself,' replied Haynes. Benoit's appearance and manner made him nervous.

'You have anything to drink?' asked Benoit, breaking another silence.

'Yes, there is some brandy I have left over from my illness. I have no soda though. You will have to take it with water.'

He poured and poured, gulped it down, and took a little water.

'Not taking one?' he asked, wiping his mouth.

'No,' said Haynes.

It was only then that he began to speak.

'Hell of a thing happened here this afternoon,' he said slowly.

'The nurse is my girl, you know,' he continued. 'Long time now; and that one in there, of late she only quarrelling. She is so damned stupid.'

But this little spurt of wrath spent itself almost at once.

'Yes, I must love the nurse, man.'

He was looking at Haynes, but absent-mindedly, and seemed to be talking chiefly to relieve himself.

'The nurse is a nice woman, man. Nice colour, straight hair and a moving woman. The nurse and me understand one another well. Everything was going so good . . .'

He curled his lip and shook his head slowly.

'If it wasn't for the nurse I wouldn't be sitting here tonight.'

He continued emphatically: 'No, I wouldn't be sitting here tonight.'

'When she first come to live here I take in one day. She was attending to a case. Lucky thing the baby was born already. She used to go and come, as they didn't want her all the time, you see. I take in in the kitchen in a fit and they lift me up. That one in there was in hell. Lucky thing the nurse come in. As soon as she see me, she say "O God! Is a stroke he getting. We have to turn it." And she started to work on me. Warm application, hot bath, she send for medicine to the doctor-shop as if she was a doctor. And she turn it back. The doctor come afterwards, but he say if wasn't that the nurse was on the spot and do everything, I might have been a dead man or a cripple. I can't forget the nurse, man . . . And you can see for yourself that she is a nice woman.'

Haynes nodded.

'And I help her, too, you know. Yes, I help her, too. When the woman first came here she was nothing. Nobody used to watch her, didn't use to give her no jobs, nothing. And then I take her in hand. I know some science, you know. And I talk to that one in there, she say yes, we take her into the house and I work on her. I put her to stand up before me naked as she born and I say the prayers over her for nine days. We boil the bath and I bathe her myself and tell her what to do. In three months you wouldn't know was the same woman. The woman start to get jobs. We lend her some money, she put in telephone, she buy glasses, she start to dress and she begin to make some good little money. I's I who fixed her up. If wasn't for me she would have been still down to the ground.'

He remained silent, looking sometimes at the walls, sometimes at the bottle on the table, sometimes at Haynes, but always with the same expression of abstraction tempered by uncertainty.

But Haynes himself had ceased to think of the Benoit sitting before him. Instead he saw the nurse standing naked before Benoit without a stitch, and Benoit performing the rites. He wondered if Benoit was naked too. Was there ever such a rigmarole? If Benoit was not there he would have burst out laughing. Benoit bathing the nurse, and Mrs. Rouse allowing it. This Benoit was a hell of a fellow though. Haynes gazed at him fascinated.

Benoit raised his head with a jerk and said sharply:

'She lie if she think this going to make me give up the nurse, though.'

'Oh! You mean to continue with her?' said Haynes, who in his simplicity had looked upon the affair as over.

'If I have to leave this one! The nurse going good. Her colour help her, you see: she does only attend to the white people. And when she leaving they give her presents, brooch and watch and sometimes ten dollars extra. If you see the presents the woman does get! And this one here, her business going bad. They ain't no money in cakes again, man.'

'But if you keep on with the nurse, Mrs. Rouse is going to be very angry.'

'Let her vex if she want. She have her husband. I ain't a married man. If she bother me I leave her tomorrow . . . But that is all right. She love me too much. I can always bring her round.'

He smiled for the first time, a confident almost contemptuous smile.

'You work it by your science?' said Haynes.

'No science, but when you see me loving a woman she never want to give me up, man, she rather die first. I am taking another drink of your brandy.'

He took it and went, a less worried man than when he had come in.

Haynes went to bed and thought of the developments of the morrow. But the next morning nothing happened. Mrs. Rouse was up early and went to market as usual, but dressed today as if she was going to High Mass. When she came back she took off the dress, but she still wore her Sunday shoes and stockings. Her hair also remained as it was on festive occasions, and she moved about the kitchen and the yard cheerfully and with vigour. Haynes, looking to see her broken or depressed, was thoroughly bewildered and slightly disappointed.

Benoit was entertaining two or three friends as on an ordinary Sunday morning and they were all talking, laughing and drinking in the dining-room. Once he came to the door and called to Mrs. Rouse.

'A., we want some more ice. Send and get some for us.'

Philomen was sent flying.

It was late before Haynes opened his door and was seen by Mrs. Rouse.

'Good morning, Mr. Haynes . . . I am well, thank you.' She smiled brightly and understandingly. 'Philomen, my girl, be careful with that rice. You know Mr. Benoit don't like it boil too soft. I hope you slept well, Mr. Haynes.'

So Benoit had been as good as his boast and had, indeed, brought her round. Haynes spoke to Ella about the affair, but Ella treated it as of no importance.

'These people, sir, don't bother with them, sir. Last night she was cuttin' the man's throat. This mornin' she lickin' his foot.'

Chapter Ten

Benoit, after that night, came in regularly for a chat. He talked of scandals in the town, of food, of women he had known, but fairly often and with a growing frequency he talked of his present position between Mrs. Rouse and the nurse. He was determined not to give up the nurse. She had established herself in a room in Kent Street, she had sent for her things, had had the telephone installed and was not in the least incommoded by the change, had rather benefited in fact, for she could now receive Benoit and enjoy his company as long as she liked without fear of interruption. Benoit spoke loudly and embarrassed Haynes, who did not want Mrs. Rouse to think that he was Benoit's confidant. And also, Haynes was genuinely sorry for Mrs. Rouse.

'But what about Mrs. Rouse, Benoit?' he asked one day when Benoit had been reiterating his determination to maintain his connection with the nurse at all costs.

'Oh! She all right, man. If she don't like it let her go to America and look for her husband.'

He was chewing as usual.

'You will soon get tired of the nurse – and—'

'Tired of the nurse! You don't know what you saying, man. The white woman is too sweet. She is like jelly. I am not going to give her up. Look! Where she work the other day they send for her, give her a big bottle of lotion, a bottle with a gold stopper and ten dollars as a present. Five was mine. Give her up! No, man. This one is too stupid. I live with you nearly eighteen years. I not going to leave you. But she ain't going to prevent me going out when I want.'

Mrs. Rouse was not going to prevent him going out. It was not long before everybody in No. 2 knew that Benoit spent every hour that he was away from home at the nurse's house. As soon as he finished work he took his lunch and left. He returned to enter the accounts in the book. He ate hurriedly, sometimes did not eat at all, and was off again, not returning until midnight, or later. Night after night he and Mrs. Rouse quarrelled. She used to sit up waiting for him, and attacked him as soon as he entered. At midnight and in the early hours Haynes could hear them, voices raised without restraint, more often than not cursing one another; so that Miss Atwell grumbled and swore that she was going to move from this 'unhaller'd' house.

One morning Haynes heard an official voice in the yard making enquiries about one Thomas Inniss, known as Aucher.

Ella came quickly inside.

'Don't look out, sir. And if 'e ask you anything you better say you don't know, sir. 'E come to see about Aucher. Aucher is a thief, you know, sir. And when they see a person like you, they always like to get them for witness, sir.'

57

Thomas Inniss was not there, so the policeman went away.

Aucher, that solemn-faced young man, was by fits and starts a well-known thief, of bicycles, goats, clothes, cigarettes, anything that he could put his hand on. Whenever he was not at 'the College', as Ella called the gaol, he worked with Mrs. Rouse.

'But why should she have such a person about her? Wouldn't he steal from her, too?'

'No, sir. 'E wouldn't steal from her, nor anybody here, sir. You know how she try with 'im to make 'im give it up, sir? She like 'im 'cause 'e don't talk too much and 'e can attend to the stove and bake the cakes well. But every now and then you hear 'e steal something. As soon as 'e didn't come to work for two or three days, Miss Atwell say she know something was up.'

'Very peculiar.'

'Yes, sir,' Ella laughed. 'Miss Atwell say that she talk to 'im and try to teach 'im, but no good. She say you can't train a common horse to win the Derby.'

'If you will excuse me, Mr. Haynes,' said Miss Atwell from next door (she was as sharp as a needle and missed nothing). 'It's no use even talkin' about 'im. 'E's a bitter black boy.'

Ella had been cooking in the kitchen at No. 2 for about a month, and during that time Aucher had given every satisfaction. Mrs. Rouse called the dull-witted but willing Wilhelmina four times to Aucher's once, and during the three following weeks she changed three boys, and all through the day she quarrelled with them. Aucher was caught after a week and sentenced to four weeks' hard labour and Mrs. Rouse was so worried about the boys and distracted by Benoit that Ella assisted her regularly, especially since, with the departure of the nurse, the scheme of getting Haynes as a boarder had faded out.

As the days passed the tension became more acute. For a time, although Mrs. Rouse and Benoit would quarrel in the night, not infrequently next morning they seemed to have made it up. But this could not last. Benoit's behaviour was too flagrant.

He now came regularly into Haynes's room for a few minutes before he took his lunch or round about dinner and, in fact, whenever he had time to spare. He seemed to avoid being with the others. By this time the relationship between the nurse and himself formed his sole topic of conversation with Haynes. He referred to her always as 'the white woman', often he talked so loudly that Haynes had to motion him to be quieter else Mrs. Rouse might hear.

'What if she hear?' he burst out one day. 'I ain't her husband, man. I am a free man to do what I like.'

One morning, opening the bathroom door suddenly, Haynes came face to face with Mrs. Rouse for the first time for a few days. There had been a fierce row the night before; she had collared Benoit and threatened to use a knife on him. When Haynes opened the bathroom door she was washing a tea cup at the sink, but she was looking into the distance and the water was running unheeded over her fingers and the cup.

'Good morning, Mrs. Rouse,' said Haynes uncertainly, unwilling to interrupt her and yet not wishing to pass without speaking.

She started and looked round at him.

'Good morning, Mr. Haynes.'

Their eyes met and held together for a few seconds. Perhaps it was because he knew of her difficulties and trials, but he seemed to read in her face all the pain and shame and weariness of the recent days. So they looked at each other without speech and Haynes, remembering his conversations with Benoit and all the laughing, suddenly felt ashamed of himself.

Mrs. Rouse's eyes filled with tears and Haynes felt as guilty as if it was he who was playing her false.

'Mr. Haynes,' she said, 'you sorry for me?'

'Yes, Mrs. Rouse,' said Haynes.

'Speak to Mr. Benoit for me, Mr. Haynes. He will respect what you say. You are young, but you are a gentleman and you have education. Perhaps he will listen to you where others fail. Do that for me, Mr. Haynes. God will bless you.'

Haynes could make no reply.

'All right, Mr. Haynes. Thank you for your sympathy. Don't let me detain you.'

In his conversations with Benoit, Haynes had always been careful not to express any opinions on the rupture in the domestic peace of No. 2. But moved by Mrs. Rouse's appeal, he decided after much anxious heart-searching to venture a word of remonstrance to Benoit when he saw a suitable opening. It would be the first time in his life that he had even voluntarily interfered in anybody's private affairs.

Very carefully he thought over what he could say without giving offence, and at last being satisfied waited a suitable opportunity. One afternoon Benoit was on his usual topic and at a pause in the conversation Haynes produced a bottle of rum and while pouring out some said jocularly:

'You know I am a man myself and we all dislike women to boss us, but you are doing this thing too openly and regularly, Benoit. Go sometimes, but go on the sly and stay home a little more.'

'Don't go so often? No, man. Things looking too good down there . . . and I have to go.'

'Have to go?'

'Twice a day. If I don't go twice that woman will kill me. You don't know her.'

His face was serious while he spoke and for a moment after. So serious that Haynes did not dare go any further. Benoit did not only remain flagrantly unfaithful. Some devil in him made him discuss the liaison openly, even in its most intimate details, not only with Haynes, but with everybody. If Maisie happened to say that she had taken a walk the evening before, he was quick to say that he and 'his girl' were on the seawall on such and such a night, or that the next night they were going for a long drive in the tramcar. The number and nature of his embraces, the nurse's reactions, all these he would dilate upon with very slight provocation. He seemed absolutely callous of the effect of all this on Mrs. Rouse. Most of his remarks she neglected, but once or twice she let drive at him. Philomen and Ella pacified her, however, when she burst out. Once Benoit left the kitchen and came into Haynes's room, his hands coated with dough.

'Let her loose off some steam,' he said. 'I don't care.'

But that was not true. Sometimes when he came into the room

he did not speak for long periods and sat deeply preoccupied and worried. On occasions he would mutter to himself. And it was always after he seemed more than usually bothered that when he returned to the kitchen he did his worst. 'After all, I ain't married to her. She not my wife. I am a free man.' He said this over and over again.

One Sunday night Mrs. Rouse collapsed. Benoit had left at about nine in the morning, and when Haynes went out shortly after eight in the evening he had not yet returned. Two hours later, when Haynes reached the house he heard a commotion in the little drawing-room. Somebody seemed to be ill. He listened and became certain. Before going to enquire he hesitated. Ella had been hinting that unless he was very careful he would soon be drawn in some way or other into the confusion which raged in the house. He listened again and distinctly heard groans and sighs. It was Mrs. Rouse. He decided to go in. He went round to the back, knocked at the door which was ajar and had to knock again and wait before anybody came. The blind between the dining-room and drawing-room was closed so that he could not see, but there were at least a dozen people in the room.

Maisie came to the door wearing a Sunday dress and when she saw him she began to preen herself.

'Come in, Mr. Haynes. Mrs. Rouse sick. She went out and she faint away in the road.'

'Did she hurt herself?'

'No, Mr. Haynes. Come right in, Mr. Haynes.'

There were some fifteen people in the room, all women, a few of whom he recognized as neighbours. There was a general chorus of 'Good evening, Mr. Haynes,' 'Good evening, Mr. Haynes,' and one or two people bent over a sofa and said:

'Come, hold up. Here is Mr. Haynes to see you. Come, my dear. Hold up and talk to Mr. Haynes.'

They made way for him and Haynes, who had only intended an enquiry, had perforce to go forward. Mrs. Rouse lay on the sofa, her face tear-stained, her vast bosom heaving like a sea. Every few seconds she shuddered and moaned. Miss Atwell knelt on the floor at her head with smelling salts and a wet towel. Everybody was saying 'Keep back,' 'Give her air,' but at any sound she made half of them crowded nearer.

Haynes's approach was hailed as if he was the doctor. Miss Atwell exhorted Mrs. Rouse to speak to him. Mrs. Rouse did not open her eyes, but with a sweeping gesture stretched out a hand which Haynes held and felt its fingers close on his.

'Mr. Haynes,' she said. 'You come to see me? You sorry for me? I know a gentleman like you will be sorry for me. Mr. Benoit living with Nurse Jackson. He leave here this morning at eight. He said he was coming back for lunch and I ain't see him up to now. Mr. Haynes, you live here and you see and know everything. He leave in the afternoon at one, he come back at five. He go again at seven, he come back at eleven. One day the rain fall and he didn't go in the afternoon and that night he never come back till three. Mr. Haynes, tell me, do you think that is right?'

'I have told him myself that he isn't behaving well.'

'Mr. Haynes, everybody knows that but he.'

She gave a convulsive wail, the grip on his hand tightened, and she almost shouted: 'Better God take me than leave me to bear this injustice,' then, more quietly but with infinite feeling: 'Lord, my burden is heavier than I can bear.'

Her passion subsided, but she still held fast to Haynes's hand.

'Don't mind, love,' said Miss Atwell, passing the wet towel over her head.

'I must mind,' said Mrs. Rouse, and she shuddered and groaned.

Haynes looked at her lying on the sofa. Forty-five, fat and age-ing, weeping, fainting, in hysterics over the defection of her paramour, a hero of forty, who was in ardent pursuit, or rather possession, of a woman who had had so long a string of lovers and in such quick succession as to justify any title which one might choose to apply to her. And he, Haynes, held her by the hand and was in the thick of it. He was uncomfortable, and wished he was elsewhere. But it was life, he thought.

'What must I do? What must I do?' she wailed. 'Mr. Benoit is living with Nurse Jackson and I am deprived.'

'Come, darling,' said Miss Atwell. 'Don't mind that good-for-nothing. Men is all deceivers. Mr. Haynes, speak to her. Comfort her, Mr. Haynes.'

There was a rush forward. Mrs. Rouse held Haynes so tight that in the hot room with the bunch of women around him he began to sweat. He could not so much as turn his head. In the close atmosphere, the smell of bay rum and smelling salts, min-gled with the smell of cheap perfume and human flesh, was almost overpowering. His hand was becoming gradually numbed from Mrs. Rouse's strong and undiminished clasp. He felt that if he were a woman he would faint. He certainly would faint if this went on much longer.

Her eyes still closed, Mrs. Rouse began to speak again, her voice deep and vibrant like that of a tragic actress.

'The woman whom I succoured, the friend I saved, the one I gave my heart and hand. Look what she has done me.'

There was a general chorus of 'Yes. True. Indeed.'

'She who I helped in her distress, she cause me mine . . . I have nourished a viper in my bosom. She was nothing when I took her.'

'Don't mind that, love,' said Miss Atwell, 'Jesus do more for Judas and look what Judas do 'im. Put a crown of thorns on 'im and spit on 'im.'

Mrs. Rouse went off into another fit of hysterical weeping and moaning, and during the attentions which were showered upon her Haynes escaped. He retired to a far corner of the room and wiped his streaming face.

Maisie came up to him and told him what had happened. That morning Mrs. Rouse prepared Benoit's lunch early and waited for him from twelve o'clock. He never came. When it was eight o'clock she had given up all hope of seeing him, and sitting by the window she started to cry. Philomen came in and urged her to take a walk. She consented at last, Philomen practically dressing her, but they had not gone twenty yards in the street when Mrs. Rouse collapsed; she had not eaten anything since ten in the morning. A policeman and a friendly passer-by had helped Philomen to get her home, and when they put her on the sofa she started to bewail and lament. All through Maisie's story blame was freely showered on Philomen, though no reason was given.

'Where is Philomen?' he asked.

'She! She somewhere outside.'

Haynes made his excuses, wished Mrs. Rouse better and went out. The cool night air of the yard was an inexpressible relief. But, still more inexpressible was the relief at having got away from playing leading man to all those women. And yet he had a feeling of exhilaration as if he had just come triumphantly through some great and exciting ordeal.

As soon as he opened his window he heard a faint sound of sobbing and could dimly make out a form leaning against the trunk of the mango tree – Philomen.

'Mr. Haynes? Is that you, Mr. Haynes? Come a little please, Mr. Haynes.'

Haynes went out to her.

'Mr. Haynes, how is Mrs. Rouse? They all blamin' me. They saying is my fault. I's not my fault. Whole day Mrs. Rouse there waitin' for Mr. Benoit. She was very distressed and by night she was in tears. I say I will take her for walk and talk to her a little bit and distract her mind. But I didn't know she was goin' to faint. I couldn't know she was goin' to faint. O God, Mr. Haynes, you will beg Mrs. Rouse pardon for me?'

She burst into a fit of wild sobbing.

'But of course Mrs. Rouse will pardon you. You haven't done anything.' They stood in the dark under the tree and Haynes began to feel dreadfully tired.

'Come along, Philomen,' he said. 'Come along. Come. I'll go in with you.'

A sudden footstep behind startled them. It was Benoit. 'It's only me, Haynes,' he said and laughed. 'I catch you fair, you fox. So is the coolie girl you like, eh?'

At the words Philomen became a different woman.

'Mr. Benoit, you must not say such things about Mr. Haynes.'

'You are quite wrong, Benoit,' said Haynes. 'Philomen was crying and—'

Maisie's voice came from nowhere.

'But, Mr. Haynes! What you explaining to the man? He not your father. Philomen, Mrs. Rouse calling you.'

'You want cooling down, you,' said Benoit, good-humouredly. 'I notice that since the other day.'

'Maybe. But you bet I not going to give you the job,' said Maisie and walked away.

'She growing nice,' said Benoit. 'Make your move quick, Haynes, or you'll be left. Boy, I was on a big time today. I reached the nurse at half-past eight this morning and I ain't put my foot outside till just now. Beef, pork and a three-pound chicken, pigeon peas and rice. Rum, vermouth and gin. She even had some nuts for me after breakfast. How this one here? She must be tearing brass, I expect. I'll see you tomorrow, Haynes. Cheerio.'

The next morning Haynes was awakened by Ella earlier than usual.

'I want some extra money, sir, to buy merinos and socks. And the black shoes, they want half-solin', sir. The rainy season.'

'Go ahead, Ella. Fix up everything. I'll give you some money tonight.'

She turned about the room.

'What is it, Ella?'

'I hear you was in the mix-up last night, sir.'

He pointed warningly next door.

67

'She not there, sir. I meet 'er goin' down the road. I's she who tell me, sir. She say you gave a lot of help, sir. She say from the time you speak to Mrs. Rouse she start to get better. You mixin' up with these people too much, sir. Murder or madness goin' to come out of this, sir. You better move, sir, and move quick. Mrs. Rouse tell Miss A. that she goin' to stop 'im goin' there, if even she have to put a knife in 'im. And if anything happen, your name sure to come up, sir, and there goin' to be a lot of trouble.'

'You think she will do anything to him, Ella?'

'I don't know, sir. But if I was you I wouldn't stay.'

'All right, Ella.'

Haynes felt her eyes on him. But she said nothing more, to his relief. He knew that Ella was right. He had been saying the same thing to himself in bed the night before. If anything did happen there would be a terrific scandal. And he might lose his job. If he did he could no longer pay the instalments on the mortgage, and his mother's house would go. Rarely did he think of the old life now. The present life was too intense. But the less he thought of his mother the more he was determined to keep his pledge to her about the house. If there was a scandal old Carritt might do anything. What was Mrs. Rouse to him or he to Mrs. Rouse? The wise thing would be to take Ella's advice and leave. And yet he felt that to leave the house would be an unbearable wrench.

Maisie stood at the door.

'Mr. Haynes, Ella gone to shop. I can do anything for you?'

She entered without waiting for an answer.

'Mr. Haynes, I heard what Mr. Benoit told you last night about me. Don't mind him, Mr. Haynes. He is a man with a dirty mind. Don't listen to anything he tell you about me.'

She sat down.

'And Ella want you to leave here. You don't want to leave us, Mr. Haynes?' She looked at him quizzingly with a touch of malice and yet with real affection.

'No, Maisie,' said Haynes.

She smiled, a friendly, intimate smile.

'I knew that, Mr. Haynes. None of us want you to go.'

In the silence that ensued a new aspect of Maisie, vaguely present for some time in the background of his mind, suddenly emerged clearly. She was a damned pretty girl, and would be very nice to sleep with.

Chapter Eleven

Next day Haynes, dreading being dragged into conversation and discussion by the egregious Miss Atwell, 'kept himself to himself', as the lady would have said. But after tea Benoit came to see him.

Benoit chewed at his nuts as usual (he couldn't eat while working in the kitchen, up to his arms in flour, so as soon as work was over he began). He looked tired. His cheeks were drawn and his eyes bloodshot as on the night after the nurse had left. But he was very cheerful.

'You have cigarettes?'

Haynes showed him the box and he lit up. He looked at Haynes's bed covered with books and magazines.

'I thought you was on a time with the coolie,' he said, 'but I find out I was wrong. But you are a funny fellow. You only reading books the whole day. A young man like you. Man, when I was your age, by the time one was out another was in. You have a nice little batchie here where girls can pass through the back without nobody seeing them. What's wrong? You sick?'

Haynes said nothing was wrong with him.

'You don't go after girls?'

'Of course,' Haynes lied bravely, 'but not very much.'

'These books you always reading,' he picked up one and looked at the title. 'About science! Ah! You read about science. Then you have books by de Laurence?'

This de Laurence was an American writer on magic and psychic science, whose books had some vogue in the islands.

'No,' said Haynes. 'It isn't that sort of science. That book is about birds and animals and electricity and so on.'

Benoit put it back on the bed.

'A man with your intelligence, if you read books on science you would do well. See now, about two o'clock, all the spirits of the air passing up and down. And if you know what to do you can compel them and make them do what you like.'

Haynes stared at him. Was the man mad?

'How can you control them?' he asked.

But Benoit, usually so outspoken, laughed uneasily. 'Not today. Another time. I hear you was in charge last night, nursing the sick.'

He chuckled low down in his throat.

'No, I just went in to see what had happened.'

'She is a stupid woman. She only making things worse for herself . . . Let her go on . . .'

'What will you do? Marry the nurse?'

Benoit guffawed. 'Marry the nurse? Not me. Take it from an experienced man. Never marry a nurse. As soon as a sick man getting better the first woman he want to live with is his nurse.

She right on the spot, you see. And that one in particular, she'll do anything, man. I living with her, but I know what she is . . . But this one, I can't understand her, she so stupid. I am still here, helping with the cake; I checking the book; I doing everything as before. All men go out. What she making such a fool of herself for?'

'She is jealous,' said Haynes, student of human nature. 'She wants you for herself alone. And you treat her very badly, Benoit. If you went down once or twice a week to the nurse. In the night— But going as you do makes her ashamed. And you neglect her.'

'Neglect her? I don't neglect her, man. Don't think so. I don't neglect any woman belonging to me, man.'

'Don't go so often and so openly.'

'I not going to give up the other one. Rouse can do what she like.'

He didn't go that afternoon: at five o'clock he checked the book, but after supper he was off again.

On the Tuesday, during lunch, the smothered fires blazed. Mrs. Rouse shrieked at him to take his things and leave the damn house and go. Either he was to stay with the nurse altogether or leave off going there. Benoit said that she could do what she liked, he was going to do as he pleased. Mrs. Rouse seemed to go mad.

'You leave me, a decent woman like me, for a whore, a woman who used to carry on her whoring in this very house. You dirty dog!' Her voice cracked with the strain she had put on it and with passion.

Somehow Miss Atwell, whose affairs had been settled now and

was out again, had been drawn, or entered of her own accord, into the quarrel, under the pretext of pacifying Mrs. Rouse. From the hour she came out of her confinement, she took Mrs. Rouse's side and fought for her valiantly.

'If Jesus Christ came down and ask me, I not giving up the nurse,' said Benoit.

Miss Atwell professed great respect for religion and had a wide if inaccurate knowledge of Biblical story and aphorism.

'Mrs. Rouse, I has to leave you,' she said in a grave important voice. 'I has to leave you. I can't put up with this ... this ... blasphemous rebel.'

Maisie's mocking laughter underscored the gibe.

'Who ask you to put up with me, you dried up old broomstick? Why don't you shut your mouth? You have a man and weeks pass you don't see him. So what have you to quarrel about?'

Maisie laughed again.

Miss Atwell's door slammed. But she continued the quarrel from inside her fortress.

'Let me keep far from you, man,' she said. 'God goin' to strike you down. 'Cause you see me as I am here you think I am your sex. In my day, you think I would have looked at anything like you? You has had no upbringin'. I has been brought up – good education and religious trainin' in my Sunday school. I know what's what. I know what's respect. If Jesus Christ come down! When God take a turn in your skin you goin' to know something. Dragging the name of the Saviour into your dirty goings-on. I am a sinner, but I know my place. Go on, Mr. Benoit, go on rejoicin' in you' evil deeds. You' Calvary is awaitin' you.'

Gradually the yard grew quiet. The quarrel seemed over. Miss Atwell remained in her room.

Haynes came outside to start for the office, but before he left the yard Maisie called to him.

'You see anything strange in the room this morning?'

'Anything strange? Like what?'

'Whole morning a dried-up old broomstick was in the yard and now I looking for it everywhere and I can't find it.'

Haynes rolled his bicycle away as quickly as he could, but before he reached the street he could hear Mrs. Rouse thumping Maisie and Maisie swearing that she hadn't meant anything.

Chapter Twelve

That outbreak took place on Tuesday morning. Tuesday afternoon and Tuesday night Benoit went away as usual, Wednesday afternoon and again Wednesday night. It was not Haynes's business at all, but he felt irritated with the man. After all he still lived at No. 2, and it would cost him nothing to exercise a little restraint. Every time, as soon as he left, the talk broke out in the yard. 'But you ever see a thing like this!' 'The man ain't got no shame.' 'If was me I'd throw all his clothes in the canal.'

On Thursday morning he did not turn out to work. At seven o'clock he came into Haynes's room dressed in his new brown suit and asked Haynes to give him a recommendation.

'A recommendation!'

'Yes, a recommendation. I am going to look for a job. Down at the West Indies Trading Company. The manager know the nurse. She attend to his wife and they like her – they make her a nice present – and she ask him about a job for me.'

Haynes said no: the idea of his giving a recommendation was

absurd. He was a person of no consequence and could not give any recommendation.

'But, Haynes, man, don't let me down. All you have to say is that I am your landlord, and you know me to be trustworthy and so on. You know how to wield the pen, man.'

'But I have no right—'

'Nonsense, man. Here is the pen. Here is a piece of paper. This is to certify . . . Come on, Haynes. It costs you nothing. Oblige a friend.'

Haynes sat down and wrote.

'Read it,' he said, giving it to Benoit.

'No need to read it,' said Benoit, folding the sheet of notepaper and taking up an envelope from the table. 'Yes, man. I am going down. The nurse told me that a man of my appearance have no right making cakes. She says she will help me to get a good job. Right-o, Haynes.'

He left, but he came back quickly.

'This is between us, eh!' he said, and winked knowingly.

'As you say,' said Haynes.

'Honour bright?'

'You can depend on me.'

Benoit had not gone five minutes when there was a knock at the door. Mrs. Rouse, thought Haynes, and it was.

'Come in, madam,' he said, and offered her a chair.

'No, Mr. Haynes. I am not for long.'

The difference between her appearance today and before when she had led Haynes into that very room made him realize more than imagination could what she had gone through. Then she was a stout housewife, slightly care-worn, but cheerful, hopeful of the future if even things were not as bright as she wished. Today she was a defeated woman – in her eyes a hunted look which she no longer took the trouble to disguise, sustained merely by the necessity to keep the wheels of her business going. And Haynes felt deeply sorry for her; and felt, too, that by talking and laughing with Benoit he was doing Mrs. Rouse a great wrong; and was aware that it was stupid of him to feel that way; but could never entirely rid himself of the feeling whenever he stood face to face with Mrs. Rouse. He waited for her to speak.

'You must excuse me interrupting you, Mr. Haynes,' she began and her voice was thin and quavering, 'but I hope Mr. Benoit has not been worrying you about anything.'

'No, Mrs. Rouse, he hasn't worried me at all.'

'I saw him with an envelope. I hope you didn't endorse any promissory note for him.'

'No, Mrs. Rouse. It wasn't that.'

'Never do anything like that for him, Mr. Haynes. He is not a man to trust.' She looked searchingly at Haynes. 'He didn't ask you to lend him money?'

'No, Mrs. Rouse, he didn't . . . He didn't, really.'

'All right, Mr. Haynes. I believe you. But I wonder what that man is up to now? God have mercy on me.'

'It is nothing important, Mrs. Rouse,' said Haynes.

'What was it, Mr. Haynes? I want to know. Tell me, Mr. Haynes. Don't mind any promises you made to him. I am the woman who, with all my troubles, have to bear the burden of this house.'

'He asked me for a recommendation. He said he was going to look for a job.'

'Going to look for a job! Today he going to look for a job. Seventeen years we have been together, he never went to look for work, and today—' She stopped short.

There was an awkward pause.

She broke it.

'Thank you for telling me, Mr. Haynes. And, Mr. Haynes, since the other day I was to tell you. Since you come here to live there is only noise and quarrelling in the place. That woman has broken up my house. I put up with her long enough. And now when I finish with her the man start. I hope all this don't disturb you too much. This isn't a house like that, Mr. Haynes . . . And all the noise I made the other morning, and all the bad words—'

'It's quite all right, Mrs. Rouse. I know how worried you must be. I am sure that everything will turn out well in the end.'

'I heard them saying that you wanted to leave.'

'Not at all, Mrs. Rouse. I am quite comfortable here.'

She looked brighter.

'We have to trust in God, Mr. Haynes.'

'Yes, Mrs. Rouse,' answered devoutly that confirmed heretic, and hurried off to work.

Haynes took his meals in town that day, for Ella was not well and he had told her to stay at home. Ella suffered from bronchitis, which was not a thing to play with when the rainy season is on. It was after ten when Haynes returned, but Maisie was standing by the gate talking to a young man – a rather unusual thing at that hour: Mrs. Rouse had generally sent a peremptory message to her long before that. The energetic and hard-worked Philomen was still moving about in the kitchen. Philomen hadn't spoken to Haynes since that night, but the warmth of her smile and her greetings were more radiant than ever. She was a simple soul with a golden disposition. Haynes went quickly to his room, locked the door and getting into bed blew out the light: he did not feel inclined for any talking, and Philomen's 'Good night, Mr. Haynes,' and the way she had come to the kitchen door had indicated clearly that she was willing.

He dropped off to sleep.

He was deep in his dreams when he was awakened by a loud screaming and yelling – Philomen's voice, and an insistent shouting of 'Mr. Haynes!' 'Murder!' 'Mr. Haynes!' and again 'Murder!' He sat up in bed and listened. He distinguished another voice – Benoit's – but could not make out what he was saying. The voices were quite near. In the yard. By Mrs. Rouse's doorstep. Philomen had ceased to call, but she still screamed. With Ella's warning in his mind, Haynes unlocked his door and looked out. There was no moon, but the night was bright with starlight, and at the bottom of the doorstep there was an arresting group. Mrs. Rouse sat on the ground limp and supported in Philomen's arms. Maisie stood near looking rather detached and leaning against the same young man she had been speaking to at the gate. On the bottom step stood Benoit, dusting his shoulder with one hand while in the other he held the long kitchen knife. Haynes's first thought was that Mrs. Rouse had been murdered and his heart gave a great leap.

'Shut your damn mouth,' said Benoit to Philomen. 'What the hell you making all that row for?'

'This is the end of it, though,' he continued, and stamped into the house.

Haynes went out to Philomen's assistance and found to his relief that Mrs. Rouse had only fainted. Philomen began to explain what had happened, but Haynes cut her short.

'Come, let us get her in.' Mrs. Rouse showed no signs of coming to and Haynes was a boy scout of many badges. 'Come on, Maisie. And you, sir, please help.'

Meanwhile from inside came two or three resounding cracks as of some heavy article of furniture being smashed to pieces. They lifted Mrs. Rouse in. She may have lost weight during the last few weeks but was still uncommonly heavy. They got her into the drawing-room and placed her on the very sofa on which she had lain the Sunday night. Then Miss Atwell appeared, as timely as if she was a character in a play, for Philomen could hardly see to do anything, being blinded by the streams of tears which flowed down her face.

'Come, Miss Atwell,' said Haynes. 'Come quickly.' He was frightened, for Mrs. Rouse lay stiff and quiet. He recalled horrifying instances of people who had fainted and never recovered. And if anything happened he was in it to the neck.

'What's all this?' said Miss Atwell. 'I went to see Ella—'

The bedroom door opened. Benoit came out with a bundle of clothes on his arm and two boxes. He went to the front door, wrenched it open with a powerful jerk and was gone without a look or word to anybody. Maisie ran to the door and followed him down the steps.

'What the—' began Miss Atwell.

'Don't mind that,' said Haynes anxiously. 'See about Mrs. Rouse.'

Miss Atwell began to open Mrs. Rouse's clothes and the modest Haynes betook himself to the dining-room and stood by the door ready to go for the doctor at the slightest word. Maisie had got rid of her cavalier and came and stood by Haynes. But Haynes was not concerned with Maisie, nor worried that she had been all those hours outside with the young man, a fact which in recent days would have given him some concern. He was thinking of himself in the witness-box explaining how he had held Mrs. Rouse's hand and Miss Atwell had told him to comfort her. But in five minutes Mrs. Rouse had come to herself. They lifted her into her bedroom, which was in disorder, the whole front of a big wardrobe being broken into and clothes scattered all over the floor. They put her on the bed and Haynes went back into his room at once. It was only the next morning he learnt how near No. 2 had been to a nasty tragedy.

Mrs. Rouse, goaded to the point of desperation, had made up her mind to kill Benoit. She told Maisie and Philomen that they were not to come into the house until Benoit returned, and Maisie had settled herself unconcernedly by the gate, knowing that she could pass the time away if Mrs. Rouse never opened till morning. Philomen, however, was uneasy, and fiddled about in the kitchen, oppressed with a vague premonition that Mrs. Rouse intended to do something desperate. That her mistress would kill herself was the thought uppermost in her mind. She had wanted to speak to Haynes about it. 'But the way you passed and locked the door frightened me off' – a stab into Haynes's sensitive conscience. Meanwhile, Mrs. Rouse dressed herself and sat by the back door with her hat, her little handbag and the kitchen knife on the table near to her; and her Prayer Book in her hand. As he opened the door she would stab him and then give herself up at the police station. The place was almost in darkness, the only light being the light of the chapelle in her bedroom and the small candle by which she was reading. From eight o'clock she sat waiting, and it was after twelve when Benoit came. He did not see Maisie, for she and her young man had wandered down the alley. Faithful Philomen, worn out by her anxieties and the labours of the day, had fallen asleep in the kitchen, her head on the dresser. When Mrs. Rouse heard Benoit's footsteps she rose, gripping the knife. He opened the door and she raised the weapon to 'stab him to his black heart'. But, poor distracted woman, she knew little of how to stab anybody.

'Take this, McCarthy Benoit,' she said, but McCarthy Benoit took nothing. Surprised though he was, he caught her raised arm. They struggled for two or three seconds, and then both pitched down the steps. How no bones were broken was a mystery. Mrs. Rouse remembered nothing else until she came to herself on the sofa.

Chapter Thirteen

That night Haynes decided to move as soon as Ella could find a room. He would be sorry to go, but when it came to knives and stabbing, however much his leaving would hurt Mrs. Rouse, he would have to go elsewhere.

Miss Atwell knocked at his door next morning and asked him about his tea.

'Ella's parting words to me, Mr. Haynes, was to see that you had everything you want. She was more worried about you than her sickness. But, Mr. Haynes, did you ever see such a thing as last night?' She seated herself without being invited and it was twenty minutes by his clock before Haynes could finally shut her off.

For tea he gave her a shilling, from which she brought back change, accounting minutely. She came in herself and laid the table, and wanted to wait on Haynes all through it, despite his protestations that he could manage by himself. He was able to stave off conversation only by pretending while he ate to be busy with a book, on the pages of which he made pencil notes even while he chewed. Mrs. Rouse was too ill to come out to work and

Miss Atwell was in charge in the kitchen; and all through the morning she was up and down, in and out, giving orders, assisting here, fixing there; though Maisie said that Philomen did the bulk of the work. This, however, might have been prejudice. Haynes forestalled her offer to prepare his lunch, saying that he had business in town and would lunch there.

On his return he heard that Mrs. Rouse had asked for him and he felt that it was his duty to pay her a visit. He spoke to Maisie, who went in first, and then came back to say that he could come.

The bedroom was quite tidy now, except for the wardrobe, which, with its gaping mouth, was a significant reminder of last night's passions and violence.

Maisie stood at the head of the bed. Miss Atwell, who received him, put him to sit down on a rocking chair and seated herself near Mrs. Rouse's feet. Mrs. Rouse herself lay on the bed covered to her neck, her eyes red and swollen, her face puffed and distorted like one of her own pastries before it was baked.

'How are you, Mrs. Rouse?' Haynes greeted her, trying his best to sound cheerful. He was stirred more than he had expected at the sight of his landlady on the bed, so ill and ugly and forlorn she looked.

'I am so-so, Mr. Haynes,' she said weakly. She held out a hand, a hot, clammy hand. The touch of it on his brought vividly to his mind that Sunday night when she had lain on the sofa complaining of how she was deprived.

'I must thank you for last night, Mr. Haynes.'

'I did very little, Mrs. Rouse. No more than anybody else would have done.'

'Indeed!' butted in Miss Atwell. 'Was a blessed thing you was there. If you wasn't there I don't know what would have happened.'

'It's Miss Atwell who brought you round and took charge,' he said to Mrs. Rouse.

'No, Mr. Haynes,' quavered Mrs. Rouse, 'it was good of you to get up out of your sleep and come out and help to lift me in. You are a stranger to me. And you took pity on me in my great sorrow. God will bless you.

'Anyway, it's all over, Mr. Haynes,' she continued. 'He's gone and all this noise and quarrelling will stop. It's better so.'

'That's exactly what I say,' said Miss Atwell. 'What you thinks, Mr. Haynes?'

'Well, it is not for me to say,' Haynes replied. 'Perhaps he will get tired of the nurse and come back. Men are like that. Of course he will be – well, a bit scared for a while, but—'

'I's my fault, Mr. Haynes. I am not making excuses for him, but i's my fault. That woman been sticking at him to leave here and he wouldn't go. I can't tell you everything, but his mind wasn't to go. One or two nights he lie down here on this bed and he say that he hope he wouldn't get up in the morning. She was after him to leave me, and he didn't want to go. If you see how he was worried, Mr. Haynes! But after I nearly kill him, he not going to come back again.'

'You didn't nearly kill him, not by a long way. He was unharmed.'

'Yes, but he wouldn't come back now . . . Mr. Haynes, I don't know what was wrong with me. I believe I must have been mad. I can't even kill a fowl. Ask Miss Atwell. Maisie kills every fowl we cook. She hold them and wring them by the neck. And I can't understand myself, waiting there with that long kitchen knife to kill the man. How you expect him to come back after that?'

'I hear Ella is sick,' she said later. 'Mr. Haynes, you mustn't let that trouble you. All the disturbance and worry is over now. I feel that you are one of us now, Mr. Haynes. You have been so kind. Anything you want call one of the servants. They will see after you till Ella come back. Maisie!'

'Yes, Tante.'

'Help Mr. Haynes if he want anything. And I'll tell Philomen myself, Mr. Haynes.'

'All right, Tante,' said Maisie and gave Haynes a ravishing look.

Miss Atwell escorted him out and engaged him in conversation in Mrs. Rouse's dining-room where Maisie joined them.

'She is passing through a great trial,' said Miss Atwell.

'Great trial what!' barked Maisie. 'I tell you if I was living with a man and he wanted to go he could go . . . I would have sent that Benoit packing long ago.'

'You is young, child,' said Miss Atwell, 'and love, a woman's true love, have not touch your heart yet. You will know in time . . . What is hurting her so, Mr. Haynes, is that she drive him.'

'Who tell you that she drive him?' said Maisie, with greater heat. 'The man was going all the time. Since Monday, every time he went out he was wearing two merinoes, two shirts, two drawers and carrying clothes and socks and things in his pocket. I see him. It ain't she who drive him. She made him go last night. But he was carrying his clothes, and when he had them I know he was going to leave her.'

'That is true, Maisie?' said Miss Atwell. 'I never heard that.'

'What I going to lie for? And Mrs. Rouse know, too. I don't like to hear people talk too much darned nonsense.' She sucked her teeth in her annoyance.

Miss Atwell had been momentarily checked, but she was not a woman to be silent for long.

'You is young, Maisie, you is still young. Mr. Haynes, you can tell her what it is to lose the loved one.'

Haynes said he was sorry, but he couldn't.

'All old women stupid when it comes to a man, I notice that,' said Maisie. 'Perhaps if she did handle the man differently from early all this wouldn't have happened. Catch me crying after any man. I tell you!'

She walked off swaggering.

'Go on, young woman,' said Miss Atwell, watching her. 'Run your run. Your time will come. You understand patois, Mr. Haynes?'

'A little.'

'Well, Mr. Haynes. *Petit cochon dit: "Gros cochon pur chee bouche ou si long?" Gros cochon dit: "Tantot, tantot."* Which being translated is: Little pig, asked big pig: "Big pig, why is your mouth so long?" Said big pig: "Wait a little, my friend, wait a little."'

Haynes laughed and went into his room, where Maisie was waiting for him.

'Now I am in charge, Mr. Haynes, until Ella come back and I am going to start to fix away the place at once. Glad I am in charge, Mr. Haynes?'

87

'Yes,' said Haynes.

'I am glad, too.'

Haynes sat and watched her moving about the room. With Ella away and Maisie constantly and in official charge of him, he felt that his affair was approaching a crisis.

Chapter Fourteen

Benoit and the nurse; the nurse and Benoit; Benoit and the nurse and Sonny; No. 2 could find little else to talk about.

'The nurse pass her exam., you know, Mr. Haynes,' said Maisie, one Saturday at lunch. Haynes came home at twelve on Saturdays and did not go back. She had been sweeping the room and now sat in the easy-chair, with the broom in her hand.

'Mrs. Rouse is sorry, I suppose,' said Haynes.

'She is bitter; she only saying i's her own fault for letting Benoit help the nurse to pass.'

'But Benoit couldn't help the nurse to pass,' said Haynes, feigning innocence.

'Perhaps. But Benoit and Mrs. Rouse believe that, though.' She lowered her voice. 'Mr. Haynes, you don't know. Benoit say he know science. He tell the nurse what to do to pass. And they write the doctor's name on a piece of paper and they put it in the nurse's boots. So whenever she walk she mash him down. And when he was talking to her, that's when she used to fail, in the talking part, she press hard on him. And they make a little image of the doctor, and all through the day of the exam. Mrs. Rouse was bathing it. That was to keep him cool. Now you can imagine how that is hurting Mrs. Rouse. To think that all day she home here bathing the image to keep the doctor cool for the nurse and now for the nurse to take away the man from her.'

'But do you believe all that about keeping the doctor cool?'

'Me, Mr. Haynes! How you expect that? Mr. Benoit call me one day to give me a bath so that I could go and get a job somewhere. I wouldn't tell you what I tell him. If Mrs. Rouse knew what she was about she would have been bathing Benoit to keep him cool, not Dr. Golding. That Benoit—!'

'You think he will come back to Mrs. Rouse?'

'I don't know. He likes two things, women and his belly. And as you see the nurse pass the exam. and things moving good with her, if she feed him up high he wouldn't leave her. He might come up here, but only to fool Mrs. Rouse and get what he could from her and go again. Now what does this one want?' She went to the door. 'Philomen, I have told you before. I am in charge here. Mrs. Rouse told me to take charge. And Miss Atwell is doing the cooking. You have a lot of work to do. Leave Mr. Haynes to me.'

Philomen took no offence.

'Anything I can do for you, Mr. Haynes? I see the room is tidy. Maisie keeping everything up to mark.' She turned to Maisie. 'You happy, eh? You in full charge. Mr. Haynes, you are a lucky man. Maisie never work for anybody in this house as she is working for you.'

'All right. That's enough. Go on.'

At this even the good-tempered Philomen felt hurt. But she said nothing to Maisie. She smiled at Haynes and went away.

'But why do you speak to her like that, Maisie? I thought you and she got on very well.'

'Long ago. But not again. I don't know her any more. She is a servant. And she should know her place. What right she has bringing letters for you to read?'

'But she says you used to read them for her and you suddenly refused.'

'I don't want to talk about her, Mr. Haynes. Let's talk about something else.'

'When will Mrs. Rouse be out?'

'Tomorrow. But don't talk about Mrs. Rouse.'

'What shall we talk about?' Haynes said mechanically. There was a new note in Maisie's voice and an inviting tenderness in her manner. His heart beat violently.

'Anything. You know your friend, Mr. Boyce, Mr. Haynes. He is a bold man.'

'What makes you say that?'

'He met me last night by the gate. He pretended he was passing, but I had seen him walk up and down once or twice before. Well, the man don't know me. I only bring some water for him the other day. But he ask me to walk down the lane with him. I didn't want to go. But I said that he is your friend, so I went. The man hold me and try to kiss me.'

'What!' said Haynes. 'Straight away like that.'

'Straight away. He was fast. So I pull away from him. And you know what he told me, Mr. Haynes?'

'No.'

'He say, "Oh, I am sure Haynes making steady love to you and that is why you don't want me."'

'But how the devil could he tell you that?' said Haynes. 'That is not true.'

'That is what I tell him, Mr. Haynes. So he say he coming here tonight again.'

'Coming here tonight! What for? I don't want to see him.'

'Not in here! By the gate. To see me.'

'You like Boyce?' asked Haynes.

'I don't exactly like Boyce, but he is a nice young man. Only he so fresh. But he wouldn't get anything from me, Mr. Haynes. I know these young men well. They very fast, you know, but I can see after myself. You make love with them for a week. Then they start: "Maisie, you love me true?" I tell them, "Yes." I know what they coming with and I waiting for them. "True, true, true?" they say. "True, true, true," I say. Then they will ask you: "I want you to prove your love for me." As soon as they come with that: "To hell with you and your proving love." I tell them and I finish with them. I am not particular about Mr. Boyce, you know, Mr. Haynes, but I talk to him as he is your friend . . .

'God! What's this?'

She sprang to the door and Haynes followed her. As he stood over her the intimate scent of her hair was in his nostrils. He had never been so near a woman before. But he had no time to savour this new and exciting sensation. Philomen had come running into the yard as if someone was chasing her. She sat, almost in pieces, breathless, on the little bench.

'Mrs. Rouse,' she called, 'Mrs. Rouse, Mrs. Rouse.'

'What is it?' said Miss Atwell.

'Ma Rouse,' said Philomen. 'Call the madam.'

'Go into her if you want her,' said Maisie.

'What is it, Philomen?'

Mrs. Rouse in an old dressing-gown, her head tied with a big handkerchief, and leaning on a stick, stood by the dining-room door, for the first time in many days. She looked dreadfully ill and weak.

'Good afternoon, Mr. Haynes. Come, Philomen. What is wrong? You sick?'

'No, madam, I not sick, but Mr. Benoit and the nurse put up their name in the Registry to get married.'

Mrs. Rouse's stick which had been standing straight swung suddenly to one side and she collapsed where she stood.

Chapter Fifteen

Though there was not a single person in No. 2 or out of it who believed such a thing possible, yet true it was. The nurse had made up her mind to tie Benoit as tightly as possible. And once the fact was irrefutably established, the mind of everyone in the house was almost incessantly occupied with one topic – the approaching wedding. It pervaded the atmosphere. Scarcely a conversation began in which it did not crop up. They would sit in the kitchen after supper whispering low, and the subject of the evening was the wedding, as it was the subject of the morning and the afternoon, and of every hour of the day. Maisie talked to Haynes about it at mealtimes, Miss Atwell whenever she could catch him, and Philomen when she had a few minutes of leisure. Haynes avoided Mrs. Rouse and thought it best when they did speak to keep as far from the subject as possible. But none of the others thought so, at least they showed no reticence that he could notice; and Haynes soon learnt that Mrs. Rouse, far from resenting, welcomed discussions of this, the culminating indignity and injustice to which Benoit intended to subject her. Philomen would bring news which in her free style she broadcast as soon as she reached the yard.

'All you ain't hear this. Mr. Benoit was talkin' to Mr. Fung yesterday. 'E say that 'e leave because Mrs. Rouse wanted to cut 'im with a knife and 'e afraid for 'is life. 'E told Mr. Thompson's clerk so, too.'

On another occasion.

' 'E say that Mrs. Rouse cake business was goin' bad. She owes so much money and the nurse makin' money and a new woman always nicer than a' old one. And Mrs. Rouse been with him eighteen years, and that is enough for her. And that if she didn't bother 'im so 'e would have stayed here, but she take 'im for a little boy and want to keep control over 'im like a little boy. An' 'e going to marry the nurse because 'e help 'er to pass 'er exam. and she is goin' to work and 'e won't have to get up in the mornin' to make no cake.'

Day after day the items of news came to No. 2. How Benoit and the nurse were strolling on the seawall one evening arm-in-arm, how they had been seen driving in the car to St. Philip's and another night to Orange Vale. How the nurse had got a two days' job and how Benoit used to accompany her to the gate of the house where she worked and how they waved hands when they parted. All this and more that Haynes did not hear, though there was not much of which he was left ignorant.

Once, after Philomen (who picked up most of the news in town) had brought up and retailed some particularly interesting item to the family assembled in the kitchen, Mrs. Rouse some time after said, 'But, Philomen, you have not told Mr. Haynes? Go in and tell him.'

Details of the preparation for the wedding began to come through.

Sunday, the 6th, at the Church of the Rosary, Father O'Donoghue was to marry them, and Dr. Price, with whom the nurse usually worked, was to give her away. A Mrs. Robinson, a sempstress of some repute, was making the dress – white fugi trimmed with beads.

'But how do you know all this, Maisie?' Haynes asked.

'I know, Mr. Haynes. The girl she buy the dress from in the store tell people. And we know plenty who Mrs. Robinson does sew for. And when they go there she tell them about it.'

Benoit was not getting a new suit. At least, a new suit was not being got for him, for he had not one cent of his own to spend. He was getting married in his grey suit, but he had ordered a pair of patent leather shoes from a shop. They still lived in the nurse's single room in Lenegan Street. The nurse had sent her son to a friend's in Orange Vale. After the wedding they were going to spend a week at the seaside.

'For the honeymoon!' commented Miss Atwell in a tone like a note of exclamation, whereat Maisie laughed noisily. Only Mrs. Rouse did not smile. When they came back they would continue to live in Lenegan Street, but at the end of the month they would move into an apartment of two rooms elsewhere.

Of Mrs. Rouse Haynes saw little. She had submitted to her fate with outward resignation. Once she suddenly screamed out that she was going to collar him and ask him if he meant to leave her for that whore, but Philomen and Miss Atwell easily quieted her. (Maisie took no part in the pacification and confided to Haynes that she would like nothing better than to see Mrs. Rouse go to the nurse's room and the three of them have a grand fight.) But Mrs. Rouse was not giving him up without effort. Three times a day the scent of incense and asafœtida burning in her bedroom poisoned the atmosphere. She was using all the science she knew to win back Benoit. But Benoit was a man of science too.

'Science *versus* science,' said Maisie, and derided Mrs. Rouse and Benoit and their traffic with the occult.

'Be careful, Maisie,' said Haynes. 'Mrs. Rouse may hear you.'

'And if she hear! Mr. Haynes, I am ready for her. She can't do anything to me.'

In addition to her own troubles Mrs. Rouse now had to deal with a Maisie fast becoming uncontrollable. As Miss Atwell put it, 'From the day the man leave the house, she take womanhood on her account.'

When it was not one thing it was another. Very often Maisie was wrong. But not always. Like most persons who are on the look out for offence, Mrs. Rouse frequently saw misdemeanour or provocation where there was none. The trouble for any arbitrator was to be able to distinguish. There was the episode of the beef.

One Monday afternoon there was a hue and cry about some beef which had been left over from Sunday. It had disappeared.

'This is not the first time,' said the exasperated Mrs. Rouse; 'somebody always meddling with it, but this time they take nearly all.'

'It isn't me,' said Maisie, emphatically. 'I ain't touch any.'

'All right. I'll wait till Philomen come and then I'll ask her. I am going to find out who it is today.'

Half an hour after Philomen came up. Mrs. Rouse met her at the kitchen door.

'Philomen!'

Philomen was scared at once. She almost dropped the basket.

'Yes, Mrs. Rouse.'

'You touch the beef I leave in the dish last night?'

'Me, Mrs. Rouse! O God! Since I workin' with you, you ever—?'

'I don't want you to tell me all that. You touch it or you didn't touch it?'

'But see my cross here today!'

'Answer yes or no. You touch it or you didn't touch it?'

'I didn't touch it, Mrs. Rouse. You know I didn't touch it.'

'That's all I wanted to hear from you.'

She turned to Maisie.

'Then it's you, you wretch! You eating me out. You don't do anything in this place, and the little piece of beef I have for people to eat you steal it.'

'But I tell you I didn't steal it. I know nothing about it. She say she didn't take it. I say I didn't take it. She is the servant and you believe her.'

Haynes knew how this would end. It meant Mrs. Rouse abusing Maisie, Maisie giving her back and a quarrel which one day might end in violence. Miss Atwell was not there. Mrs. Hart, one of the boarders, observed the scene contemplatively from the dining-room doorstep. Quite instinctively he felt it his duty to make peace, as Miss Atwell would have done if she had been there. He had a short but sharp battle with himself. Hitherto

98

whatever part he had taken in the upheavals at No. 2 had been inadvertent and, in fact, against his will. Should he go out or not? His old timidity was still strong upon him, but he knew the respect with which they listened to anything he said. After all, why shouldn't he? He went to the door.

'Mrs. Rouse, don't worry about it. I know it is vexing. But you'll only get into a temper with Maisie and you'll be unable to do your work.'

Before Mrs. Rouse could answer Maisie broke out:

'Yes, everybody is against me. Hear what Mr. Haynes is saying now! Everybody prefer to believe the servant instead of me. I ain't take any beef.' Her voice was shrill and tearful. 'I ain't take any beef, I say. Give me my clothes, let me go from this house. Better I die than to go on living here.'

She leant her head against the mango tree and sobbed from deep down in her chest. The whole yard stood still and listened to her. Haynes overcame the temptation to retire into his room. He could not leave things like that.

'Well, you see, Mrs. Rouse,' he said, 'not to say I think Philomen has taken it; but perhaps Maisie hasn't taken it either. Of course,' he continued hurrying on, 'it's very mysterious, but you must give Maisie a chance. I don't like to hear those quarrels between you and her.'

'I am sorry I disturb you, Mr. Haynes.'

'No, no, Mrs. Rouse, it isn't that. But Maisie is your only relation and I am sorry that you and she don't get on better. Give her a chance this time.'

'I don't want any chance,' said Maisie, wiping her eyes. 'Chance what! I say I didn't take the beef. What! I am any cat to go snatching stale beef out of a pot?'

'Treat the gentleman with more respect,' said Mrs. Rouse sharply to Maisie.

'All right, Mr. Haynes,' she continued in a calmer tone. 'Perhaps she didn't take it and I am judging her wrongfully.'

Maisie came into Haynes's room and sat down with her hands before her face.

'Now take care,' said Haynes. 'When you go out don't start that quarrel again.'

'No, I wouldn't. But,' she whispered to him, 'I took the beef, you know.'

'You took the beef?'

'Yes, I was hungry and I took it . . . But I say I didn't take it. The coolie girl say she didn't take it. Why she must believe the coolie girl instead of me?'

She would not listen to Haynes's remonstrances.

'I am Mrs. Rouse's niece. Why she always taking up for the coolie? Everything is only Philomen, Philomen, Philomen. If I and the girl have a little disagreement, Philomen always right, I always in the wrong. Philomen is a servant. She shouldn't have more privilege than me.'

'Don't speak so loudly, Maisie. You see, Mrs. Rouse says that Philomen helps her. And you don't give her much assistance.'

'But, Mr. Haynes, Philomen working. She must work. What I must help Mrs. Rouse for? For the scraps of food and clothes she give me?'

'Philomen works very hard. She is a good girl.'

'Good girl, she! Mr. Haynes, what you saying?' Maisie laughed shortly. 'All those clothes you see her putting on on a Sunday, I could get it if I want to get it as she get them. She is the worst little prostitute in Victoria.'

'Now, Maisie—'

'But I have to speak about it, Mr. Haynes. If I don't tell you you wouldn't know. All of you only holding up Philomen as if she is a model. I'm speaking the truth. That same Philomen you praising up so much she used to live with Mr. Mill, the druggist, and Bennett, the assistant. And when old Mills find out he sack Bennett. Two of them the same time. All these lawyers and solicitors and clerks, she pass from one to the other. A little before you come here whenever you see a motor-car draw up in the night was Philomen they come for. Everybody know her. Ask Mrs. Rouse. I's only that stupid Sugdeo who see her and his eye catch fire, and he as if he want to get married. I tell you. The nurse was the first one and she will be the next. Marriage! Jesus wept! Look what marriage coming to, my God!'

Chapter Sixteen

It was only on the very morning of the wedding that Haynes had any direct talk with Mrs. Rouse about it. First Maisie and then Miss Atwell left for the church, Maisie heartlessly excited and eager. Haynes had no work to do and stayed at home. He would have been glad to go himself, but he decided that his dignity did not allow it. Mrs. Rouse was waiting for him. As soon as he showed himself, she came to the kitchen door.

'Today is the great day, Mr. Haynes, Mr. Benoit's wedding morn. Ah, Mr. Haynes, that man is making a fool of himself. He does not know what he is doing. He is going to rue the day, the hour, the minute. And he nearly kill me too. My heart is like lead. He leave me to marry that woman. She is no better than a prostitute, Mr. Haynes. One of these days I will tell you some of my history, Mr. Haynes, and you will see how Mr. Benoit and the nurse have treated me . . . I went to Mother Superior and told her everything. And she console me. I will be able to go back to my Church now and live a straight life. Mother Superior told me everything is for the best, but it's hard, Mr. Haynes, it's hard.'

'You must keep courage,' Haynes said.

It was a wonder how any work was done that morning. It was Sunday, but nowadays No. 2 worked almost as hard on Sunday as on other days. Benoit's absence made a heavy gap. Philomen went up and down on her usual errands, leaving Mrs. Rouse at home. At every footstep she came to the kitchen door, looking anxiously. What desperate hopes of motor accidents, sudden illness, or even miraculous intervention must have flitted through her brain during the last hours. Some of her hair had escaped from its controlling pins and a stray lock waved about her forehead. Whenever she appeared at the kitchen door she was putting it back in its place. Once when Philomen came in she could restrain herself no longer.

'They ought to finish by now, Philomen. They ought to finish long time, now. Why Miss Atwell hasn't come yet? Something happen!'

'I don't know. Perhaps something prevent the wedding.'

'But nothing could happen, Philomen. What could happen? But why Miss Atwell haven't come yet? She say as soon as they finish she was coming back. Go and see the time.'

It was a quarter past ten. The wedding had been fixed for nine.

A few tense minutes passed. Not a word in the kitchen from either of them, only the sounds of pots and pans, and the swish of water and squelching of clothes from Wilhelmina washing at the sink. Haynes tried to read but could not. He had a feeling that something was going to happen to prevent the wedding. The idea was absurd, but he could not rid himself of it.

The clock had just struck eleven when there was a cry in the yard.

'Ma Rouse!' It was Miss Atwell.

Mrs. Rouse came out into the yard followed by Philomen and Bruce, the latest yard boy, a little good-for-nothing who had started to work on the Sunday previous, and was sure to be dismissed that very night.

'What happen, Miss A.?' said Philomen.

Miss Atwell, slightly out of breath, for she had been walking fast and fanning herself from the heat, was nevertheless happy, for she held the centre of the stage.

'Well, it's all over, Ma Rouse,' she announced. 'Nurse Jackson is now Mrs. Benoit. The happy couple was made man and wife at nine this morning at the Church of the Rosary, Father O'Donoghue officiatin'.'

'Mr. Haynes!' This was Miss Atwell. Haynes showed his head at the door. 'You doesn't want to hear about the wedding?'

They all were looking up at him.

'Come and hear, Mr. Haynes,' said Mrs. Rouse in a thin voice.

'I can hear from here,' Haynes replied, coming down to the second step.

Miss Atwell began. 'The church was full o' people. A lot of idlers. I suppose they had come to see the Jezebel married at last – 'cause everybody know what she is, you know, Mr. Haynes. And people was only whisperin' about the way the snake come into you' house and take the man away. There was a strange woman next to me and we was talkin' about it all the time. Then everybody begin to say "She is comin'," and she walk up the church with Dr. Price – I don't know how 'e find hisself in that.' Miss Atwell fanned herself a little.

'The bride was in white with a lot of beads,' she continued, 'but although the cloth was expensive she didn't look well.' Miss Atwell shut her eyes, shook her head and repeated, giving emphasis to each word: 'She didn't look well. And one foolish little hat on 'er head, and as for he, in the old grey suit. I look to see what kind o' shoes 'e had on, if was new ones in truth, but where I was sittin' I couldn't see. Then they ring the bell little bit when they was goin' away, but the whole thing was tame, tame, tame. You could see was a pick-up wedding. The man did look too shame. Well, Mrs. Rouse, to tell you the truth, it did look to me as if 'e just wakin' up out of a dream. I sorry for 'im, Mr. Haynes. When 'e realize, when 'e realize 'is mistake, it will be too late. Man ties the marriage rope, but only God can unloose it. Truly when I look at 'im I could see they fix 'im up.'

'How do you mean fix him up?'

'What? You a Creole and don't know these things? Mr. Haynes, you are a young man and should take my words to heart. You has to be careful what you eats and where you eats it. If you is visitin' a house and makes you'self very familiar in the place, and then doesn't show marriage intentions, they puts a little thing in you' food, and I tell you, you never gets away. Whatever was you' previous intentions you finds you'self married. And is so the nurse catch Mr. Benoit, I'll bet my bottom dollar.'

'Tell Mr. Haynes you' dream, Ma Rouse,' said Philomen.

'I didn't tell you, Mr. Haynes?' said Mrs. Rouse. 'One night a few days after he leave I dream, and he appear to me in the dream and he say, "Alice, don't vex with me. I's not my fault. She catch me in fish."'

There was a long pause. None of them had anything to say, only looked at Mrs. Rouse. Then Miss Atwell spoke:

'Don't mind, Ma Rouse. In God we trus'.'

' "In God we trus', but in man we bus' ". All you still talking about that worthless Benoit,' said Maisie, coming round the other side of the house. 'Miss A., how you reach so quick?' She sat down on the little bench.

'Lord, the sun is hot! Mr. Haynes, if I had seen you this morning I must have asked you for a tram-ticket. But I don't like to wake you on a Sunday morning. Oh, but, Mr. Haynes, the nurse had a sweet little wedding. She wait long time for it, but I tell you it was worth the waiting.'

There was an indescribable ejaculation from Miss Atwell. Maisie continued:

'The dress, gosh! The fugi fit like if it grow on her. Mrs. Robinson is a class sempstress. You know how the nurse thin. Well, she make it a little full; silver shoes, white silk stockings and a little georgette hat. Everybody agree they never see the nurse looking so well. She came in with the doctor, stepping high, and you know how she stylish already, and she had the glasses fix on her bosom, so aristo, and when the priest start she unfix it and put it on her nose, and she hold up her head in style.'

The look of strained attention was gone from Mrs. Rouse's face. She stood erect, her head thrown back, disbelief in every line of her attitude. But Maisie continued to direct her remarks to Haynes.

'Mr. Benoit look good, too, Mr. Haynes. He didn't have a new suit. But the grey suit press, you know – razor crease – and he had a silver-grey shirt and collar to match, and the nurse brooch below the tie and the patent shoes. And one stylish trim. And the moustache trim, too. And when he was coming down, after the wedding, his face was serious. But I was waiting for him, you know. I was at the end of a seat and when they pass the people began to follow behind them. So I walk down quick and I pull him and I say, "Pappy!" and he look round. I tell him: "I's so you do it, then?" He laugh and he was going to say something and the nurse look round and see me and pull him. And then they went in the car. And that is the way my story end.'

'Your story in truth, you little devil,' snarled Mrs. Rouse. 'I don't believe you, you confounded liar!'

'Don't believe me,' said Maisie, jumping up and taking off her hat. 'Miss Atwell was there. Ask her.'

But Miss Atwell declined.

'Ask me nothing. I wishes to get into no contention with you, young woman.'

'To besides, I went to see the wedding for myself,' said Maisie. 'And what I see, I see. I ain't no newspaper.'

However much the point of view might cause the commentators to disagree, the wedding was an accomplished fact. Mrs. Rouse and the servants went quietly back to work, while Miss Atwell went into her room. But after ten minutes Mrs. Rouse said: 'Philomen, my child, carry on for me. Here is my purse. You know all what to do.'

Philomen came to the kitchen door and watched her as, eyes on the ground, she walked slowly up the steps and into the house. She went into her bedroom and the yard did not see her again that day.

Chapter Seventeen

'Mr. Haynes, is that you?'

'Yes, Mrs. Rouse.'

'I have been waiting for you, Mr. Haynes. I want to see you for a few minutes. I suppose you must be hungry. It's that girl Maisie. She is going to come to you with a long story about Philomen. But don't believe her. She is a terrible liar.'

It must be something serious, for Mrs. Rouse always waited until after supper before coming to talk to him.

'Some quarrel about your comb,' Mrs. Rouse explained. 'Maisie says that Philomen was using your comb and brush and she had no right to. Philomen say she wasn't using it, she was moving it from the table to the shelf. I don't know the right of it. But if even Philomen was using the comb that was no reason why Maisie should go on as she go on. She called Philomen so much coolie dog, so much lousy head, ask her what she know about comb and brush in the village where she come from. Maisie have no right to behave like that, Mr. Haynes. She tell her, too, that she is a servant, that if she want to use the comb and brush she could use it because you and she are friends, but Philomen should know her place. And a lot of things. Well, Philomen answer her and they had a big row in the yard. And Philomen cry. Now Maisie say as soon as you come she is coming to tell you about it, and she speak in a way as if what she tell you, you will believe before anybody else. That is why I stop you.'

'I am very sorry to hear all this, Mrs. Rouse.'

'Mr. Haynes, Maisie is too aggravating. The girl is a burden to me. When I spoke to her this afternoon she answer me in a way I had to chase her out of the yard. She is going to bring me in trouble. One day I am going to lose my temper with her and the police going to have to come for me. I send and tell her uncle to come for her. I don't want Maisie in my house any more. She is the root of all my trouble.' Lately Mrs. Rouse had said more than once that Maisie was the root of all her trouble and the sentence had no meaning that Haynes could see.

'I know it grieve you to hear this because I see you and Maisie are good friends, but I can't have her worrying Philomen like that. Philomen loves me, Mr. Haynes. Mr. Benoit desert me and leave me to perish, but Philomen wouldn't do me that. Look at the work Philomen does here up and down the whole day. Sometimes my temper bad and I quarrel, but she don't answer me back like Maisie. Gomes at the parlour, who see how Philomen work for me, offer her four dollars a month and a room in the yard to work for him and his mother, two of them alone, very easy work. Another lady, a Mrs. Clarke, is after her, but Philomen wouldn't leave me. She see me struggling with my troubles, and she remain by my side. And Maisie, who do me so much already, she don't help, and now she wants to make my life a burden by driving Philomen. All your soap and tooth paste, Maisie use it regular. I tired speaking to her. She will go and play your gramophone when you not there. I warn her, I haven't forgot the day she break the bike. When you miss anything or anything break is Maisie, Mr. Haynes, not Philomen. All right, Mr. Haynes, I wouldn't keep you back from your supper any more. Everything is on the table.'

Mrs. Rouse was hardly out before Maisie came boisterously in. She was eating ice cream from a cone and she was in high spirits.

'If you know what happen, Mr. Haynes.'

She sat on the bed and sucked at her ice cream and laughed.

'What happened?'

'Mrs. Rouse didn't give me no dinner, but I had six cents so I went up to the parlour, the one the Chinee man keeping by the drug store. So I tell him, "Hey, Chinee, give me three ice cream cone." That is six cents. He look at me and he say something to his friend in Chinee and then he ask me where I come from. "No damn business of yours," I tell him. "Give me the cones quick." He give me them and I see him go to the drawer and stop as if to give me change. So I stand up, although I know no change for me. He give me three cents. I say, "Ah-ha, let me get out of this, quick." "You nice gal," he say when I was going. I ain't watch him. I go down the road. I eat the cone (my head hurt me, I eat them so fast), and then I go back to the parlour. As soon as he see me, the ugly Chinee dog, he say, "Ah, you nice gal, you come back, you like me? Me like you, too." I was mad to spit in his face, the man so ugly, but I tell him, "Yes. You nice Chinee man. I want three more cone." I eat two of them on the spot and I walk off. I ain't pay him a cent.'

'What did he say?'

'He say: "You nice gal, you come back tomollow. Buy mo' cone." I tell him, "Yes, me nice gal. You nice Chinee man. I come tomollow, you give me mo' cone".'

'But, Maisie!' Haynes was horrified.

'But, Mr. Haynes! Since the man so fresh! I going tomollow. I will eat his cone, too.'

'But you are begging for trouble.'

'Trouble! All he is going to get out of me he get already. And when I'm ready I'll put him in his place so quick!'

'Anyway, Maisie, let us forget the Chinaman for a bit. I want to talk to you.'

She looked up quickly at him.

'Don't raise your voice though, for Heaven's sake. Miss Atwell is in Mrs. Rouse's bedroom, but still you know when you get excited what happens.'

'All right, Mr. Haynes,' she said submissively. She seemed to be expecting some revelation.

'Something happened here this afternoon between you and Philomen.'

'Oh, that!' she burst out. 'That lousy-head coolie girl!'

'Steady, Maisie. Remember what I told you.'

She quieted down, but she was now all resentment.

'The girl come in here and start to use your comb and brush, and I stop her. She have no right. All coolie head have lice. And she is too nasty.'

III

This was an out and out slander of Philomen, who, as is customary with Indians, bathed often, more often than anybody in the house, getting up at extraordinary early hours to do so before her work began. Mrs. Rouse took her weekly all-over wash on Sunday after breakfast; Maisie sometimes three times a day when the weather was hot, but was inclined to avoid it on cold mornings. Miss Atwell went to the bath only at long intervals, but Haynes always heard. Maisie made a public affair of Miss Atwell's bath. Miss Atwell hit upon the plan of going to the bath only when Maisie was out. Maisie countered by always enquiring as soon as she returned whether Miss Atwell had had a bath.

'And she always using your soap and toothpaste,' continued Maisie. 'If you miss anything, Mr. Haynes, it's she who take it.' But Haynes knew even without Mrs. Rouse's exhortations that this was not true. Philomen was as honest as the day, proud of it, too, and deservedly so. All No. 2 knew it and trusted her implicitly.

'Now, Maisie, forget about Philomen for a while. What is wrong between yourself and Mrs. Rouse?'

'What is wrong between Mrs. Rouse and me?' she said slowly. And then more briskly: 'I going to tell you, Mr. Haynes, what is causing the whole trouble. Mrs. Rouse is telling everybody that I am the cause of all this business with Mr. Benoit. But she lie—'

'Not so loud.'

He motioned to her to come and sit nearer to him. She came obediently.

'That Mr. Benoit! You know he bring his freshness to me, Mr. Haynes.'

'What!' said Haynes.

'Not so loud,' said Maisie, and laughed uproariously.

'Yes. But that isn't what Mrs. Rouse vex with me for. She vex because I know all the time this thing was going on, and I didn't tell her.'

Maisie chuckled, and though Haynes did not know what she was going to say, he started to chuckle too. Maisie's laugh was infectious, and of late she was always telling him things that set him chuckling.

'Let me tell you from the beginning. On mornings, long time ago now, I used to see the nurse and Mr. Benoit, whenever Mrs. Rouse and Philomen gone to market he always talking in her room, they talking and shu-shuing and so on. Then sometimes they used to be in the front bedroom. They had lost the key to the door and as was a bedroom nobody used to worry to open it. So I unlock it early one morning and shut the door just as usual. I was preparing for them.'

Maisie's good temper was quite returned.

'Well, I open the door sudden and catch them fair and square on the bed. So I start to laugh. Mr. Benoit jump up and he start to curse, but the nurse (that is a woman, you hear, Mr. Haynes!) all she say is: "Well, what you laughing at? I sure you doing the same thing already." So I laugh at them and went outside. Little bit after Mr. Benoit come out and he call me. He say, "Hey! You! You better don't tell your aunt anything what happen this morning. She will corn your behind for you." "I's mine she goin' to corn?" I tell him. He wanted to frighten me, but it take better than him to frighten me, Mr. Haynes. So I went on laughing. Then at the same time the ice cream man was passing. So I tell him, "Look here, buy an ice cream for me or you live in pickle." He say, "I ain't have no money, I tell you, and she ain't have." I tell him, "I's nearly nine o'clock. Just now Mrs. Rouse coming. And if you don't buy twelve cents ice cream for me, I sell you." So he buy it. After that, Mr. Haynes, I live fat off the two of them. Whenever I wanted ice cream cone, six cents, twelve cents, anything, they used to give me. Now Mrs. Rouse find out that. She say I am the cause of the whole thing. She say if I had told her, all this wasn't going to happen. But it was all her fault, Mr. Haynes. She knew what she knew and she should have been on the look-out. The man was her man. Was her business to watch him, not mine. I saw my chance to make my little coppers and I make them. You don't think I was right, Mr. Haynes?'

Haynes did not reply.

'You think I was wrong, Mr. Haynes? It wasn't my business. Coppers or no coppers, how could I go and tell Mrs. Rouse that I see Benoit in bed with the nurse.'

'Quite, Maisie, I agree.'

'So I wasn't wrong, Mr. Haynes?'

Her face was half in the shadow from which her eyes shone out, sparkling into his, appealing, and yet with a confidence, half-amused, half-satirical.

'Say I wasn't wrong, Mr. Haynes.'

'No, I can't blame you, Maisie.'

She smiled a happy, triumphant smile and looked more handsome than he had ever seen her look before.

'I am going, Mr. Haynes. It's half-past eight. I have a date. Let Mrs. Rouse say what she like.'

'Mr. Boyce?' said Haynes.

'Yes, Boyce. He want me to prove my love. But let him wait.'

She left, but returned after a minute.

'If you are lonely I can stay with you, Mr. Haynes.'

'No, Maisie. I have work to do. You run away to your date.'

And long after she had gone he sat cursing himself for the fool that he was to have missed that chance of keeping her away from the dangerous Boyce, even if he were not himself ready to speak to her.

Chapter Eighteen

One Sunday morning Mrs. Rouse sent to tell Haynes by Maisie that she would be glad if he could spare a few minutes after breakfast.

'Certainly,' he told Maisie, and then more quietly: 'What's up?'

She shrugged her shoulders.

'Don't know. One thing I know she going to talk about Benoit. That man always in the house. When he was living here you couldn't turn round in the bedroom without seeing him, and now that he gone an hour of the day don't pass you bound to hear his name.'

After breakfast, with the sun as hot as fire, Haynes waited for Mrs. Rouse, who did not come at once. When she did, she was full of apologies for having kept him. In her hand she held an oblong Japanese box. Haynes gave her a seat, she drew the chair nearer, and unlocking the box took out a bundle of papers, old receipts, a few letters and some little account books, which she placed on the table. She wanted some help in her calculations, and Haynes consenting willingly, she put her position before him.

No. 2 Minty Alley was mortgaged for six hundred dollars at twelve per cent. She was supposed to pay forty-three dollars a quarter – eighteen dollars interest and twenty-five dollars on the principal. But the interest did not lessen as the capital was paid off.

'But why, Mrs. Rouse?'

'Mr. Rojas said it wouldn't pay him, Mr. Haynes, and we wanted the money, so we took it like that.'

No more than a hundred dollars had been paid on the capital. After the first year they had paid nothing but interest. She wanted to know if she reduced the quarterly amount to twelve dollars and fifty cents, how long it would take to clear the house. About eight years, Haynes told her – if she did not miss.

'Eight years!' she said blankly. Eight years of this cake-making business with herself and Philomen.

'Can't you make him lower the interest?'

'No, Mr. Haynes. It is on a Bill of Sale on the house. And I can't tell him anything. We haven't paid the principal so long that he have us in his hand. He could take it over at any minute. I tell you he safeguard himself good when he made that mortgage. I am surrounded on all sides . . . All this persecution, you see I suffering from Benoit and that woman, it's the house they after, you know.'

'I don't quite understand you, Mrs. Rouse.'

'The house is what they want to get. This house, No. 2, Minty Alley.'

'I thought it was your house.'

'Yes, but let me explain.'

She took off her glasses. 'I thought you knew. The house is on his name and mine.'

'I see.'

'And he and me sign the deed of mortgage to Mr. Rojas. Now Mr. Rojas angry with him how he behave, but Mr. Rojas tell me to be very careful how I do anything because the house is not mine, i's only half mine. Mr. Benoit fighting to see if I could fail and have to sell out. If Mr. Rojas have to sell me out, we can't do anything unless Benoit's name come in. And then he will have to get his share and will spend it on the woman. That is why you see he moving heaven and earth to see me fail in business. Gomes is my chief customer. I can make a little money out of Gomes's business now that the man is not licking out every spare cent. But once we borrowed a hundred and fifty from Gomes. Benoit and I sign. Whenever I borrow, Mr. Haynes, I always arrange to pay back principal and interest together. Every quarter I giving Benoit the money to pay. I think the man paying. Mr. Haynes, he spend nearly every cent. And now that he leave me the man go to Gomes and tell him if he want his money he better come down on me quick. Gomes send for me and tell me. Now nearly every cent I make is going to Gomes for debt I pay already. You don't think that is hard, Mr. Haynes?'

Haynes said nothing.

'Tell me, Mr. Haynes,' she insisted.

'Yes,' he said.

'And they haven't stopped there. The woman believe she is a doctor and know everything. I tell her that I have an uncle in the lunatic asylum, and when I had my first child seventeen years ago I lose my nerves and I talk a little wild. You know how it is at a time like that. Well, I tell her so. And she and he, she put it up to

118

him that if they work their business well, I will go mad. She say I have it in the family. And if I go mad and go up in the asylum he will be in full control of the house and everything as they wish. But I am protected. They can't harm me. He, the man himself, come and tell me how much they pay him to send me off my head or even kill me sudden. And Mr. Benoit himself is a man that knows things. But when he was with me he tell me one or two things that make it impossible for anybody to harm me, least of all him. The man tell me that when he do his business he see at once that I was too powerful for him. He come and tell me and ask me if I want to send it back where it come from. I tell him, "No. I am not going to do Mr. Benoit evil, I leave him and his wife in the hand of God." That is what that devil in the shape of man is doing to me, Mr. Haynes, me, the woman who have done so much for him.'

She sat at the table with her arms resting on it, her hands holding some of her papers. Her eyes, fixed on Haynes while she spoke, she suddenly withdrew, and looked for some seconds out of the window, so that it seemed as if she had quite forgotten he was there. Then she heaved a deep sigh and saying, 'Ha, God,' she spoke again.

'That nurse, Mr. Haynes! If you know what she was, the life she used to carry on in that room next door, where Miss Atwell is. I take her and make her something; and look what I get for it. Mr. Haynes, it is hard, hard, hard. I sacrifice myself for both of them, and I lose both of them at one time, my husband and my best friend.'

'But, you know, Mrs. Rouse, I have often wondered why, as

soon as you found out what was going on, you didn't turn her out?'

She didn't answer at once.

'Well, Mr. Haynes, I saw them kissing one day. They swore that was all and I believed her. You see I had got to like her. She was a woman who had nice ways. You have to give the devil his due. She was a nice person to have in a house. She could do nice little things, you know, and keep the house happy. And when I saw them that day she beg so much pardon, and promise so hard not to do it again that I forgive them.'

Haynes shook his head in disapproval.

'Yes, Mr. Haynes,' she admitted regretfully. 'Plenty people blame me. But look at it this way, Mr. Haynes. From the time we take the nurse in we all live like family. And I had liked her little son a lot. When the nurse went out I was in charge of him. Mr. Benoit and Maisie, and his mother, too, all used to ill-treat him, so he clung to me. Well, about May last year I saw them in the dining-room. Mr. Haynes, I didn't know what to say. And then, you see, I had endorsed a note for her for a hundred and twenty dollars. And she was paying back, but she didn't pay back as much as half yet. So I had to study my head or else I would have had to pay the money. I make up my mind to wait a little bit and do as if nothing happen, as if I know nothing. But I couldn't help showing it, Mr. Haynes. She see it too. Anyway, she tell me one morning: "Mrs. Rouse, it seems as if you in distress and I am the cause." I ask her: "You do me anything? If you do me nothing your conscience is clear." And nothing more happen that day. But the Sunday night the three of us was eating at the table. I wasn't

120

saying anything. I couldn't talk, Mr. Haynes, my heart was too full. He too was frightened 'cause he had a guilty conscience. Well, all of a sudden she burst out crying—'

'The nurse!'

'Yes, Mr. Haynes, that nurse. You wouldn't think she is a woman like that, eh? But she is a funny woman. You never know where you are with her. He ask her what she crying for. And then the whole thing come out. Mr. Haynes, she cry, she cry, she beg my pardon, she say after all I do for her is so she recompense me. She went to the nuns, to Mother Superior, to ask Mother to beg my pardon. Mother send to call me and beg me to forgive her. Mr. Haynes, she spend all Monday afternoon and Monday night in her room crying. She was doubled up under the bed. Yes, she, that same nurse you see always as if nothing trouble her. People tell me was to fool me for me not to put her out. But I don't think it was that, Mr. Haynes. Still you can never tell – and look what happen now. Anyway, she cry so much I feel sorry for her and I make her get up from where she was on the floor. She fall on me begging pardon, and I comfort her and I tell her I forgive her. I tell her I see that her repentance was sincere and I wouldn't bear anything in mind against her. This is my words to her, "Nurse, I been living long in the world and I know. Men ask the questions and women have to say 'No,' but sometimes the women is weak and they try to refuse and they can't." I call Mr. Benoit by himself in the kitchen and I tell him what I had to tell him. Well, everything quiet down. He come to me after and he promise nothing wouldn't happen again. He said it wasn't the nurse fault. It was he who held her and kiss her. And that stop for a long time. I am sure it stop, Mr. Haynes. I used to keep an eye on them and I had a servant used to watch them for me.'

'Wilhelmina?'

'No, not Wilhelmina. Another one. It really had stopped. We all live good. Until about October so, somebody tell me they were meeting outside. And the man leave me and get married so quick, Mr. Haynes, that I can't realize it. I sit down sometimes and wonder if it is true.'

'The temptation was too great to have them living in the house together.'

'So everybody say,' agreed Mrs. Rouse, sadly. 'But the man, Mr. Haynes, the man should have remembered all that I do for him, all I have been to him. All my youth and strength I devote to Mr. Benoit and look how he recompense me. Mr. Haynes, I have been an unhappy woman in my life. Twice I make a venture with a man and twice I fail. I married, as a young woman of nineteen, to Mr. Rouse. I grew up as a young lady in my mother's house, Mr. Haynes. I used to sing in the choir. I didn't used to work. I used to make cakes and I was a good hand at it. But that was for my home, Mr. Haynes, and for my friends. It was not to sell.

'After I was married eighteen months, my husband start to be unfaithful to me. He used to be living with a woman before he marry me, and the woman went away when he got married. But she came right back to Trafalgar, where I come from, and she wasn't there a month before he go back to her. And then was constant quarrelling. He come home night after night one, two, three o'clock. Ah! Mr. Haynes, women have to suffer too much from men. And my temper was always hot. Sometimes he didn't used to come at all. Then the woman start to throw remarks at me when I was walking in the street and my mother tell me to leave him. I leave him and went home. I didn't ask him for no support, Mr. Haynes, and he and the woman leave and go to America. I stay home for two or three years and then I started to make cakes and bread and send out. Once you married you know, Mr. Haynes, you can't go back as a young lady doing nothing. And I wanted something to do. Well, I was getting on very well when Mr. Benoit propose to me. At first I didn't want to take him, but afterwards I tell him, yes. I had some money, and he had some, too, not much, and we open together. Mr. Haynes, the man write for me, yes! and write my mother too. He promise to do all in his power to make me happy, and to be true and kind and faithful all the days of his life. A little before he went I show him the letter and tell him: "You didn't only tell me. You write it. And words pass away. But black and white remain forever." He say: "Oh, that's old talk!" You see at men, Mr. Haynes!

'Mr. Haynes, my poor deceased mother dead and gone but she was against it. She tell me: "Alice, he is a man who you will have to help. He isn't a man who will help you."

'She was against it, but my life was spoilt already. I couldn't stop a widow all the days of my life, and I went with him. My mother wouldn't have anything to do with me after that. She died and I didn't see her. When I wanted to go, the man keep me back, and when I went up it was too late. Poor woman, I glad she didn't live to see me as I am today. She wanted me when she was dying and was only calling for me. She died and I didn't see her. All on account of this man.

'She leave the little property, the house she used to live in and two others for me. Little houses, but, still, something. Well, Mr. Benoit and me was getting on good. I made one baby for him and I lose it. Working, yes, Mr. Haynes! When I should have been lying down I was working. I nearly died and the doctor say I wouldn't have any more.

'It was bitter for me, but now I see that God in his wisdom knew better. Where I would have been today with a long string of children to support?'

'Perhaps that might have kept him.'

'Perhaps. But nothing was going to keep him, Mr. Haynes. Not that man. Anyway, as I was telling you, we work hard together. He help me well and we made some money and we live a happy life. We had our little troubles, but the King and Queen have them, and he was always a man who like a frock. But all men are like that, and when you married a man and get to know him well there's plenty of things you must see and don't see. He make me sell the property. As if he didn't like me to have anything by myself. He worry me till I sell it. Then we start to build this house. Trouble, Mr. Haynes? We start just as the war break out. Prices went up. I can't tell you the trouble we had. At last we finish it. And all the time Mr. Benoit living high. He used to dress. When he step out people take him for a barrister or a doctor. He eat the best and drink the best, and whenever he was going out, five, ten, fifteen dollars in his pocket. I see that man go to races one year and spend a hundred and forty dollars in the three days. We used to rent out the house, but after a time things went so bad, you remember the bad times – we had to come and live here.

Then the restaurant-parlour we had went down. We give it up and we start this cake business. Mr. Haynes, all this time the man wouldn't finish paying off the mortgage. If things get bad, live a little quiet, give up luxuries till they get better and then you will live as you used to. No, he wouldn't do that. When he want money he make a row if I didn't borrow it. He borrow here, he borrow there, and now when things really turn bad he leave me. But God will punish him, Mr. Haynes.'

She held her head back and it quivered on her neck. Indignation, justifiable, shone in her eyes and transfigured her face. Over the lips towered the Roman nose. She spoke with power.

'God will punish him, Mr. Haynes. He can't escape. I am going to see him suffer. I am going to see Mr. Benoit suffer. You can see the wrong he have done me. I can see it. Everybody can see it. You don't think God can see it, too? He watching, He seeing, He saying nothing, but He not sleeping. God don't like ugly, Mr. Haynes, and tears of blood going to run from Mr. Benoit's eyes for the misery he have caused me. His heart hurting him where he is. If things was going nice and easy it would hurt him, much less now that he seeing trouble. His mind going to come back to me. As I tell him one day when we was quarrelling about the woman, he say he was going. I tell him, "Go, but you will never forget me."

' "Where ever you may be, by land or by sea
My spirit before you, you will ever see."

'Mr. Haynes, I have been more than a wife to him. I have been a mother. I nurse him in sickness. I shield him from harm. And he gone and leave me. But let him go with that woman. The day will come when he will call for the one he leave behind.

'Mr. Haynes, if my little child that died was alive today so that I could hold her to my bosom and cherish her, or if Maisie was a different child, a girl who could comfort me, it wouldn't be so hard. What hurts me is that I have nobody.

'But, Mr. Haynes,' her voice which had softened rose again, 'Maisie not going to stay in my house after I put my business in order. I can't keep her here. She brings back all my wrongs when I see her. You see I leave her alone. I don't ask her to do anything. I leave her to do what she want. All the work I have I fight with it, me and Philomen. She knew everything, Mr. Haynes, and she used to be standing by the gate on a Sunday morning looking to see when I coming up while the two of them carrying on inside. The girl betray my honour for vanilla ice cream and sugar cake. And the man didn't have no shame. Look who he had assisting him in his nastiness. A child who used to call him Pappy, and who he held in his arms as a baby. I well rid of him. Yes, Mr. Haynes, I well rid of him. Men change. They all right in prosperity, but when adversity come, then you see the bones of them. You are a gentleman, Mr. Haynes, and I can tell you this. If you know what Mr. Benoit ask me to do a few months before you come to live here! Races was coming on and he wanted a suit and money to go. He tell me to go to town and see Mr. Nesfield who carry on that grocery in Main Street. We used to deal there long ago. He tell me to go and tell Mr. Nesfield we in difficulty and if he could lend us fifty dollars. I tell him: "McCarthy, try and do without the money. Let us keep down a little and then we will have times as before."

Mr. Haynes, the man make such a row that for peace I had to go. And when I dress the morning to go he call me and tell me: "A., you know if Mr. Nesfield scrupling to lend you the money and he offer to you, that wouldn't be nothing if you take him. As long as you don't do it in secret behind my back i's all right." That what he tell me, Mr. Haynes. After we live sixteen years and I was a true and faithful— I was true and faithful. You don't see the man didn't have any respect for me? I was only his convenience.'

She dropped a tear or two on the table. A gust of wind blew some of the receipts out of the box all over the room and some into the yard.

'No, Mr. Haynes. Leave them. Maisie!'

'Yes, Tante,' said Maisie, immediately, from Miss Atwell's doorstep.

'Go outside and pick up those receipts and then come in here and pick up these.'

She was standing and did not sit down again.

'Mr. Haynes, I leave them to the will of God. He will deal with them in his good time. I have them in the hollow of my hand, but leave them to Him. Yes, Mr. Haynes, in the hollow of my hand. The nurse is a famous thief. Wherever she go to, the nurse steal something. Links, gold stud, gold watch, gold-stoppered bottle, cigars, brandy. Don't laugh, Mr. Haynes, it's true. Everything that woman put her hand on she steal. And she bring them here. She used to say it was presents they give her, but once when she thought they was going to lock her up she telephone to him and tell him where the key was, and to open her press, and take all the jewels he see and hide them. She was expecting the police to

127

come. But they didn't come. And after that the man used to wear the links and the stud. I used to tell him: "McCarthy, don't do it." He wouldn't hear. And they have the things down there, Mr. Haynes. I only have to go down to the Constabulary and lay my information and the two of them will sleep in the cell tonight. Because reports been made to the police already about the missing things. But I wouldn't do that, Mr. Haynes. Perhaps my principle is too high. But she told me in confidence when she was my friend and I wouldn't use it now she is my enemy.'

The clock struck three.

She was a little hoarse. She had been talking for nearly two hours. But Haynes was far from tired and could have listened to the subdued passion of her voice and watched the working of her face until dark.

'Mr. Haynes, I been here since one o'clock. I keep you back from your work. You must excuse me. Sometimes I feel if I don't speak to somebody I will die. I have everything here,' she laid her hand on her bosom.

'At any rate, Mrs. Rouse,' said Haynes, striving to rise to the occasion, 'you must keep your spirits up. You mustn't think of your troubles too much.'

She smiled gratefully.

'All right, Mr. Haynes. As you see, I am fighting. And I have the Great Helper of the afflicted. God is there for all those who need him. I would have sink to the ground already, but prayers sustain me. They wouldn't get my house, Mr. Haynes. And I not going to go mad. Let them wait. Four times a day I kneel to my Maker. Six in the morning, midday, six in the evening and at midnight.

Whatever I am doing I leave it when that hour come. I go to my bedroom, I compose myself, and then I speak to my God.'

'At twelve in the night too!' Haynes, remembering the woman's labours in the day, wondered at the heroic vigils she must endure to fulfil this voluntary programme.

'At midnight,' she said proudly, conscious of the powers it displayed to keep so exacting a tryst. 'And I don't go to sleep, Mr. Haynes. I am sleepy and tired, but I sit in my rocking chair, dozing and waiting till the clock strike twelve every night before I think of going to bed.'

'And one night, Mr. Haynes,' said Maisie, appearing on the doorstep with some of the receipts in her hand. 'One night Mrs. Rouse fall. Every night she only nodding and nodding in the chair and this night she was nodding and when the clock strike she start up and the rocking chair tumble over and she come down flat.'

Maisie was enjoying her own joke, but Haynes dared not smile and he kept his eye on Mrs. Rouse, whose face darkened as the tropical sky before rain.

'Excuse me, Mr. Haynes.' She turned to Maisie and shook her finger under her nose. 'Move aside and let me pass. Go on, young woman. Whether anybody there or not, you have no respect for me. But if next year meet you in this house you lucky. You will find out if those you join with to kill me want you now.'

Chapter Nineteen

Haynes went to see Ella one day and came back to No. 2 rather grave. Ella was no better and was going to the country to be taken care of by her mother. She had not wanted to go, had held on to the last minute. But Haynes insisted, for her condition was obvious. Ella had hinted that he should move. She said she had a friend who would be able to take her place.

'You are afraid, Ella, that they will take me away from you. But don't be afraid. That is impossible. You remember how the nurse tried and I put a stop to it.'

Ella had left it at that, but slyly and respectfully (yet very firmly) she had examined Haynes about how much money he gave Mrs. Rouse, and what she gave him to eat and how long the money lasted and all the various things which she used to manage.

'Everything is all right, isn't it, Ella?' And Ella had had to admit that everything was.

But walking home Haynes had been driven to think of a few things which had never crossed his mind before. Mrs. Rouse, he knew, was in great straits. Where formerly Benoit, Aucher and

Wilhelmina helped, now there was only Philomen, and a Philomen who had more to do with every succeeding day. Now and then Mrs. Rouse engaged a boy, but usually he stole the cakes. Some of them complained of the heat of the kitchen, and they were sometimes very rude when Mrs. Rouse asked them as she often had to do to wait a few days before they were paid. And then, too, there was no denying that Mrs. Rouse was a difficult woman to work with in these days. Haynes recalled certain frantic efforts on mornings to borrow a shilling here or eighteen pence there, to help in the making of cakes. There were times when Mrs. Rouse would be walking up and down the yard waiting anxiously for Philomen to find out if her efforts to secure credit for flour or sugar had been successful. He had no right to be adding the burden of his business on hers. And once he began to think that, he thought over it with ever-increasing dissatisfaction with himself and a feeling that he should put his business right at once.

When he reached home he called Philomen and told her that he wanted to speak to her about something – something rather important. Philomen asked if it would take long. Haynes said he thought it would. He would thrash the matter out thoroughly with Philomen and then speak to Mrs. Rouse. Philomen said that Mrs. Rouse had friends – Haynes could hear them in Miss Atwell's room next door. She was busy cleaning up the kitchen, but in half an hour she would be finished and then she would come.

Haynes had barely finished talking to Philomen when Maisie came into the room.

'By the way, Maisie,' said Haynes, 'Mrs. Rouse's business is giving her more trouble than before. Business is going worse.'

'What is that to me?' said Maisie. 'Business could go smash as far as I care. And to besides, Mrs. Rouse is all right, Mr. Haynes. She has a man running after her now.'

'What!' said Haynes.

'Yes, he's a policeman.'

'What sort of a man is he?'

'A man, Mr. Haynes. What sort of a man, you expect him to be? Some old frump. I often wonder how old people make love. Love is a matter for young people, people like you and me, Mr. Haynes.'

'And Mr. Boyce,' said Haynes.

Haynes had surprised himself by the good temper and generosity with which he had drawn aside and allowed himself to be defeated by Boyce in the race for Maisie's affections. Maisie did not answer at once. She merely shrugged her shoulders.

'But I haven't seen him round here for some time, Maisie.'

'And you're not going to see him either,' said Maisie. 'I suppose now that he has got what he was bothering me for he is not coming back here again.'

And having said this almost with anger, Maisie's mood changed and she smiled mysteriously to herself, with a touch of scorn, and gave Haynes time to consider it.

Haynes, after the first shock, reacted strongly. He considered what Maisie had said. He also considered Maisie. Her confession of Boyce's success fired his imagination. And now Boyce was gone. There was a touch of repulsion at the idea of so quickly succeeding someone else, and that person, a friend of his. But Haynes badly wanted to start making love to someone. And he was as certain as could be that Maisie would not repulse his advances, was inviting him to make some. There she was, leaning forward in the rocking chair waiting. Her lower lip pouted a little in vexation. But that was as it should be. Haynes saw himself soothing the scowl into a shy smile of acquiescence and at the end Maisie sleeping peacefully in his arms. Why not do something now? But she was too far away. He was sitting on the bed. If she were sitting next to him no one would be able to see. As it was if he went over to her, then Philomen might be able to see them from the kitchen. Hard lines. He glanced at the door and considered the angle.

'Have a cigarette, Mr. Haynes,' said Maisie. 'Let me light it for you.' And she brought it for him and sat down on the bed beside him.

She lit the cigarette, but did not move. Haynes puffed twice and then put it on the table. Now he was in the very lists of love. Maisie lifted the cigarette from the table and put it in the ash tray. When she brought her hand back she put it on the bed. Haynes could feel it resting against his leg. She left it there. Now certainly was the time. Better hold her hand first so as not to startle her. If he acted too suddenly she might scream or utter a cry and those next door might hear. Yes, he had to guard against that. There was a lot of talking and laughing next door, but if he startled Maisie in any way and she shrieked they would certainly ask what was that. His hand moved furtively towards hers.

There was a sudden lull in the conversation next door. Haynes stopped at once. Better wait until they began again. He stole a glance at Maisie. She was leaning forward, her eyes on the table before her, but as he looked at her, although she did not look at him he knew that she had seen him for she swayed towards him, and he felt her body lean slightly against his. The talking and chattering started next door. Haynes looked at Maisie's hand. He would hold it first and then not say a word, but merely put his arm round her waist and draw her to him. He would do it. He would.

'Mr. Haynes,' came Philomen's clear voice from outside, 'I'll be ready in five minutes.'

'Very well, Philomen,' said Haynes, 'as soon as you are ready.' He got up quickly from the bed. 'Have a cigarette, Maisie,' he said.

He held a match for her with fingers that trembled. Maisie had given no sign, but as the match shook in Haynes's fingers, she held his wrist to steady it.

'Thank you, Mr. Haynes,' she said without looking at him. 'If Philomen is coming in here I am going out. Is she going to stay long?'

'Not too long,' said Haynes.

'I'll come back later,' she said, and she left. But before she left she gave him one long, farewell look which was at once a reminder, an invitation and a promise of good things to come.

Haynes began by referring to Ella's continued absence. Philomen had brought in some sewing, but she put it aside and stopped him at once.

'I hope you not thinkin' of gettin' somebody in her place, Mr. Haynes.' And when he did not answer she shook her head decisively.

'No, Mr. Haynes. Busy as you see Mrs. Rouse, if you stop the cookin' it will hurt her too much. She will think something displease you.'

They could talk freely as the laughing, animated conversation still went on next door.

'Mrs. Rouse happy,' Philomen looked up and smiled. 'I glad to hear her laughin'. She have enough trouble, poor woman.'

'That is why—'

'You have nothing to do with that, Mr. Haynes. We are all glad to do anything for you. But things are really bad all the same. Christmas comin' and I don't know what sort of Christmas the madam goin' to spend.'

'What about you and Christmas?'

'Me, Mr. Haynes? I all right. As long as Sugdeo don't get jealous and cause me anxiety nothin' trouble me. I's Mrs. Rouse I studyin'. Mr. Benoit gone. She goin' to miss 'im this Christmas. And then no money to buy anything at all. Mrs. Rouse like nice wine and stout. She don't eat much, but she like to drink on a spree day. Christmas long ago she and Mr. Benoit used to have champagne and Guinness stout mixed.'

'Do you drink?'

'Me! No. One Christmas, the first Christmas I spend with Mrs. Rouse, I drink some champagne. I get sick, I throw up, I couldn't eat for the day. And not me again.'

'You eat well though?'

'Long time; but my appetite goin' now. I can't eat the stale cake, you know, Mr. Haynes. And Mrs. Rouse does cook only once a day. Sometimes she don't cook at all for the day.'

'Not cook at all for the day!' It was incredible.

'Why! That is nothing.'

'But hasn't she to cook for me?'

'Yes, but that is different. She must cook for you. You give her money.'

'And what do you all eat?'

'Any little thing. We cook sometimes. But if we only get money to make cake for the parlours we can't get anything. You know how Gomes can quarrel if anything wrong! We make tea every morning, and we credit milk from the coolie man to pay at the end of the month. If I feel hungry I credit ice cream cone when I goin' down the road and eat it. I like ice cream, you know. But often I so busy I haven't time to think about food.'

'But why don't you credit at a shop?' said Haynes, and knew even before he was told that he had asked a stupid question.

'Credit at a shop? If you know the messages the man at the shop does give me to bring to Mrs. Rouse if she owe him a dollar! I don't tell her because I don't want to worry her.'

'Philomen!'

It was Mrs. Rouse calling.

'Comin', Mrs. Rouse. Good night, Mr. Haynes, I hope you sleep well.'

As soon as Philomen had gone Maisie came back again, closing the door behind her.

'Mr. Haynes, I heard them next door giving Mrs. Rouse jokes about her new sweetheart.'

But Haynes had other things than Maisie to think about now. 'I'm sorry, Maisie, but I find I have something very important to do.'

136

He bustled about the table with pen and paper.

'You will finish soon, Mr. Haynes?'

'I'm afraid not, Maisie.'

'All right, Mr. Haynes, see you tomorrow night, Mr. Haynes?'

'Yes, Maisie.' Haynes would not look round, glad to be rid of her.

When she left he locked the door and put down his pen. He was genuinely shocked at what Philomen had so casually revealed. To the burden of Mrs. Rouse's own overwhelming difficulties, he had with unpardonable carelessness added his own. It was all very well to throw his personal affairs upon Ella. That was Ella's job. He paid Ella far more than the average servant got. She was ill and he still paid her her money. But Mrs. Rouse and Maisie and the rest did between them everything that Ella had done. With Ella he still had no regular system but merely gave money, and when it was finished gave some more. He always paid the money due on the mortgage from his weekly income and lived on the balance and the rent. Haynes was in a state of abject self-blame. And with good cause. Often when money was finishing Mrs. Rouse, just as Ella used to do, would say:

'Mr. Haynes, how are things with you?'

If it were late in the week Haynes might say, as he did with Ella:

'On Saturday morning, Mrs. Rouse,' and perhaps it might be late Saturday night before he gave it to her. Sometimes he would draw money on the Saturday and go off to the country, not returning until Monday morning. But never once (except one day when it rained from three in the morning to ten o'clock without a break) was any meal late, and although his meals varied in quality, yet, judging from Ella's standard, he got good value for the money. Morning, noon and night everything was ready punctually on the table for him. Now and then he did not come for supper and the food stayed till morning, some of it having to be thrown away. He had gone on his way, taking it all for granted. To what sacrifices had he put the good woman to feed him regularly while the rest of the household starved. He would have to do something about it. He would go into details with Philomen and then talk about it with Mrs. Rouse. He would do it as soon as possible. Of course he had never intended to do it that night. He had only wanted to get rid of Maisie. Maisie! Maisie liked him obviously. But tonight was not the time for that sort of nonsense. When he had settled his business with Mrs. Rouse. He felt that Maisie was as good as his.

Chapter Twenty

Benoit got married early in October, and it was in December that Haynes met him for the first time after the marriage. He was sauntering home along the pavement with his hat over his eyes, reading a newspaper, when he heard footsteps behind him and felt a hand on his shoulder.

'Haynes!'

It was Benoit.

'Hello, it's you.' They shook hands and watched one another. At the first glance Haynes saw that all he had heard about the failure of his life with the nurse was true. In health and appearance at least his change from Mrs. Rouse to the nurse had not been for the better. His face was blotchy, which, with his black skin, gave him a particularly unhealthy look. His cheeks were hollow, his eyes were a dirty brown colour and he was unshaven. His paunch, a sign of his well-being much admired at No. 2, except by Maisie, was almost gone, and the white suit was dirty. The trim and slick Benoit, who used to be such a delight to the eye of

Mrs. Rouse when he took the street was no more. And the man had not been married two months.

'How is the nurse?' Haynes enquired after the first greetings.

'Well, thank you. She out on a job. How everybody home?'

He continued to grin at Haynes uncomfortably and Haynes was uncomfortable himself. He knew what was passing in both their minds, but he left it to Benoit to begin. For once, however, the fighting cock could not flap his wings.

What a fool he had made of himself! Haynes felt he ought to have known that the wife living with him in two rooms would be less desirable than the woman whom he could hold in his arms only in stolen interviews. The material advantages which he had hoped to gain he had lost. Maybe Haynes had met him at a particularly bad moment, but so dispirited was the man's appearance that if even he had not been caught in fish, his mistake had been realized quite as early and as disastrously as Miss Atwell had predicted.

'I hear Mrs. Rouse wasn't too well.'

'No, she is all right.'

Mrs. Rouse, though thinner, had not had a day's illness since the wedding.

'I hear her nerves was troubling her.'

'Not that I know of. Though it may be so.'

'I heard she was sick,' Benoit repeated.

'Perhaps she may have been,' Haynes said. 'I know very little of what is happening there, for I am away most of the day.'

'No, man. I hear you writing letters, making receipts, giving advice and so on. In fact you take my place.'

He laughed and spoke more like himself than since they had met.

'Going anywhere particular?' Haynes asked him.

'No.'

'Let's go over to the bar and have a drink. There is a private room at the back.'

The private room was empty. Haynes ordered two beers, and they sat down on opposite sides of the little table.

'Well, how do you like your new life?' said Haynes.

'Not bad.' But he avoided Haynes's eye. 'Of course we haven't settled down yet. The nurse out working and I have to fix up at home, you know. But we will move soon and get a servant – by the New Year, you know.'

If there was money he wasn't getting much of it. He hadn't a cent in his pocket and let Haynes know as much.

'You have cigarettes?'

'No,' said Haynes, feeling in his pocket. Benoit asked him to buy some.

'Let's have another beer.'

'Yes, man. Liquor is helpful.'

He smacked his lips after two or three mouthfuls and lit a cigarette.

'I sorry we don't meet sometimes to have a little talk, Haynes, as long ago.'

'I miss you myself. I often remember the good talks we used to have.'

'Yes, man . . . I's her fault, you know, that this happen.

'I's her fault,' he reiterated. 'She used to bother me too much.'

'I didn't know that.'

'Yes, man. I used to tell her to let me go out and do a little business. I have good luck. I understand science, as you know, Haynes, and I know when to start a business and make it successful. Some things, if you start on a Friday must turn out bad. And some things, again, Friday is your only day. And little things I know. But she always hamper me. She never want me to go out. I could have made money as a commission agent. She could have got another servant to do the cake business. But no, whatever she doing, parlour cake, everything, I must be there.'

Haynes saw his point, an aspect of the matter he had never seen before.

'And she make such a fuss about me and the nurse. If she didn't take up knife and all that, this thing would have died down, man, and me and she would have been still together.'

Haynes wasn't so sure of that, but he nodded.

'After all, Haynes, a man is not a little boy . . . I's all her fault . . . You would have done the same in my place. She always was a jealous woman. And that spoil everything. I's her fault.'

He seemed quite melancholy now, but soon he was lively again.

'I hear you and the little one nice,' he said.

'No,' Haynes replied. 'You ought to know that that is not true.'

'I don't believe in truth. I was only joking you. But I hear she in your room the whole day?'

'That's true. But I am not her sweetheart.'

'She is a hot little thing, you know.'

'Well, I can't say.'

'You can't see that for yourself? If I had stayed there a little longer she wouldn't have escaped me. I used to kiss her and

142

squeeze her when I get the chance; playing Pappy, you know. But how the nurse and me was nice, I didn't trouble her too much. And as she was young, I was in no hurry. I hear she filling out pretty. I wish I was you. She like you, you know.'

'How do you know that?'

'Man, any girl like Maisie will like a nice young fellow like you. Ask for what you want. If you don't ask, you don't get.' He drained his glass. 'Though, by Christ, plenty of them today don't even wait for you to ask.'

'She likes somebody else,' said Haynes.

'Who you mean? That fellow Boyce? She prefer you to Boyce, man. I hear her say so. And if even she like him what you have to do with that? A woman isn't like a loaf of bread, where you share you only have half. Haynes, man, you are afraid. She always in your room. Choose your chance, hold the girl and kiss her. You needn't even tell her anything. You just hold her and kiss her well. Boy, if I was up there I'd show you.'

Haynes said he had to go.

'All right,' said Benoit, and as they shook hands he added: 'Don't be surprised to see me up there one day, you know.'

'What!' said Haynes.

'Sure. Why must I give up up there like that?'

'You will give up the nurse?'

'No. I am man enough for two.'

'Nothing doing for you up that way again, Benoit. I know. She'll not look at you.'

'You don't know, boy,' said Benoit, and they parted.

Haynes had been hearing rumours that things were not going

well between Benoit and his wife, but had rather discredited them considering the biassed sources from which they came. But lately they had been more insistent. Philomen often met Benoit in the street, and she first brought the news how he wasn't looking too well – 'he lose all the pig punch he had.' Miss Atwell also brought some news from where she worked. (Haynes saw little of Miss Atwell now. Mr. Cross, her keeper, was so remiss in his visits and paying of rent that she had sought and obtained employment in a shirt factory, where she worked twelve hours a day.) She heard from a co-worker who lived near to the pair that they had come to blows two or three times already, the chief source of contention being the little boy. Benoit was not in the least the cherished darling. Indeed, Miss Atwell reported that he walked about the yard 'with 'is naturals on the groun',' that is to say barefooted, which was a bad thing for a man who had been so ill.

'I see already his slippers go bad and he quarrel about wearing his good boots in the kitchen and I give him mine, and I stand up in this kitchen three whole days in my high heels till the Saturday night I buy a pair. But it serve him right.'

The nurse had failed to get the promised job for him and he was still unemployed.

The first sight of Benoit had been sufficient to confirm the rumours. Benoit had himself told Haynes in the past of the kind of disposition the nurse had.

'I must like the nurse, man. She nice to me. And you see her there, she don't care for nobody – only for herself and the child.' He had spoken wiser than he knew.

Why had the nurse married him? He had told Haynes once he

144

could do as he liked with her. 'As soon as I kiss her, man, she can't say no to anything I tell her.' Had he wanted to marry her? Or she to marry him? Haynes did not know. It had been all very well when Mrs. Rouse ran the house, saw after the food and clothes, and all the nurse and Benoit had to do was to contrive meetings. But either the nurse had discovered how to say 'no' even after kisses, or perhaps he didn't kiss her so often. Six weeks was a very short time. Still, as Maisie said, 'that was his funeral.'

Haynes thought at first of telling Mrs. Rouse that he had seen Benoit, but at the last minute he changed his mind. There had been more than enough talk about all this business lately.

But the very next evening Mrs. Rouse stopped him.

'Excuse me, Mr. Haynes. I hear you and Mr. Benoit was drinking together yesterday, Mr. Haynes.'

There was a smile on her face, but a rather wry smile, and the lips were drawn tight. Was there a hint of reproach in her voice and manner?

'Yes, Mrs. Rouse, I met him. We started to talk and we had a drink for old times' sake . . . He doesn't seem very happy with the change he has made.'

'Doesn't seem happy! I's so you put it? Doesn't seem happy! Ha! Mr. Haynes, you heard the latest? She calling on him to find work.'

'He didn't tell me that.'

'No, he wouldn't tell you that. But I hear everything. Every day they quarrelling. But he ain't start to see trouble yet for all he have done me and still doing me. You know what she tell him the other day? She tell him' (Mrs. Rouse drew herself up), 'she tell him "I marry you. And it's true I promise to find employment for you. But if I fail haven't I do enough for you? I give you the boots you married in, the hat, the ring, the shirt, the collar, the tie, the motor car. I pay for you to go down to Rockville Bay. I do everything for you. You do nothing for yourself. I's time you get some work to do." And, Mr. Haynes, you mark my words, the time going to come when she going to put him in the District Court for maintenance. He going to have to find work. He sit down here, Mr. Haynes, but he not going to sit down there. She going to drive him out and make him work, and as long as he work she going to get her share. One-third the Court allow you, Mr. Haynes, and she will get her one-third. She is a woman like that. And he know her. He ought to know what kind of woman she is. But his punishment ain't begin yet.'

'He isn't the man he was here.'

'How could he be, Mr. Haynes? How could he be? I used to see after him here. If he wanted this I get it for him, if he wanted that I got it for him. But she, when she out on a job, she getting everything she want; he at home. Things bad with them. All that money you see she was saying people give her presents and giving him his share, was money she borrow. Borrow to fool the man, Mr. Haynes. But now she have to pay it back. They have no servant. He got to cook. I hear they have to share a little kitchen with some other people, and in a place like that the man cooking food for him and the nurse little boy. But I going to see him worse than that, Mr. Haynes. I going to see him go flat down to the ground.'

Mrs. Rouse had worked herself into a passion. Nobody spoke when she made one of these outbursts, just kept a respectful and sympathetic silence and waited for her to cool down. But this afternoon the voice of the invisible Maisie singing softly to herself broke the stillness.

'Sometimes I is up, and sometimes I is down,
Yes, Lord, down, Lord, down to the ground.'

Mrs. Rouse exploded into wrath. 'You, young woman, always there to make a joke of everything I say.'

'Me! What I doing?' said Maisie, in an innocent voice coming round the house. 'I only singing what Mr. Haynes play on his gramophone. Look, let me get away from trouble, eh?'

Maisie went into Haynes's room and Mrs. Rouse returned to the kitchen.

While Haynes was eating, Maisie began to wind the gramophone.

'Thank you very much, Maisie. But what have you got there? Let me see.'

She laughed.

'You are too smart, Mr. Haynes.'

It was as he thought. 'Nobody knows de trouble that I see', a Negro spiritual, with the words she had sung a few minutes before.

'But Maisie, you are a devil. Why do you worry Mrs. Rouse like that?'

''Cause I don't like to hear people talk such confounded non-sense and lies all the time.'

'How do you mean?'

'You hear all she saying about the man? I tell you, Mr. Haynes,

147

and you mark my words. If Mr. Benoit come back here tomorrow morning, Mrs. Rouse will take him back.'

'I don't believe that,' said Haynes, but remembered Benoit's words.

'You don't believe that! I live here. I know her. You don't mind all that she is saying there. If he had two wives she'd take him. She can't do without him. He have her like a little puppy. You remember what the nurse tell her, "Doggie! Doggie! Look bone." Well, with all that big talk, she talking there, she is no more than a little dog to the man. And especially as you hearing how he and the nurse can't get on. Wait and see. If you live here long enough you going to see him come here and you going to see her take him back.'

But Haynes was not listening to what she was saying. Maisie, he noted, was looking exceptionally well. And Benoit's words had come back to him. Just hold her and kiss her and all would be well. He decided he would choose his opportunity and do the job soon. He had fumbled long enough. He knew Maisie liked him, was always giving him openings.

'Come on, Maisie,' he said, heartily. 'You are impeding my progress.' Boldly he held her shoulders ostensibly to move her aside. She twisted her head to give him a brilliant and encouraging smile. They stood like that for a few seconds. Haynes squeezed her shoulders. She remained passive. Then, 'Take care,' she said, 'someone is coming.' And this time Haynes was disappointed.

Chapter Twenty-One

Christmas came and was not nearly as gloomy as had been anticipated. A fortnight before, Mrs. Rouse went to Gomes and made a desperate personal appeal to be allowed to draw all her money for at least ten days. She succeeded. Then there were some private orders for cakes. And altogether life looked brighter.

Early one morning of Christmas week Aucher came in. He had been serving His Majesty for another short period. He was warmly welcomed and came to tell Haynes good morning, no doubt sent by Mrs. Rouse, for in his case such an act of politeness unprompted by authority was impossible. He greeted Haynes gravely, as innocent-looking and as quiet as ever. He came into the yard at about nine o'clock and ten minutes after he was attending to the stove. This unexpected assistance gave Mrs. Rouse more freedom and also relieved Miss Atwell, for after all it was Christmas week. Though the nurse was not there, yet there was scrubbing of floors, cleaning up of furniture, etc., to be done. Miss Atwell, who had been helping in the kitchen, was switched off to cleaning as soon as Aucher came. Work, work, work, everybody was harder at work than ever before. But there was a cheerfulness and happy anticipation about No. 2 which was in strong contrast to the hard, tense atmosphere in which the everyday work had been done during the past few months.

After tea Miss Atwell came fussing to Haynes about the condition of his room. But Haynes begged for a respite.

'I am going to the country tomorrow for three days.'

'For Christmas Day and Boxing, Mr. Haynes!'

'Yes, Miss Atwell, I have a holiday and shall spend the time getting a little ozone.'

'Of course, Mr. Haynes.' Her agreement was apologetic. 'But, anyway you was saying?'

'When I go you can take charge. I know you'll be busy on Christmas Eve. The room is small, though, and it wouldn't take you half an hour. But for the time being give me a chance.'

'Of course, Mr. Haynes, of course. That is a very excellent arrangement.'

But she looked crest-fallen and Haynes surmised that they had counted on having him with them over Christmas. Nor did he want to go away. But he was somewhat tired and for his health's sake thought it would be good to go to a quiet country village by the sea. He wasn't particularly anxious to go, but he had made all arrangements already. In the evening Miss Atwell laid his table and gave him his supper herself. (He couldn't see Philomen, she was so busy up and down, and Maisie, having put her mind to work, was working unremittingly.) When supper was over and she was taking away the things, Miss Atwell remarked to Haynes how much she regretted that he was going. Mrs. Rouse and she had planned to invite him to lunch with them on Christmas Day, as Mrs. Rouse's guest, in her part of the house.

'You is one of the family, you know, Mr. Haynes, and Mrs. Rouse is very, very, sorry.'

When she went Haynes thought it over for a few minutes and then called Miss Atwell.

'Yes, Mr. Haynes?'

Her eager face was at the door.

'I am sorry to call you so often, Miss Atwell,' Haynes began in quite unconscious imitation of her usual manner to him.

'That's quite all right, Mr. Haynes, quite all right,' she answered in her high-pitched voice, still looking expectantly up at him.

'I have to be in town on Boxing night. I can come down on Boxing morning, spend the day here and at least take lunch, and go out in the evening. Ask Mrs. Rouse if that will do.'

'That's too, too, too excellent, Mr. Haynes. That will do most perfect. It's very nice of you, Mr. Haynes. We appreciates it very much. Thank you very much, Mr. Haynes.'

Later in the day Mrs. Rouse saw Haynes.

'We are very glad you have accepted our invitation, Mr. Haynes,' she said, smiling almost shyly, like some poor young woman thanking a rich lover for some splendid gift.

The Boxing Day lunch was a quiet but successful affair. Four of them sat to table, Mrs. Rouse, Miss Atwell, Maisie and Haynes; everybody officially dressed. Philomen served, but joined freely in the conversation. She helped things to go with a swing at the start, for Maisie, so glib in Haynes's room, was silent, and

Mrs. Rouse's thoughts were elsewhere, though for once never a word about Benoit crossed her lips. Also she was tired. But fatigue and Miss Atwell's wiry body never seemed to have made acquaintance and the early constraint disappeared before her briskness and bustle.

It was a very good meal. When it had been eaten, Miss Atwell produced, as if by magic, a quart of champagne which had been in a bucket of ice all the morning. Philomen opened it with a dexterity which made Haynes envious and it was poured into four glasses, Philomen refusing to have any.

'Not me, Miss A., I have to go out with Sugdeo. No cakes today. And if this thing don't agree with me look what a pickle I'll find myself in!'

When the glasses were filled Miss Atwell rose and Haynes realized she was going to make a speech. Maisie started to laugh and only a sharp, 'Maisie, I'll make you get up,' from Mrs. Rouse recalled her to order; Philomen stood with her fat face wearing a fine grin, full of interest and importance. Mrs. Rouse smiled and looked brighter, but she maintained her air of abstraction. Miss Atwell waited and when perfect silence was established, she began. She spoke with fluency and without the slightest nervousness.

'Mr. Haynes, we is all highly gratified that you has honoured us with your presence here today. We has all liked you from the day you come here. You sits in your room, you doesn't go out, you reads your book, you writes your paper, you plays your gramophone, you troubles nobody. And we wish you long life and prosperity.'

After applause (chiefly a great burst of laughter from Philomen and loud 'Hear, hear's' from Maisie) Haynes rose to reply. On the few occasions in his past life that he had been called upon to speak he, having prepared carefully, had made rather a mess of things. (There was that never-to-be-forgotten occasion on which he had begun with, 'I – personally – myself—' and then could go no further.) Now he rose to his feet, and confident of his intellectual superiority got going from the first sentence. The champagne also helped enormously. He spoke of Mrs. Rouse's hard work and patience in her troubles, of Miss Atwell's staunch friendship, of Philomen's devotion. Then he again thanked them all for their kindness, making individual references, and ended by wishing them all a happy and prosperous New Year. It was up to that time the speech of his life.

There was a sustained burst of applause, and a chorus of 'excellent' from Miss Atwell. Ever afterwards one of her favourite remarks was that Haynes should stand for the Legislative Council. She then got up, rummaged in a drawer and produced a cigar.

'We knows that you ask Philomen to buy one sometimes, so we got her to buy one of the same kind, Mr. Haynes.'

Haynes lit up at once, Philomen removed some of the dishes, a pint of whisky and some well-iced soda were placed for Haynes, and vermouth for the ladies, and they were all very much at home.

'It's very hot, Mr. Haynes. I see you is perspirin'. You can take off your jacket, Mr. Haynes. Push that curtain away, Maisie. Philomen, take Mr. Haynes's jacket. You is no stranger, Mr. Haynes. Whisky for me, Mr. Haynes? Thank you, I likes a little whisky.'

After a general conversation and two whiskies and sodas, Haynes said goodbye and went over to his room, full of food and drink and vaguely conscious that of all the Christmas eating and drinking, this had been the best. Maisie, who had followed him, somewhat damped his satisfaction by saying that he had spoken too long, but he knew Maisie too well to let her think he was affected by her criticism.

'Jealous, Maisie. That's what you are.'

'If you say so, Mr. Haynes.' She lay back in an armchair, her hands behind her head.

'Mr. Haynes,' she said suddenly.

'What is it?'

'I want a cigarette.'

'What will Mrs. Rouse say?'

'I wouldn't let her see. All those white ladies smoke. I don't see why I shouldn't smoke.'

'Look in my pocket. But mind, I didn't give them to you.'

'No, Mr. Haynes. You light it for me.'

'Sure,' said Haynes. 'Here you are. I give you with a kiss.' And if he did not seek to implement them, the words at least were bold.

'Oh, Mr. Haynes! One glass of champagne and two glasses of whisky.'

But it was more than that. Haynes was feeling exhilarated by the unexpected fluency he had found in his tongue. And that had given him a new confidence.

'Hold her and kiss her,' Benoit had said. And now he felt that he could do what he liked with Maisie when he pleased.

She, too, seemed aware of a subtle change in Haynes's manner. She did not seem dissatisfied and lay back puffing with an ease which bespoke practice. Maisie in the armchair, Haynes sitting across his bed, with his back on the wall. Their eyes met and

Haynes did not withdraw his as often hitherto. A film seemed to draw over Maisie's. 'Why are you looking at me like that, Mr. Haynes?' she whispered.

'Because I want to. You are very nice to look at.'

'You have suddenly become a great speech-maker, Mr. Haynes. I didn't—'

A sudden knock at the door startled them both. It was Miss Atwell come to borrow a book to read.

'Mr. Haynes, the last one was good, a little high for me, but good. I is not a person of much education and I knows nothing about stories and so on. I used to be a great reader of novels in my day. That is a long time now. And novels isn't serious books. Though some of them has good morals. But I pass through the Universal Spelling Book at school, Mr. Haynes, and when you pass through that you knows something, you can take it from me. And I can tell you, Mr. Haynes, it was a real good book. A 1 and no mistake. High, high class. But how do men think of these things, Mr. Haynes? Education. That's what it is. Education. If I had a child I would sacrifice anything to give him education. Thanks very much, Mr. Haynes. I'll take every care of this one.'

She had barely disappeared before Maisie's lip curled in a rather bitter sneer.

'But listen to the withered old monkey. If she had a child! Well, my God, if she make a child—'

'Quiet, please, Maisie,' warned Haynes.

But Miss Atwell must have heard. Usually she did not carry news on Maisie, and if not on the side of quiet was always on the side of peace, but she was the only person who could have told

Mrs. Rouse that Maisie was smoking a cigarette. And even if she mentioned it, she could hardly have foreseen the consequences. Mrs. Rouse suddenly appeared at the door and caught Maisie in the very act of emitting smoke from her lips, head thrown back, face to the ceiling and underlip extended.

She walked quickly in.

'Mr. Haynes, you must excuse me. I have to disrespect you today. So is that you coming too, eh, young lady? You smoking? Not in my house.' And she boxed Maisie right and left about the face until to save herself Maisie ran from the room.

Haynes had no time to say a word even if he had thought of something to say, Mrs. Rouse had been so expeditious. Then he heard Maisie's voice outside raised.

'You old advantage-taker! But I am not going to take this so, though. By Christ, I am not going to take it so.'

The incident ruined the day. Maisie had undoubtedly been hardly treated. Although Mrs. Rouse had never actually caught her she knew that Maisie smoked. And Maisie was not smoking in her house. The room was Haynes's room. As Maisie said, it was a piece of advantage-taking. Maisie complained to Haynes that he ought not to allow Mrs. Rouse to treat his room as if it were her own house. But when Mrs. Rouse later apologized profusely, Haynes brushed her apologies away. He was one of them now, sharer of joys and troubles. He knew it and not so much welcomed it as took it for granted. It was the quarrel between both his good friends that worried him. And what reason was there for it? Maisie answered at once.

'Why she do that? Why? Because her heart hurting her that

Mr. Benoit spending Christmas with the nurse instead of here. But that is no reason why she must beat me as if I am pudding. If she want to beat somebody let her go down to town and beat the nurse. I didn't steal her man. Benoit, Benoit, Benoit. That man is an evil spirit haunting this house. But I am not going to take this so, I not going to take it so.'

She spoke loudly so that Mrs. Rouse could not fail to hear.

'You not going to take it? Do what you like. And to besides, don't give me too much of your cheeks out there. What can you do?'

'You'll see,' said Maisie.

'Look here,' said Mrs. Rouse and came to the door, but Miss Atwell told her not to bother.

Haynes was troubled, not only by the incident, but by a certain open defiance in Maisie's attitude of which he was now fully aware for the first time. He knew Mrs. Rouse's temper and he now was beginning to be aware of Maisie's. He felt that he had to be on the alert to prevent trouble. He realized that whatever he said would carry weight with them, and with this realization came a sense of responsibility and increasing confidence. Miss Atwell, too, was his abject slave and admired his appearance, his clothes, his speech and everything about him with a personal pleasure and a desire to please that overbore embarrassment.

How these women centred round a man.

'It's good to be a man,' said Haynes to himself, and girded himself for the task of showing both Maisie and himself what a man he was.

Chapter Twenty-Two

On Old Year's night Miss Atwell paid Haynes a visit. She wished him profuse compliments of the season and came straight to her point. She said that she hoped he wouldn't be vexed but she had taken it upon herself to ask him about his boarding. Mrs. Rouse had not sent her, but Haynes could see how things were in the house, and if he could manage to let Mrs. Rouse board him at about twenty dollars a month it would be of 'mateeral' assistance to their kind landlady. She assured him a second time that Mrs. Rouse had nothing to do with her asking. Haynes told her cautiously that he had been thinking of 'coming to some new, temporary arrangement with Mrs. Rouse' for some time and at least would be glad to 'discuss the matter' with her. It would be easier for him and he was sure it would be easier for her also. But Ella had been his servant for so long that he would not do anything which hurt her feelings in any way. He might perhaps board with Mrs. Rouse until Ella came back, but yet—

'Ella is the person I am considering, Miss Atwell,' he concluded.

'We knows that, Mr. Haynes. But Ella is sick and she is gone so long.'

'But still you know, she may be better.'

'I heard from a friend of hers whom she wrote that she was still pretty bad. I thought she had wrote to you to tell you, Mr. Haynes. She has not written?'

'No, she hasn't; but she wouldn't write.'

Ella would have died rather than expose her writing and spelling to her master.

'Mrs. Rouse knows that you have come to ask me?'

'Yes,' admitted Miss Atwell. 'We was talkin' over the New Year and how bad things lookin' and I tell her I am goin' to speak to you.'

Haynes had a bad two minutes. The old attempt by the nurse had made him wary on the question. But the way they all flew to do anything for him, Mrs. Rouse's kindness to him, the kindness of all of them, his authority in the house. On the other hand, Ella's long and faithful attendance to his every wish, her trust and confidence in him.

'Help the poor soul, Mr. Haynes. She need it.'

Miss Atwell sat motionless, her hands crossed in her lap; her shining eyes met Haynes's whenever he looked at her.

'Very well, Miss Atwell,' said Haynes, with decision. 'Tell Mrs. Rouse I shall start with her tomorrow. In the morning we will make arrangements.'

'You is doin' her a good turn, Mr. Haynes. God will bless you. Good night, Mr. Haynes, and sleep well.'

That was December 31st. Mrs. Rouse and Haynes concluded

arrangements on New Year's Day and inasmuch as he had the money and boarding meant her spending, he paid her twenty dollars in advance for January. That was January 1st. On January 4th (Maisie's birthday) Haynes learnt that Ella was in town. She had come in on the morning of the second, but by some means or other had heard that he was boarding with Mrs. Rouse. How she and her set managed to be so well informed about anything in which they were interested was a marvel, but heard she had and, accepting the circumstances, had not even come to see him to discuss the question. Haynes would never have known that she was back in town at all if Maisie had not told him, and told him with relish that she heard Ella was looking well and had come back to work. Haynes waited a day or two wishing that Ella would come and get the interview over.

On the second afternoon as soon as he reached home he asked again. Had she been? Maisie was quietly superior.

'No, Mr. Haynes. You ought to know Ella well enough to realize that she will not come here again.'

'Then I shall have to go to see her and explain,' said Haynes.

'Why bother?'

Haynes knew the interview would be awkward, but knew, too, that it had to take place. 'And I must stop putting off things. I'll go immediately after supper.'

Ella did not receive him coldly. She laughed, and he told her he was glad to see her looking so well.

'You lookin' well, too, sir,' she replied. 'Mrs. Rouse and them takin' good care o' you, sir . . . I hear you boardin' with them, sir, and you don't want me, sir. That's why I didn't come.'

'It isn't that I didn't want you any more, Ella.' He explained to her as best he could. When he told her that Miss Atwell had assured him that she was still ill, she rapped out:

'That's a lie. I was well before Christmas and I was comin'. But everybody tell me to stop and spend Christmas, especially as I know you used to go to the country for Christmas.'

Ella was taking it easily, but her resentment was plain. She had stuck to him all through his mother's illness, had helped in ways for which he could never repay her, and now when she was ill, he had allowed these strangers to take him away. And yet he knew that Ella was not blaming him, but was wrath with them.

Haynes said goodbye.

'Goodbye, sir. I sorry the day I ever take you to No. 2, sir. I know from the first that they was goin' to try and get you away from me, sir. That Mrs. Rouse! She don't look it, but she is as deep a tricker as the rest, sir. Beware o' them people, sir.'

The next two or three days were difficult ones for Haynes. The household with remarkable sensitiveness avoided him – even Maisie, probably on Mrs. Rouse's stringent orders; perhaps, however, she was on some intimate affair of her own. Haynes felt that he had been had. And it was the feeling that Mrs. Rouse had been concerned in some low conspiracy against him that worried him. He found himself thinking of it at meals, at work, in bed; and some of his old timidity and distrustfulness came creeping over him. The awkwardness over Ella he had been able to overcome without difficulty. But he had been fitting himself into the home life at No. 2, and now this thing had come to upset him. He felt surprisingly desolate. Was all this good will and kindness merely to catch him? Was he a trusting Simple Simon? He did not know what to think and was surprised how much he worried over such a little thing. After all, he lived there, was very comfortable. They were as nice as ever. Why bother? But still he doubted and brooded until, chiefly through Maisie, his doubts were resolved, or at least he worried about the matter no longer.

Maisie was determined to get even with Mrs. Rouse. Haynes heard Mrs. Rouse say once or twice that Maisie was doing her best to pick a quarrel. He thought that the expression was only a figure of speech for Maisie's usual mischievousness. But the words were literally true, for Maisie exerted herself until she had deliberately brought about a tension. On the Sunday after New Year's Day the quarrel broke at last.

'Yes,' she screamed from the alley, whither she had retired after the early exchanges, 'all you only have eyes for me, all that I doing, how I bad. But God going to punish all you for your wicked deeds. All you take away Mr. Haynes from Ella. From the first day the gentleman come here all you been trying to take him away. And when all you couldn't get him, all you invite him and give him a lot of food and things to drink to fool him. You lie on Ella and say she sick? Elsie Daniel come here and I hear her tell all you that she see Ella in Hastings and that Ella well and coming back, and all you lie and lie and lie until all you take him away to get his money to spend.'

Mrs. Rouse emerged from the kitchen, hatchet in hand: 'I going to kill her this morning,' she said. 'This is the end. Nobody tell me anything.'

Since that night with Benoit and the knife Haynes had always treated Mrs. Rouse's histrionics with a measure of seriousness. He did not wait for Miss Atwell, but went straight out and held Mrs. Rouse by the arm.

'Don't worry yourself, Mrs. Rouse. You think I believe all that rubbish Maisie is babbling out there? She is only doing it to worry you. I know it is not true. Maisie knows it is not true. But all she wants is to get you into a passion.'

Mrs. Rouse allowed herself to be disarmed and led back inside.

'Thank you, Mr. Haynes. It is good you are a gentleman like that. If was somebody else they would believe all the lies that flowing out of that girl's mouth.'

But all the demons of doubt and suspicion were once more active in Haynes's mind. He had been reading when the disturbance occurred, but now he put his book on the floor beside him and sat up in the armchair thinking hard. If all this had been mere pretence and he had been the prey of designing people he would go back to his mother's house, send for Ella and shut himself away from the world again. Suddenly Mrs. Rouse appeared at the doorstep.

'Mr. Haynes,' she said. 'Here is your twenty dollars.' And she held out the four green notes in her hand. 'Take it back. You have been too much of a help in my great trouble for that child of evil to say the things she is saying. I am old enough to be your mother, Mr. Haynes, and God is my witness . . .'

She broke down and Haynes rose to his feet and held her hand and closed her fingers over the notes.

'No, no, no, Mrs. Rouse. I believe you. I believe you absolutely. If I didn't I wouldn't stay here. You have my fullest confidence as I know I have yours.'

'Them is noble words,' said Miss Atwell, who had been listening just outside the door, and came in to add her quota.

Five minutes after both had gone and Haynes was left alone. He wanted to tell the spiteful little bitch, yes, that's what she was, a spiteful little bitch, exactly what he thought of her. He felt implicit confidence in Mrs. Rouse now, a confidence which nothing that Maisie said would ever shake. He felt a load lifted off his shoulders and only then knew how much the good will and sincerity of No. 2 meant to him. And Maisie. He felt an itching in his tongue to tell her that she was a spiteful little bitch. Never in his life had Haynes used such words or applied them to anyone even in his mind. He had heard the expression used once by Benoit months ago and now he remembered it. How it would startle Maisie! Curious that though he was certain she was lying and wanted to curse her for it he hadn't the slightest ill-will towards her. He made up his mind to greet her with the words if she came. It would help. But Maisie did not come.

Chapter Twenty-Three

It was about this time that Benoit started to show himself round No. 2, walking up and down, standing at the corner, even talking to Maisie on the side-walk. Contrary to the general expectation, Mrs. Rouse never stirred an inch to see him, though some of the family peeped through the front window. Mrs. Rouse had never met him and said she didn't want to. She said she had been living in sin, God had punished her and shown her the way out and she prayed to Him for courage and strength to live a decent life. Once, however, when Maisie raised a wolf cry of 'The nurse! The nurse!' Mrs. Rouse left a slipper behind in her dash to catch a glimpse. She said she wanted to see how the prostitute was faring as a married woman.

Although the town was small, neither Haynes nor Mrs. Rouse had ever seen the nurse since the day she had left No. 2. Maisie had stolen away once or twice to see her, Philomen had met her and they talked, Miss Atwell saw her and passed her as if it was she and not Mrs. Rouse who had been deprived of Benoit. But Mrs. Rouse and Haynes, who most wanted to see her, never.

When they did see her, they saw her together, the day she was sentenced.

About four o'clock one afternoon Haynes was driving in the tramcar, on the firm's business, when he caught a fleeting glimpse of the tail-end of a crowd above which towered a policeman's helmet. Many heads turned and there was a buzz of conversation in the tram. At the next stop someone came into the tram and, as is the habit in the West Indies, started to tell the conductor all about it. The crowd was following a nurse, a thin little white woman, married the other day to a black fellow, Benoit. Some report had been made to the police-station about her stealing things. A policeman had arrested her and was taking her to the station. The news had created a sensation in the town, for many people knew the nurse, especially since the romantic marriage.

Haynes hurried through what he had to do and sped home as fast as he could in order to be able to give the news to Mrs. Rouse. Had she succumbed to temptation and informed the police? He did not think so. But he wanted to know and to hear what she would say when she heard. But with all his haste, Philomen forestalled him. He was just in time for the tail-end of her account. Maisie, Miss Atwell, Aucher and one or two neighbours formed a group in the yard while Philomen told what she had seen. As soon as Haynes appeared she stopped.

'Mr. Haynes!' said Maisie.

'You heard, Mr. Haynes?' said Mrs. Rouse. 'If you were in town, you heard.'

'Yes,' Haynes replied, 'but don't let me interrupt Philomen. Go on, Philomen. You said you saw her coming down with the parcels—'

'Yes, Mr. Haynes. She had a big basket of clothes on her hand as when you carryin' a baby, and the two police one on each side and the inspector behind. And one crowd of people! But she wasn't crying nor nothing, you know. She had on the uniform and the glasses and her head straight up. And so she pass into the station. I was going close, but they had too much people, so I make my round as fast as I could and come back up to tell Mrs. Rouse. I just reach.'

'If was me I would 'ave died,' said Miss Atwell.

'I know I wouldn't have carried any basket,' said Maisie. 'To go down I would have had to go down, but they couldn't force me to carry any basket. If they wanted any basket they could have carried it themselves.'

Mrs. Rouse looked at her, but decided to say nothing. She spoke to Haynes.

'You see what I was telling you that day was no lie, Mr. Haynes. God let it work round so. That is my revenge.' Her lips were a piece of wire and her eyes shone like steel. 'God is great, Mr. Haynes, look what she come to. Down Main Street like the common thief that she is, carrying all that she thief before her. And Mr. Benoit! Where he going to hide his head, Mr. Haynes? Where he going to put it? But let him look out for himself, too, Mr. Haynes. See if they don't work him into it. She is his wife. He have to stand responsible for her; he cannot shirk his duty now. He went in the church with her. For better or for worse. And, Mr. Haynes, he used to wear the things. People used to see him.

You watch and see whether they don't bring him in with her before the case finish.'

She paused for lack of breath.

'But if you did see her goin' down!' said Philomen. 'All the barristers and solicitors and clerks in Court Street comin' out to watch her goin' down with this big parcel. And the police! And the people! God, if was me, I would have died.'

'Poor thing!' said Maisie.

There was scarcely an occasion Haynes could remember in which Maisie either through inadvertence or malice, or both, did not with infallible instinct say or do the thing most calculated to ignite Mrs. Rouse.

'Poor thing! It would take a dog like you to say "poor thing." Yes. You and she is the same breed. That's why you say "poor thing." You didn't say "poor thing" when you was helping she and the man to stab me in my back. All the persecutions the woman persecute me you didn't say "poor thing." When I working here day and night to get food to give you, you don't say "poor thing." But when God give this one what she deserve – look here, girl, move.' Mrs. Rouse was already in a frightful passion and advanced a step towards Maisie. 'Move, before I strike you down.' Miss Atwell rushed dramatically in between them. Miss Atwell, though sincerely deploring the quarrels, enjoyed the part of peacemaker, especially when it came to rushing in 'to save Mrs. Rouse from trouble.'

Maisie walked quietly off.

'Strike me down, eh? You think is so people does get strike down? Try it and see if both of us don't sleep with the nurse tonight.'

'Don't bother with her, Mrs. Rouse,' said Miss Atwell. 'Don't mind. Words don't break bones. I's all right.'

And Mrs. Rouse, who had shown signs of following Maisie, sat down on the bench.

'Mr. Haynes, God is too good. Pray to Him and He will never desert you. Mr. Haynes, today is Thursday. Saturday gone I get a letter. Look, if you knew my distress when I read it.'

'Whom from?'

'From that woman. Who else?'

'Show Mr. Haynes the letter,' said Miss Atwell.

'No. I can't show Mr. Haynes that,' said Mrs. Rouse.

'But why not?' said Miss Atwell. 'Mr. Haynes is a big man. He ain't no little boy.

'Show Mr. Haynes the letter,' insisted Miss Atwell, who had no hesitations nor reticences whatever with anyone, and once when Haynes noticed that she was at home for a few days and unsuspectingly enquired what was wrong, embarrassed him horribly by telling him that, of course, she need not tell him what it was that kept her, but she hoped before long that the change of life, 'you know, Mr. Haynes,' would rid her of her difficulties.

Mrs. Rouse took from her pocket and handed him a cheap envelope addressed to 'Mrs. A. Rouse, 2, Minty Alley.' Inside was a piece of foolscap paper on which Haynes read as follows:

'You son of a bitch, you not ashamed. You dog, you bitch, you son of a bitch. You still encouraging the man. You think you going to take him away but he leave you. Why don't you leave him alone. He had your latitude for eighteen years and he leave you because he don't want you any more. You have no shame.

You wouldn't get him away no matter how you try. What an old bitch like you want with a man. Why don't you take Aucher or Mr. Haynes. You dog.'

Haynes handed it back without a word.

'Mr. Haynes, she and the man been quarrelling since a week after they married. I hear last week he leave her for good. She hear he is coming round here so she must think he coming back to me. But I don't want him, Mr. Haynes. I trying to make my peace with God. And then for that woman to write me this!'

'But I shouldn't have let such a childish letter worry me,' said Haynes.

'Same thing I tells her,' said Miss Atwell.

'Oh, Mr. Haynes! You not a woman. Look at the things the woman write in the letter. If you know how I feel when I get it. But, Mr. Haynes, God not sleeping.'

She stood up and she raised her right hand in the air, with the forefinger pointing upwards.

'No, Mr. Haynes, He not sleeping. I get the letter on Saturday. Sunday morning I went to church. I say: "God, the protector of the widow and the fatherless, You know I have nobody else but You. Look down on me with the eyes of pity and give me my revenge on the one who have done me this injustice." Mr. Haynes, that was Sunday. Monday, Tuesday, Wednesday – three days – and look where she is. And let Mr. Benoit look to himself. His turn coming next. Let him look to himself.'

The nurse got bail and her case was called and adjourned. Again No. 2 was in a fever. The general expectation there was that she would get three months at least. But Haynes heard in town that she would probably be heavily fined. The charge was a serious one, but it was whispered that many of the people she had attended did not wish her to go to gaol, and strong influence would be brought to bear on her behalf.

On the day of the case, however, Haynes was in Court. He had carefully arranged, days before, to be away from the shop that morning. Mrs. Rouse had got up at three o'clock to make the cakes, and she and Miss Atwell (who had sent an excuse of illness to her shirt factory) had gone long before him. Maisie, too, was there. Philomen hoped to get a chance to look in sometime. Aucher, sojourning at No. 2 for a while, was left in charge at home. Aucher went to the house of justice too often on business to go there for pleasure.

When Haynes went into the court house that morning the place was crowded. He saw Miss Atwell and Philomen in the front row of spectators and wondered where Mrs. Rouse was. Maisie he did not see at once, but soon discovered her in animated conversation with a young solicitor's clerk. At five minutes to nine – Court began at nine – those who were to be tried walked upstairs from the marshal's room, a constable in front and one behind. Today the nurse, whose case came first, headed the procession. She came up the steps, 'thin as a string and flat as a board' (Miss Atwell) and very pale; but she carried herself erect, and Haynes could not help admiring the courage with which she was at least beginning the day. She saw him and gave him a slight smile and an inclination of the head. Haynes had just replied when Mrs. Rouse, who had concealed herself in an alcove in the passage, suddenly jumped out. There was a little space between the policeman in front and the nurse. Mrs. Rouse moved quickly into it and barred the way of the nurse, who fell back and threw the line into disorder. Mrs. Rouse had an umbrella in her hand, but contrary to the expectation of those who were looking on she did not attempt (nor had she ever had in mind) any assault on the nurse. Blocking the nurse's way she struck the umbrella two or three times on the concrete floor and throwing her head back she said:

'Doggie! Doggie! Look bone!'

Luckily she had no more to say. The two policemen threw her roughly out of the way. But she did not mind. She had done what she had planned to do. She went to Philomen, who had been holding her seat for her, and put on her glasses to follow the case.

The nurse was fined fifteen pounds or three months. Mrs. Rouse, who had confidently expected and freely predicted that she could not escape gaol, was disappointed, but not too much so. Her triumph of the morning filled her heart.

All the afternoon at No. 2 they discussed the case, saying over and over again to one another what each had seen.

'You remember when he ask her . . .'

'And you remember how she look at Benoit when he . . .'

Mrs. Rouse: 'All you notice when they ask him about the links how he look at me before he answer?'

After supper, Mrs. Rouse, Miss Atwell and Philomen came to Haynes's door.

'We are going for a little walk on the seawall,' said Mrs. Rouse.

'To talk over things,' said Haynes.

'Yes, Mr. Haynes,' said Mrs. Rouse. 'I feel happy. I know that God have not deserted me.'

'And this is you' vindication before the public,' said Miss Atwell. Philomen laughed gaily.

'Isn't Maisie going too?' said Haynes.

'No, I am tired. I don't feel to go for any walk tonight,' said Maisie. 'I going to bed early.'

Something in her voice, and in the way she stretched herself as she spoke, touched chords in Haynes. He realized that his moment had come.

Chapter Twenty-Four

It was a very simple affair after all. When Haynes thought of all his longings and doubts and hesitations, he was amazed that possessing Maisie was so easy a business. 'Hold her and kiss her,' Benoit had said. So he held her and kissed her, and then to his astonishment did what he liked with her. He could not look her in the eye the next morning, but gradually that awkwardness wore off. Maisie was the soul of discretion. 'Mrs. Rouse must never, never know,' she said, and as Haynes would also have been ashamed for Mrs. Rouse to know, they kept their secret. Maisie's manner scarcely changed. She told him risqué jokes which formerly she had declined to do. They never made love except when they were about to go to bed together. The affair was not altogether what he had expected it would be, but as he wanted no more than Maisie gave, he missed nothing.

But day by day they became better friends. Intimate conversations they had only when lying in bed together, all passion spent. And then they scarcely talked about their relationship, but about No. 2 and the people who lived in it. How Mrs. Rouse hated Maisie because she had seen Benoit looking at Maisie and knew that Maisie could have taken him away with one wink. Of what a dirty dog that Benoit was and how Mrs. Rouse had slept for years with her lawful husband and thought that sleeping with a man was a duty as a wife and that was all; and then Benoit had taught her differently and made her his slave for eighteen years. Of what a liar Miss Atwell was (when caught fairly she would beg to be excused and called it her 'magination), but that at heart she was a good soul; of all the shifts of the household to live; all sorts of details, general and personal, about the whole past history of No. 2. She told him how they all liked him from the first day he came because he was so polite, and how Mrs. Rouse had sneered at Maisie and told her that she thought so much of herself, but that a young gentleman like Mr. Haynes would never look at her! There was a smile in her voice.

'Why did you take so long, Mr. Haynes?'

'Well, you see, Maisie, I didn't know.'

'The nurse was after you, you know, Mr. Haynes.'

'What!'

Haynes nearly jumped out of the bed.

'Yes, you didn't know? She told Mrs. Rouse one day that you were still a baby, that she had never seen such an innocent as you and that she would like to take you away to the seaside for a month, and when you came back you would be a man.'

'And what did Mrs. Rouse say?'

'She said. You wouldn't get angry, Mr. Haynes?'

'Not at all.'

'She said: "Leave the poor darling alone, nurse. You don't see them often like that today. If I had a son like that I would work my fingers to the bone to see him somebody in the land."'

'And what happened?'

'Nothing.'

'And did you think I would have anything to do with the nurse?'

'Not at all, Mr. Haynes. I knew you liked me.'

'Oh you did, did you? How did you know?'

'I knew.'

One night she told him that Mrs. Rouse had pawned her last piece of jewellery that day.

'Heavens! I wish I could help her,' said Haynes, 'but I have no money, Maisie. I am always hard-up.'

'But why, Mr. Haynes? You have a good job. People come here and tell us that you are a very bright young man and have a future.'

'Maybe. Do you know what my salary is?'

'Ten dollars a week at least.'

'Five. And I do more work than the boss, who draws forty. He leaves everything to me.'

'Tell me about it, Mr. Haynes.' And Haynes told her to her rising indignation. She sat up in bed.

'But what are you going to do, Mr. Haynes? We all thought you were getting ten dollars a week at least. Miss Atwell said fifteen. Ella knew?'

'Yes. Why?'

'Because she said she didn't. The nurse tried to pump her. Mr. Haynes, why don't you go and ask for a raise.'

'I asked him and he said later he would consider it and let me know.'

'How long ago was that?'

'When I first came here.'

'And you haven't asked since?'

'No.'

'If was me I would ask him and threaten him with a week's notice.'

Maisie said no more, but a few days after, when they were in bed together again and talking, she said:

'Mr. Haynes, listen to me. I have friends in the offices in town, and was speaking to one of them. Go and tell Mr. Carritt that you feel your salary is too small, that you think you have waited long enough and want to hear something from him.'

'But suppose he gets angry and sacks me.'

'He wouldn't do that. People don't get sacked like that. I ask all my friends. "How much you think Haynes is getting?" And the least they say is ten dollars. Everyone says that you are valuable to the firm. And they say you are conceited and stuck-up because you are getting on so well and Carritt can't do without you. But I know that isn't true about your being stuck-up.'

Haynes said he would think it over.

Day after day Maisie stuck at him. She abused Carritt with a personal animus that astonished Haynes, who could not understand why Maisie should so hate someone she had never even seen.

'He is an old advantage-taker. And if i's one thing I hate i's people taking advantage.'

At last one Sunday night (on Sunday evenings Mrs. Rouse and Miss Atwell usually went out together) with her arms around him and her lips on his, Maisie dug a promise out of him.

'Mr. Haynes, you were afraid to ask me. And I was only waiting. Go and tell him.' She held him tight and shook him, and Haynes promised. He would ask the next day. Next morning she saw him to the road. 'And mind you, Mr. Haynes, be serious with the man. Don't tell him if he don't give you will leave, but let him see that you mean business. Talk to him like the day you made the speech. He wouldn't say no. God, I wish it was me.'

That afternoon as soon as he turned the corner he could see Maisie standing by the front of No. 2. She came running to meet him.

'Don't tell me you didn't ask him, Mr. Haynes.'

'I asked him,' said Haynes, gravely.

'And what happened?' asked Maisie, apprehensively.

'He asked me what I thought I required,' said Haynes, still gravely.

'And what you said? Five, I hope, Mr. Haynes.'

'I said five.'

'And what he said, Mr. Haynes?' Haynes put aside his gravity and held her by the arm.

'Said that was exactly what he was thinking. And he intended to let me have it at the end of the financial year. The liar. I should have asked him before. I saw the old sinner go pale when I looked at him. I am going to manage him in future. I'll never forget you, Maisie.'

'Me, Mr. Haynes. You'll never forget me? You mustn't say such things.' She was smiling, but she was serious.

'Why mustn't I say such things?' said Haynes, but he spoke mechanically.

'Because they aren't true. Come, let us go in. Give me the bicycle.' And giving herself a vigorous kick-off with one foot, she rode on the pedal along the side of the house and turned in between the kitchen and the cistern with a grace and dexterity which were the wonder and admiration of the yard.

Chapter Twenty-Five

Haynes lent Mrs. Rouse twenty dollars to be paid by six monthly deductions from his board and lodging. He and Maisie planned it. Somewhat to his surprise Maisie raised no objections to his helping Mrs. Rouse. She said she didn't hate Mrs. Rouse that way. She wasn't going to stand any damned nonsense from her and that was as far as it went. She didn't want to pull the old bitch down. Haynes wanted to write a letter. Maisie said: 'No, go and tell her, Mr. Haynes. No need to write any letter. You are not begging for anything.'

So Haynes went up and spoke his piece and felt so happy after that he was glad he had taken Maisie's advice. And after that he was the master of the house. Nothing was ever done without consulting him. He made up Mrs. Rouse's accounts, told her what to pay, and wrote letters to the more difficult creditors, endorsed a note for her (the business simply would not go well), and as Mrs. Rouse told him one day was of far more help to her than Benoit had ever been in his life. About Maisie's intimacy with Haynes she appeared not to know. And even if she did know! As

Maisie was always saying, it was his own business. But he made arrangements and met Maisie elsewhere.

One morning Mrs. Rouse brought Haynes a letter she had received from her admirer – a formal proposal, asking her to live with him. This admirer, who had materialized at last, was a retired police-sergeant and a man of some reputation. The wife of the Inspector-General, the Colonial Secretary, the Governor's aide-de-camp and some others formed a very fast set and used to rush away for one-day parties to a little island off the main coast. There had been very nearly some drowning once, and ever afterwards the Inspector had sent Parkes on the launch with a personal request 'to keep an eye on them.' Parkes was discreet until he left the service; only then did he speak, and being no man of letters but a good Christian, his references were to Sodom and Gomorrah instead of Boccaccio and Rabelais. There was no doubt that Parkes was a proper man. He wrote that he had always loved Mrs. Rouse, but couldn't address her as she had somebody already. But now the way was clear he sent to assure her of his love and to say that he would always cherish her. Then came a most convincing piece. He had heard the house was mortgaged. He had some money saved and would pay off the mortgage if Mrs. Rouse would put the house on his name and hers. His pension was forty-five dollars a month, and together they would be able to live like Isaac and Rebecca to a green old age. He promised to treat her kindly, and she could be sure he would never do her what the venomous reptile had done her. It was an honest and sincere letter. It had come by first post, and Mrs. Rouse being busy and not knowing the handwriting, had asked one of the boarders, a Miss Hart, who happened to be in the kitchen, to read it for her, so that everybody heard and laughed at it before Mrs. Rouse brought it to Haynes. When she came to Haynes's step work was suspended and they all stood round in the yard while he read.

'And what are you going to do, Mrs. Rouse? Accept him?'

For some reason or other, to judge by its effect, this question was thought extremely funny. And Philomen's 'But hear, Mr. Haynes,' contained not only amusement but surprise.

'Mr. Haynes,' said Mrs. Rouse, 'he don't want to cherish me as he put there. He have six children and i's them he want me to mind. That is what he want.'

The group became aware of Maisie almost in hysterics on the little bench.

'But what's wrong with you, Maisie?' asked Miss Hart.

The laughter which Maisie had been trying in vain to suppress overflowed and she wandered across the yard, her head thrown back, her hands on her hips, laughing so that she could be heard at the end of the alley.

'But what's wrong with her?'

Mrs. Rouse's face hardened.

'She is laughing at me because somebody write me a love letter,' and Maisie's extra loud cackle proved that Mrs. Rouse was right. 'She think that an old woman like me i's a joke for me to get a letter. I tell you I wouldn't want any letter from those nasty little good-for-nothings I see you talking to by the gate every night.'

Mrs. Rouse went back into the kitchen, swearing that she wasn't going to stand Maisie much longer.

For the next day or two there was a lot of talk about the offer.

Miss Atwell said if it was she he did ask she 'wasn't goin' to let 'im pass.' She had seen him in the street and he looked a steady, respectable man, and with a person like Mrs. Rouse and with Mrs. Rouse's nice and takin' ways, they was sure to get on well. Another thing was that he wouldn't prove the 'venimous reptile' that the other had done. She asked Haynes what he thought of it. Haynes said that he could not express an opinion.

Mr. Parkes was coming for his answer on Friday morning, and what Mrs. Rouse intended Haynes did not know. She said nothing to anybody. Once or twice in the yard her eyes and his happened to meet and she gave him a self-conscious smile and a blush. That was all, but she was brighter than usual that week, her temper was better, and the general opinion, doubtful at first, veered round to the view that she would take Parkes. On the Friday morning she was up early and dressed herself better than she had done for a long time. Haynes thought she was preparing for Parkes, for whom things seemed to be moving well. She looked quite fresh and there was a brightness in her face. Parkes was serious, as his offer to pay off the mortgage showed, and Haynes could not believe that bare-faced as Benoit was he would have the courage to fight a case in court, especially as by some lucky chance, for the eight years that they had owned the house, the duty of paying the taxes and the rates had always fallen to Mrs. Rouse, and all receipts were made in her name. Late one night she had slipped into Haynes's room and they had talked the matter over. She couldn't decide. Haynes asked her if she still cared for Benoit. She repudiated the idea. 'Well, I don't see why you shouldn't take him, Mrs. Rouse,' said Haynes. 'I am glad to hear you say that, Mr. Haynes,' said Mrs. Rouse. 'I felt that I should, but I wanted to hear what you had to say first.' He was rather dubious now that his opinion had turned the scale.

'But suppose it doesn't turn out well, Mrs. Rouse.'

'I wouldn't blame you, Mr. Haynes,' said Mrs. Rouse. 'I know that whatever you advise me you are thinking of my interest.'

Mrs. Rouse had a surprise in store for No. 2. For even before Haynes left for work she said she had business to do and went off to town.

When Haynes came back to lunch she had not yet returned. He surmised that she was evading the issue and was pondering on the eternal coquette that sleeps in all women when Maisie startled him by jumping into the room in a state of high excitement.

'Mr. Haynes! He came, you know.'

'Who? Sergeant Parkes?'

'Yes, and I fix him up. When I see Mrs. Rouse leave here this morning I was only hoping she wouldn't come back in time.'

'What have you done now, Maisie?' Haynes asked in some alarm, for Maisie was as reckless as a runaway horse, and had made it known that she was against Mrs. Rouse having anything to do with Parkes. She said she didn't want any old man in the place and having made it her business to see Parkes, animadverted on his whiskers, which she said would turn her stomach every morning she got up and saw them.

'What have you done, Maisie?' Haynes asked her again. 'Come, speak up.' He was frightened.

Maisie was laughing, but she was frightened too.

'I chase him away.'

'Who? Mr. Parkes?'

'Who? Mr. Parkes? Of course, Mr. Parkes. If he have the face to come back again—'

'Well, this is the end for you.'

Haynes was in a state of absolute consternation, for he realized what would be the probable consequences of Maisie's escapade. But the elation of action was still with Maisie.

'Let me tell you, Mr. Haynes,' she said. 'About nine o'clock the bourgeois come. He dress up in a tweed suit and waistcoat. So I carry him inside and ask him to sit down. Mrs. Rouse tell me if anybody come to say she gone to town and she will be busy the whole day, but will be here after supper. But I ain't tell him so. I say: "You are Mr. Parkes? Come in." I knew Mrs. Rouse wasn't coming back early. So I tell him, "Come and sit down, sir." I give him a nice sir, you know, to fool him off. "Mrs. Rouse will be here just now. She is having a bath." Mister sit down, you know, and I go in the bedroom peeping at him. He only fixing his tie and smoothing down the whiskers. I say to myself: "Boy, if you ever come to sleep in this house and I don't clip off those tiger-cat things you have there, I don't know." So, mister there, sir. Quarter-past nine. I tell him: "Mrs. Rouse coming just now. She taking a little time to dress herself nice, you know, sir." I tell him so and he laugh. He must be say to himself: "Ah! Things good!" The old fool! As if a lady will dress herself in a bathroom and anybody would bother to dress for an old ape like him. Half-past nine he begin to fidget. He call me. He say: "Young lady, Mrs. Rouse is staying long." I tell him: "Sir, a neighbour down the lane send to call her urgent. She coming now." But he get suspicious. I only praying to God now that Mrs. Rouse don't come by accident, for I have some more waiting for him. Then mister get up, vex' now. He say: "But this is all nonsense. That is not the way to treat—" I tell him: "Excuse me, sir, but you seem dull of comprehension." He say: "What!" I tell him: "Can't you see your presence here is not requested?" He jump up. He say again: "What!" and he went out to Aucher. Aucher in the kitchen. But Aucher will do anything I tell him, you know, and I have Aucher ready for him. So he say: "Boy, where is Mrs. Rouse?" Aucher tell him in his big voice: "Who you calling boy?" He say: "Excuse me, but where is Mrs. Rouse?" Aucher say: "Don't ask me anything." And mister take up his hat and he stamp off.'

'My God, Maisie,' cried Haynes. 'Mrs. Rouse is going to murder you.'

'I don't care a damn,' she said. 'I don't want any old man with whiskers in this house.'

'Where is Mrs. Rouse?'

'I don't know, I suppose she coming just now.'

Haynes pondered for a second. 'You must leave this room, Maisie. I don't want Mrs. Rouse to come here and catch us talking. This is the end of you, you know.'

'I don't care,' she said.

Her wilful blindness to the consequences of her madness infuriated him.

'Damn you to hell, Maisie. Couldn't you think of other people a little? Couldn't you think of me?' He had been so happy, life was moving so smoothly and now—

'You haven't done anything. What is it to you? I didn't want him here and I wouldn't have him here. And don't damn me, Mr. Haynes. I have never heard you damn anyone before. And you mustn't begin with me.'

'I'll damn you when I please.' He looked at his watch. 'Come on, dress yourself. I have to be here when Mrs. Rouse learns about this. If I am not here she'll kill you.'

'Kill who? She! All this hatchet and knife business is only a lot of style she makes.'

'Don't argue. You have to leave the place with me. Here is some money. Go to the pictures. And mind you, don't you show your nose in this house until after five.'

'All right, boss,' said Maisie.

'Hurry up. I am not leaving here until I see you out of this place.'

'Yes, cap'n,' said Maisie, but she moved quickly away. In three minutes she was out.

'Don't pass by Argyle Street. You may meet her. Go down the Avenue.'

'All right, Mr. Haynes. But before I go, Mr. Haynes—' She was in one of her rarely serious moods.

'What is it?'

'I am sorry, Mr. Haynes, to cause you all this trouble. You are not vexed with me?'

'I am; damned vexed. Don't stop here talking. You make all this trouble and I have to get you out of it.' Maisie turned and walked away with slow steps and head down. Haynes began to be sorry for her, but hardened his heart and rode past her on his bicycle without turning to look. He had to teach her a lesson.

Chapter Twenty-Six

He worked that afternoon with feverish haste and anxiety. Maisie rang him up and he answered, telling her that if she went home before he did he would never speak to her again. She gave a very docile 'All right,' and he slammed the receiver down. If she was wretched she had every right to be. He would make it up with her some time, but not until this business was settled. He rode home as fast as he could, but when he reached did not go straight in but leant his bicycle against the side of the house and reconnoitred.

There was no sound of any disturbance. As he was going quietly across the yard to get into his room, Mrs. Rouse called to him from the dining-room and he stopped, nervous but ready.

'Mr. Haynes, you will not guess what happened here today.'

But there was no sign of anger on her face. Triumph, rather.

'Mr. Benoit come back here this afternoon.'

'Benoit!' said Haynes.

'Yes, sir, Benoit. Come right back like a dog to eat his vomit,' said Mrs. Rouse. 'Go in, Mr. Haynes. I am coming to tell you.'

She followed him into the room and sat down. She didn't know yet at any rate.

'Yes, sir. Come right back here this afternoon. But I knew he was coming, you know. He had to come. But let me tell you. I went to town to see my solicitor about some business I had been trying to fix all the week. They keep me there longer than I thought, you know how these solicitors disgusting, and up to now the man ain't tell me anything, tell me to come back next week. I drop off the car here about half-past one and I come straight in. Well, as I reach to go up the step, I hear, "Alice, Alice!" I turn round, and I see the man standing up in the yard. Mr. Haynes, you could imagine! From the day the man leave here I haven't seen him up to that hour. You could have knocked me down with a feather, and if you had run a pin into me I don't think you would have got a drop of blood. Anyway, I pull myself together, you know. God give me courage, and I ask him: "What you want here? You have no right here." And I watch him. He say: "I come to see you." I tell him: "Go to your wife. She is the one you have to see now." And I turn my back on him and walk into my bedroom. I sit down on the bed. I was feeling upset, you know, Mr. Haynes. So I lean my head on the bed like that. Then I suddenly feel somebody standing over me. And when I look up was he.'

'Into the bedroom?'

'Into the bedroom! You ever could imagine, Mr. Haynes, that the man so bare-faced? I face him stern. "You have no right here," I say. "I will call the police to put you out if you don't go." He say: "Yes, I know you will call the police. I hear you and the police very nice. I's that that bring me up here today." Sergeant

Parkes he mean, you know, Mr. Haynes. I tell him: "Yes, I have a protector now, so don't think you can take advantage of me." He tell me he hear I was going to take somebody and he come to find out if i's true and not to do it.'

'Well, I never,' said Haynes, and seeing Maisie standing in the yard, felt his heart sink. She had just reached; her hat was still on.

'Imagine that man, Mr. Haynes! But that is not all. I am telling you. I tell him: "You not ashamed McCarthy Benoit, to come here and come into this bedroom to ask me questions? Man, you ain't afraid God will strike you down?" He say: "If God ain't strike me down already he wouldn't strike me down again." I tell him: "Ah! I's your conscience pricking you now? But your troubles ain't begin yet, boy. Wait!" He talk a little bit, then he turn the conversation. He say: "But tell me, Alice——" "Alice to my friends," I tell him, "not you." He ain't say anything to that. He only stop a little bit, then he went on: "Tell me you not going to take him." Mr. Haynes, I look at the man. All his big punch gone. His eyes red, his clothes dirty, his face with a lot of hair on it. He look like a fowl that fall in a barrel of molasses. You know, Mr. Haynes, how bright Mr. Benoit used to be when he step out from here long ago. But where I reach? Yes. He ask me if I going to take Parkes. I tell him: "It's no business of yours. What you have to do with that?" He say: "Alice, wherever I go I see you before me." I tell him: "And you will see me to your dying day." And then I went for him, Mr. Haynes. I tell him all I was to him and all I do for him and how he treat me. I tell him: "Look at your condition. What care is the woman taking of you? You think when you was with me I would see you leaving this house looking as you looking now? Never.

When you was with me you was somebody. But look at you now. Who respects you? You are nobody. You have an old prostitute for your wife. You can't walk a street in the town without meeting a man who live with that woman you take and give your name." Mr. Haynes, I give him good and he ain't say a word. He hang his head like a dog. So when I finish he say: "Tell me, A., promise me you not going to take him." "I going to take him," I tell him. He say: "I'll prevent you." He catch a little spirit now. "You are mine until death," he say. "Never in this life," I tell him. I stand up, you know, for he rouse my spirit.'

Haynes could guess how she stood up and how she looked at him. But if she had driven away Benoit for Parkes she would rend Maisie limb from limb when she heard.

'I cow him, Mr. Haynes. I cow him down, for I had God on my side. Then he try to come near me to hold me. But I tell him that if he touch me I will bawl the house down. So he stand up looking sheepish and then I call for Aucher, and when I call he pick up himself and walk out.'

'So you have triumphed over both of them,' said Haynes.

'God will it so,' said Mrs. Rouse. 'He haven't kept me long.'

At half-past five, to Haynes's surprise, Miss Atwell, who never got home until long after seven, came hurrying into the yard.

'I am in at Mr. Haynes, Miss A.,' called Mrs. Rouse. 'What you doing here so early?'

'Hey, my dear! Good afternoon, Mr. Haynes. Excuse me, Mr. Haynes. So, Ma Rouse, I hear the man come back.'

Philomen had come up, heard the news, and the overworked girl had gone half a mile out of her way to tell Miss Atwell.

'As soon as she tell me I tell the boss that I get message somebody very sick at home and I come up to hear.'

Beads of perspiration covered her face and she fanned herself vigorously. Mrs. Rouse repeated the interview almost word for word, Miss Atwell making the appropriate ejaculations of astonishment, execration, admiration and here and there suggesting what Mrs. Rouse should have said or what she, Miss Atwell, would have said.

'God was testin' you, Mrs. R., to see if you have learnt you' lesson. But if you hadn't you would have been chastened with whips and scorpions. The owdacity of that man. 'E want to come back now and think 'e have only to wiggle his finger for you to come runnin'. 'E run 'is run and now, like the fox who lose his tail, 'e want to come back. The venimous reptile. Mrs. Rouse, I used to hear them girls in the kitchen say that if 'e did come back here you was goin' to take 'im, but I know you had better sense than that. But you are a good woman. You talk to 'im. But I'd 'a see him in the gutter with the dogs lickin' his sores and I wouldn't notice 'im.'

'Take him back, Miss Atwell! I take him back! The whole island would laugh at me. I wouldn't know how to walk the street. And if I take him back now after what he do me he have a right to kill me this time. Take him back! Never see the day.'

Haynes heard Aucher's deep voice at the door.

'Madam, the sergeant say 'e here to see you.'

Sergeant Parkes had returned.

Haynes braced himself for the ordeal. What would happen he did not know. All he knew was that he had to stand by and use his influence to stem the foaming torrent of Mrs. Rouse's righteous wrath. There was going to be a hell of a row. But he felt that difficult as it might be and awkwardly as the situation might develop, he could manage Mrs. Rouse. It would be hard, damned hard, but he could do it. He was watching her face intently. Did she know? Hardly. How would she greet her future partner? To his astonishment a slight expression of annoyance flitted across her face.

'Why that old man only bothering me? Tell him I am busy and I can't see him.'

But Sergeant Parkes, hat in hand and whiskers in evidence, was already by the door. A grey, but well-preserved military-looking man in the late fifties. His whiskers were certainly not attractive, but Haynes liked his face. Nor did he look like one who had come to complain about his ill-treatment of the morning. He had more important matters in hand. Suddenly Mrs. Rouse cut him off from Haynes's view. With a sudden movement she went and stood in the doorway.

'I am sorry, Mr. Parkes,' she said decisively, 'but I am afraid that we wouldn't be able to come to any arrangement.'

Haynes could not see Parkes, but the others told him afterwards what he looked like. Miss Atwell raised her hands in horrified amazement.

'But, Mrs. Rouse—' said Parkes.

'I have considered everything, Mr. Parkes,' said Mrs. Rouse, firmly. 'I am sorry.' And she turned back into the room. 'Man only bothering me,' she said. 'I don't want to have anything to do with any man.'

'He is gone?' Haynes asked.

Miss Atwell looked out.

'Yes, it looks as if 'e gone. Aucher, the gentleman gone?'

'Yes,' said Aucher.

There was a silence. Mrs. Rouse's hands lay idle in her lap and her eyes were on the floor.

'But I thought you was going to take 'im,' said Miss Atwell at last.

'I am too old for that sort of thing now. I had two experiences and that is enough for me. I's the third attack that kills.'

Maisie coming to the door on some pretext chose her moment skilfully, and under Mrs. Rouse's unsuspecting nose gave Haynes a wink of exquisite triumph.

Chapter Twenty-Seven

Benoit, defeated in the attempt to re-establish a footing in No. 2, began another series of persecutions directed against Mrs. Rouse. Once for a period of two or three weeks scarcely a day passed without somebody coming in and offering to buy No. 2 at some absurd price. It was in vain Mrs. Rouse protested that she was not selling. All told her that it was freely rumoured in town that the place was now for sale. Next, Mr. Rojas came up to see her. He said that a woman had come to see him and asked him to lend her some money to buy a property in the suburbs. She did not have all the money, but she would give him a mortgage on the building she was about to purchase. Asked where the house was she named it as No. 2, Minty Alley. Rojas told her he was sure she had made a mistake. She said no. She had sent someone to value the place and interview the owner, who was anxious to sell as she was leaving the island soon. It was easy to prove that Benoit had sent her.

It was all stupid, as Mrs. Rouse could not possibly sell without Mr. Rojas knowing. But Mrs. Rouse said that the idea was to maintain a lot of talk and bother about No. 2 so as to get Mr. Rojas annoyed, when to end everything he would probably sell her out.

The day she told Haynes about it, she seemed discouraged and inclined to give up the struggle.

'I have it all around me, Mr. Haynes,' she ended. 'I don't know where to look. I have to fix my eyes above to keep my courage.'

Miss Atwell, who slept with her, said Mrs. Rouse still cried at nights. And her temper during the day was tempestuous. Once or twice when he heard her fly out at Philomen, Haynes really thought that she should try to keep more control of herself. Until one day, nearly a year after he was living in the house, he went into the kitchen for the first time. As soon as he was fairly inside, he felt that he was in the mouth of hell. The big three-decked stove was going, the coal-pots with food, the concrete below so hot that he could feel it through his slippers, and above, the galvanized iron roof, which the tropical sun had been warming up from the outside since morning. He could scarcely breathe and involuntarily recoiled.

She came to the door smiling as usual.

'You find it hot, Mr. Haynes?'

'How can you stand it, Mrs. Rouse?'

'Poor people have no choice, Mr. Haynes. It's hard, but it is better in the hot season. When it is raining you have to leave the hot stove to go out into the wet yard and so you catch cold.'

He stood at the kitchen door wondering how any mortal could stand that for so many hours every day for so many days.

'Ha, Mr. Haynes,' she said, mildly self-satisfied, 'now you

know. But it isn't that which troubles me. I's the thoughts. They hurt me more than the heat.'

He looked at her and it struck him how much more she had changed during the months since the marriage. She still carried herself well – she was made like that – and though she had lost flesh she remained a big woman. But it was her face which really showed most the effect of all she had undergone. It was thinner, so thin that he could see clearly the contours of the cheek-bones, the hollows in the jaws and the long, thin chin. Now that all the flesh had gone it was a different face. Had he never seen her after that first morning, he might have passed her in the street today. But in the thin face the strong Roman nose was more prominent than ever, the lips tighter and more firm, especially when she paused during recitals of her woes. The hair on her forehead and temples was very grey. Thin and worn she might look, and she might complain at times, but if her courage was ever fundamentally shaken Haynes never saw it. Hour after hour all through the day and every day she was on her feet, up and down the yard and kitchen, in and out of the house, working, directing, exhorting her helpers to increased efforts. Frequently she was unjust. How she quarrelled! But he could forgive her this as did everybody (except Maisie) when he realized how powerfully she was struggling to stem the tide that threatened to overwhelm her.

'You have courage, Mrs. Rouse,' he said to her one day after they had made up some accounts.

She smiled a grateful smile.

'But I have a good friend, you know, Mr. Haynes,' she said, looking at him quizzically.

'Who is that, Mrs. Rouse?' Surely he knew all of Mrs. Rouse's friends who mattered.

She threw her head back with pride, almost with exaltation, and pointed upwards.

'God, Mr. Haynes. He is my refuge and my strength.'

Side by side with her, with less responsibility but with equal interest and spirit, worked Philomen. Strong as was Mrs. Rouse, Philomen was stronger than she, was indeed of exceptional physical strength. But she too was getting thinner and thinner and Haynes spoke to her about it one day. Her explanation was unexpected.

'It's Sugdeo, Mr. Haynes. The man is troubling me. I lose twenty pounds in the last two months.'

She went off into a long rambling story of her love affairs, the intolerance of her lover and his exorbitant demands upon her patience. Nothing pleased Philomen more than to get an opportunity to chatter about her sweetheart. If Maisie was near, however, Philomen was soon cut short. Maisie would come in and sit down very quietly, giving the impression that she was above being interested in what Philomen was saying. But that always meant the end of Philomen's confidences for the evening. And frequently Haynes longed for Maisie to appear.

But it was not only love but work which was causing Philomen to lose weight. All the rushing up and down to get money, the marketing, the goods from the shop, the messages here and there, all this Philomen did expeditiously and cheerfully. And she did her share in the kitchen, mincing the meat, helping in the making of the jam, attending at the stove, down to the town in the broiling sun with one half of the cakes (to keep Gomes quiet), back again, down with the second lot, helping to make the afternoon despatch, down to town with that, too, on one arm, and on the other her own basket to see what she could sell to bring in a few cents. Then came dinner and the preparation of the cake pans and the kitchen for the next day. (Mrs. Rouse was frequently out at nights to church, or to see the various persons whom she owed money, either to pay or to make excuses for not paying.) Sometimes Philomen would leave everything to go out with Sugdeo till eleven and then when she came back would set to work to put the kitchen to rights.

Maisie did some of the washing for the household, but refused to wash Philomen's clothes.

'I will wash and starch and iron,' said Maisie, who liked to play in water and did not very much mind doing jobs where no one interfered with her. 'But I'll leave this house now, before I wash the clothes of any damn servant. And a coolie beside!'

'You will wash them or leave,' said Mrs. Rouse. But Maisie had her way.

So that sometimes after going to bed at eleven or twelve Philomen would rise in the morning at four o'clock to do her washing. Money, too, was scarce. She did not dress nearly so well on Sundays as before. And often Haynes met her treading the burning roads on the soles of her own feet. The slippers worn out and no money being forthcoming to buy more, she wore the tops for respectability's sake and went her way as cheerful as usual. Her lightest day was Sunday. She did not have to go up and down, but she worked in the house the whole day until about five, when she started to prepare for her evening out with Sugdeo. She never complained. Whenever she was called it was: 'Comin', Mr. Haynes.' 'Comin', Mrs. Rouse.' And it was a long time before she ever hinted to Haynes that she found Mrs. Rouse's temper trying. Whenever she spoke of Mrs. Rouse it was to express sympathy. Mrs. Rouse on her side always talked of Philomen with love and gratitude. (When the atmosphere of No. 2 changed as it did change with almost catastrophic suddenness, she never spoke of Philomen at all.) Mrs. Rouse would sometimes give Haynes a joke about one of the lodgers or somebody in the house.

Philomen came out of the kitchen one evening, well-dressed, scarf around her head, and gave them both, standing by the door, a happy good evening.

'Off to meet Sugdeo, Philomen?'

'Yes, Mr. Haynes. We are going for a drive to Rockville.'

'All right. Don't let me keep you back,' for she would stand there and talk about him for ten minutes.

'That is another one,' said Mrs. Rouse, when Philomen had gone. 'All that drive they going for i's Philomen's money, Mr. Haynes.'

'Sugdeo is not paying?'

'Not a brass farthing. Philomen buy socks for him, shirts, tie, every time they going in the car she give him money to buy tickets. She draw a little chitty and lend him all the money. Love him! But she is not going to get it back. And Philomen is not a little girl. Philomen has carried on a lot of life already. As long as she don't bring it into the house where I am, I don't bother her. She is not a child after all. But now she hold on to this man and you would believe he is the first man the girl ever love. All right, Mr. Haynes.'

Mrs. Rouse had not left a minute when Maisie came in.

'I heard you and Mrs. Rouse talking,' she said, taking a cigarette.

'Yes.'

'I can't bear to hear her. She laughing at Philomen and Sugdeo. She have eyes to see them, but she haven't eyes to see herself. I am sure if I wanted to laugh, she and how Benoit treat her would be the first thing I would laugh at.'

Mrs. Rouse could struggle with cake-making, disorder in the house, persecutions from outside, everything. But one person was too much for her. That was Maisie, and by any form of trial Mrs. Rouse would have been acquitted if she had long ago driven Maisie from the house. Warfare was open and every succeeding week saw them more bitterly at it than ever. Mischievous as she had been before, the audacity of her escapade with Sergeant Parkes and evasion of the consequences seemed to tap new sources of devilry, and Mrs. Rouse and Philomen paid. Haynes remonstrated with her, but the antagonism between herself and Mrs. Rouse was fundamental. Maisie was, to Mrs. Rouse's brooding and distorted imagination, the origin and immediate cause of the tragedy of her life. Maisie fought back tooth and nail. It was no use Haynes telling her that she must make allowances. Haynes enumerated all that Mrs. Rouse had undergone, the work she had to do, the struggle against creditors, the annoyances of Benoit and the nurse which never ceased. Maisie never even listened seriously. She would keep silence and then invariably reply that it was no use.

'So you were saying, Mr. Haynes. But you don't understand Mrs. Rouse. Whatever I do, we will always quarrel. She have no use for me, I have none for her. I have one or two friends trying to get a job for me and when I get a job she will only know that I gone when people tell her.'

She was barely seventeen, but big and strong, and she grew taller and stronger and more attractive every day. With the lack of any check, except Mrs. Rouse's futile eruptions, she grew as fierce as a young tigress. After a time nobody in the yard could tell her anything. There were days when she would fly out at even a glance. 'What you see on me to look at? I wearing anything belonging to you?' Haynes alone could keep her quiet.

The quarrel might start with Miss Atwell or with Philomen (a singularly inoffensive person) or with a neighbour. But however it started the end was always the same. Mrs. Rouse was drawn in and then, with seconds off the stage, the principals would have it out. And all Mrs. Rouse's very real dignity would be of no avail against Maisie's barbed darts. If Haynes was there he called her into his room and she always came, pausing on the top step to fire a parting shot. Otherwise she raged unchecked.

Night after night she held court by the gate, the centre of half a dozen young men.

'Don't mind me talking to those boys, Mr. Haynes,' she told him once quite unsolicited. 'I laugh and joke with them. But no further. As long as we are together, I wouldn't risk picking up anything and give it to you.' But all the boys came to talk to Maisie and they carried on till late. Many a night Mrs. Rouse would lock the door, and it was Miss Atwell who got up to open for Maisie. Miss Atwell spoke to Maisie about it, but the girl answered with a vigour that silenced criticism.

'What do you expect me to do? I mustn't have friends? I can't bring them in here, so I have to meet them in the road.'

'Bring them in here!' said Mrs. Rouse, overhearing, as Maisie had intended her to overhear. 'I wouldn't tell you what I will throw on them if I catch one of them in my house.'

'Yet when you finish you say I am common,' said Maisie. 'Who have no respect for Mr. Haynes, now?'

'Look here, young woman, mind your stops with me.' Mrs. Rouse came to the kitchen door. 'Mind your stops or I'll bathe you down with this boiling pot of jam and mark you for life.'

'I'll sleep in the hospital, but you'll sleep in the gaol.'

Mrs. Rouse advanced into the yard with the cauldron in her hand. Maisie had her back to the mango tree, ready, even to be marked for life. Miss Atwell came out of her kitchen and held Mrs. Rouse's arm. 'Leave her alone, Mrs. Rouse. You have enough troubles on your shoulders. Don't put yourself in more. God, I wish something could happen and this girl would go away from this house. Go in to Mr. Haynes, Maisie. God have bless him and give him that power over you. Otherwise, child, I don't know where you'd be this day.'

And as the quarrels increased in number and fierceness it became clear that sooner or later a split was inevitable. And the mere idea of this hung over Haynes like a sword. For, accustomed to thinking about himself and seeing his own life very clearly these days, he realized that much as he liked and admired and respected Mrs. Rouse, No. 2 without Maisie would now be unbearable. It wasn't only the sleeping with her. They met elsewhere for this purpose and that could continue. But for the first time in his life he had a friend. If she left this life was over. He knew that he would leave. But if he left because Maisie left no water would wash it that he had only stayed there on account of Maisie. That was not true and yet would be a final and bitter disillusionment for Mrs. Rouse. He set himself to keep the peace and ward off the impending catastrophe.

And yet it was Philomen, the good, the faithful and the true, who went first.

Chapter Twenty-Eight

The break between Mrs. Rouse and Philomen developed with alarming suddenness. Though Maisie devoted her attention to Mrs. Rouse as the chief enemy, she did not neglect Philomen, whom she hated quite as much as Mrs. Rouse and found it far easier 'to dig' or 'to grind'.

Philomen had her hands full. The work in the house and in the kitchen. The up and down in the sun (that year eighty-seven in the shade), Sugdeo. Even Mrs. Rouse forgot all that Philomen was doing and began to speak to her so roughly that Philomen complained to Haynes once or twice with tears in her eyes. She did not have much time to speak to him now, but still she managed to let him know that Sugdeo was not only moody and overbearing, but unfaithful. This, she said, was because she never had time to go out with him as before. Often, even on a Sunday, she had work to do. And Maisie's persistent pin-pricking, planned and executed with ingenuity, care and discretion was directed chiefly against Philomen's having one peaceful moment with Sugdeo at No. 2.

Philomen slept on a bench in the kitchen as there was no room for her in the house now. Late at night Sugdeo would come up to No. 2, pass through the window, and Philomen would entertain him. They were very quiet about it and nobody knew. But somehow Maisie got a hint and one night complained suddenly of a pain and said that she wanted a kettle to boil tea. She got up, rushed outside, opened the kitchen door and made a tremendous fuss because she saw a man in the kitchen. It was nearly twelve and Mrs. Rouse was still awake, waiting for midnight to say her prayers. She came out to see what had so startled Maisie and was very annoyed with Philomen. Poor Philomen could scarcely hold up her head the next morning, Maisie was laughing all the day, and the air was thick with remarks about thieves and kitchens and others more suggestive.

That morning when she was cleaning Haynes's shoes, Maisie asked innocently if he had heard the noise the night before. But Haynes was waiting for her. He told her he had not got up because he knew she was no more frightened than he was and he didn't want to hear anything about it because he wasn't interested.

'But on the dresser, Mr. Haynes, where people cook food.'

'That has nothing to do with it at all. You had no right. You and the girl don't agree. She leaves you alone, you should leave her alone.'

'Leave her alone? Never. Every chance I get to dig her, I will.'

'Yes, but look at the result. Everybody hates you. Mrs. Rouse, Miss Atwell, Philomen.'

'You, too! Don't forget to put yourself in.'

'Now you are trying to put me off. But unless you—'

'All right, Mr. Haynes, all right.'

'Yes, but you must listen.'

'No. I am not going to listen. I don't want to hear.' She rubbed a shoe vigorously. 'Don't go on. If you go on I will clear out of the room and I won't come back until you stop and you will have to go with one shoe clean and one dirty.'

'I'll clean it myself.'

'I'll take the polish away,' and she grabbed the tin.

'Come back you wretch.' And Maisie sat again on the top step and continued to clean the shoes, whistling tunes from Gilbert and Sullivan with great speed and justice of intonation.

To complete poor Philomen's discomfiture, Sugdeo, with the unfairness of men whose women love them too much, threw all the blame on her and wrote to say that he was finished. Haynes could understand his annoyance, for, according to what Maisie told him later, Sugdeo had cut a rather ludicrous figure, when after a quick knock she slammed open the kitchen door and held up the candle.

Philomen brought Haynes the letter to read for her.

'What to do, Mr. Haynes?'

'My dear girl, what can I tell you?'

'But it isn't my fault.'

'I know it isn't. But that has nothing to do with it. If things only happened to you in life when it was your fault, life would be comparatively simple.'

'Mr. Haynes, if I take a knife and run it in that girl—'

'The police will lock you up and you'll get hanged or something. You mustn't think of that. If he loves you he will come back.'

'He may, Mr. Haynes, but I don't think so. This No. 2 is an

unlucky house. All who come into it get a curse on them. Don't you think so, Mr. Haynes?'

Haynes thought it over.

'It certainly looks so, Philomen. But I hope it isn't true.' And he was surprised at the gravity with which he spoke.

The Sugdeo incident of itself was a trifle. What made it remarkable, however, was the attitude of Mrs. Rouse. Where under ordinary circumstances she would have taken Philomen's part, she rated Philomen soundly, Maisie escaping almost blameless. And, however Maisie might rub it in, Mrs. Rouse took no notice. Aucher was away (and was likely to be away for a long time; the City Magistrate was quite tired of him) and Mrs. Rouse had to attend to the stove herself. Of late when that happened she was always much worse than usual. When Philomen complained to Haynes he always did his best to console her. And Philomen did not need much effort to be consoled. But Mrs. Rouse's behaviour to Philomen grew so unjust and overbearing, and that so quickly, that in less than a fortnight Haynes could not even with honesty and sincerity make excuses to Philomen for the injustices which she was made to suffer. It was not so much the work that Philomen complained of. She would have worked until she dropped. But the insults. If she did anything wrong, and if Sugdeo came to see her (as he did very soon) and Mrs. Rouse saw him, she would throw remarks about coolies and call Philomen to do something inside the house or send her out on some message. Haynes could not understand it at all, and the way Philomen stood it was a wonderful proof of her feeling for Mrs. Rouse. Especially as Gomes, who saw what a good servant Philomen was, always told her that if she wanted a job at any time she could come and work for him. And not that Mrs. Rouse didn't know that the Gomes job was still open. Maisie told Haynes that she knew, and although Maisie's hatred of Philomen still continued, yet she continually brought instances of Mrs. Rouse's treatment of Philomen to Haynes.

'That is the Mrs. Rouse you want me to go and friend up with. Look how she treating Philomen. If you know the things she tells that poor girl. Sugdeo really like her in truth. I don't know how he have stomach to come back here.'

Haynes decided to talk to Mrs. Rouse about her treatment of Philomen. For if Mrs. Rouse allowed her temper to drive Philomen away, the business would fall to pieces. Never again would she get a servant who would work and understand the business as well as Philomen.

One afternoon at about six o'clock Mrs. Rouse told Philomen who had been at it since five in the morning that if she didn't want to do the work she should leave it. Philomen went crying down the street. Haynes called Mrs. Rouse into the room to talk to her about some money and when he had done so, he said: 'Philomen is giving you a lot of trouble, Mrs. Rouse?'

The question took her by surprise. Haynes spoke gently, but the words meant far more than they said.

'Don't tell him if you don't get it you will leave, but look as if you will.' Since the day when Maisie's advice had proved so successful and he had felt himself a stronger man than old Carritt, Haynes had always borne it in mind and used it at critical moments.

For a few seconds Mrs. Rouse could not answer. Then she said, turning her eyes away: 'Philomen and I can't agree any more, Mr. Haynes. The quicker she leave the better.'

Haynes was struck dumb for a minute. He had not visualized a deliberate break from the side of Mrs. Rouse. She was not in any sort of temper.

'But, Mrs. Rouse,' he said, 'can you afford to lose Philomen?'

'I'll have to do my best without her, Mr. Haynes.'

But the sigh that followed the words showed that she realized to the full the implications of what she was saying. And she could not face him. Haynes felt that she was hiding something. He leant forward and put his hand on hers which lay loose on the table. 'Tell me, Mrs. Rouse, is anything wrong?'

'No, Mr. Haynes. I'll be sorry for Philomen, but how things are I'd prefer her to go. I won't tell her so. But I hope she will go when the month is finished.'

But still she could not look at him and he left the subject there. She went, but ten minutes after came back to say: 'It has nothing to do with Mr. Benoit, you know, Mr. Haynes. I hope you understand that.'

'I would never have thought that of Philomen,' said Haynes, who had just privately decided that that could be the only reason. Maisie had no solution. Miss Atwell had none.

Two or three days before the end of the month Philomen told Haynes that Gomes had agreed to take her on at the beginning of the new month.

'It is a good job, Mr. Haynes. Mrs. Rouse does pay me three dollars a month and he will pay me four. I wouldn't have to sleep in the kitchen. I will have a room in the yard and Sugdeo will be able to come and see me as he like. I wouldn't have to go on any message except to the shop to buy food. And i's only he, his mother and his sister. And he is away workin' the whole day.'

'Well, Philomen, if you and Mrs. Rouse can't agree it's best that you go. It is very strange I admit. But you are lucky. You are going to have a much easier job and better pay. And you are sure you have done Mrs. Rouse nothing. Don't cry about it.'

But her eyes were streaming already.

'But, Mr. Haynes, I can't understand it. I do Mrs. Rouse nothing. You see how I work here. Nine years I live with Mrs. Rouse and I serve her faithfully. I love her, because she take me from nothing and make me something. And she always treat me kindly. She used to quarrel and so on, but you used to tell me: "Don't mind, she has troubles," and I used to bear patiently with her, and when her temper pass she used to tell me: "Philomen, my child, don't mind when I bawl at you. Sometimes when I think of how that man and woman treat me, I feel I am going mad." And I used to tell her: "That's all right, Mrs. Rouse. I's the same thing Mr. Haynes tell me." And suddenly so she take behind me, and everything I do she quarrel with me and now she as good as tell me to go.'

She was sobbing in good earnest.

'But Philomen,' Haynes tried to cheer her, 'don't cry. You are going to be better off where you are. How long has the man been asking you to work with him?'

'Nearly a year, Mr. Haynes,' she sobbed. 'But it isn't that I am studyin'. Why Mrs. Rouse treat me so? I ain't do her anything, Mr. Haynes. Speak to her for me. Ask her. If i's anything for me to do I will do it. I ask her if I do anything. She wouldn't answer.'

Philomen could not summon enough courage to tell Mrs. Rouse that she was going, but Mrs. Rouse had heard already. The first of the month was a Sunday and all the Sunday morning Philomen was moving her things over to Gomes's house and continually wiping her eyes in her apron. Then she came in to say goodbye.

'You must come and see me sometimes,' said Haynes.

'Yes, Mr. Haynes.'

The tears flowed more and more.

'Don't cry, you silly girl. You will have more time to see Sugdeo.' She smiled at the mention of her lover's name.

She went outside and he heard her tell Miss Atwell goodbye. She went to the kitchen door, apron to her eyes, and said in a faint voice: 'Mrs. Rouse, I am goin'.'

Mrs. Rouse came to the door. And she was crying too. Then (Haynes could hardly believe his eyes) she took Philomen in her arms and Philomen fell on her shoulder, weeping loudly.

'Oh, Mrs. Rouse, Mrs. Rouse.'

'You going, Philomen. God will it so. You wouldn't forget me and I wouldn't forget you.'

Mistress and servant, and a mistress who had practically driven away the servant, they held each other tightly like mother and daughter who are about to part and do not know when, if ever, they will meet again. Philomen had entirely lost control of herself and her sobs could be heard in the street.

'Don't cry, Phil. Don't cry. You must keep courage.

'Don't mind, don't mind. I am going to come and see you at Gomes as soon as I get a chance.'

Philomen went at last and it was as if a pillar of the house had gone. Mrs. Rouse continually called her and spoke of her as if she were still working at No. 2. Even Maisie confessed that she missed Philomen.

For the life of him Haynes could understand neither head nor tail of this strange business.

Chapter Twenty-Nine

And with the departure of Philomen, Maisie, who had maintained some sort of relationship with the Indian girl through all her malicious dealings, almost gave up going into the kitchen, and spent every spare moment in Haynes's room. And Haynes on his part found himself liking her more and more and spending hours talking with her where formerly he would have been reading. She called him in the mornings and gave him his tea. After tea she would fetch the bike and ride on the pedal to the street. One morning as he was turning the corner he happened to look back. Maisie was standing looking at him. When he returned at lunch she said: 'But, Mr. Haynes, you look back and saw me and didn't even give a little wave.' Next morning Haynes looked back, saw Maisie and waved. Thenceforward every morning he looked back at the corner and waved. Little by little she was making a human creature out of him.

On Sundays, however, it was a different story. Haynes slept late and Maisie would sleep late also. She would not get up until nine, sometimes ten o'clock. She went into the bedroom and locked herself in — said she wanted to be private. (Mrs. Rouse raged for six hours the day Maisie said this.) Now that Philomen was gone Mrs. Rouse needed all the help that Maisie could give. But Maisie would not assume any obligation.

Mrs. Rouse undertook desperate measures. The morning Maisie did not get up in time, she got no food for the day except what she could steal. Money for shoes and clothes, little enough before, dwindled to nothing. She was sometimes in desperate straits for money. She could always depend on Haynes for money to buy food and Haynes always enquired first thing every afternoon whether she had eaten. But she was young and good-looking and she wanted pretty things. No. 2 began to suffer from a series of petty thefts, growing in size. A penny, four cents, a sixpence, a shilling, then back to sixpence again; but on the whole mounting steadily. Mrs. Rouse accused the yard boy, accused the servants, hinted even once or twice at some of the more disreputable lodgers; but Maisie covered her tracks so skilfully that Mrs. Rouse was compelled to stop short at thinly disguised innuendo. It was strange how she hesitated at accusing Maisie outright. Then one Sunday morning Mrs. Rouse lost a dollar note and accused Maisie point blank with such certainty that Haynes knew she had her at last. Maisie gave her a very cold 'Search me,' and took refuge in Haynes's room. Miss Atwell was at home, one or two of the boarders joined in and the waves of dispute rolled up to his step.

'Miss Atwell,' said Mrs. Rouse, 'if she don't give it back to me this morning I go for the police.'

Maisie leant back in the armchair inhaling deeply at a cigarette.

'Took the beef?' Haynes whispered. She nodded an affirmative.

'Give it back. I'll make things right.'

'I'll go to gaol first.'

It was no use arguing with her in this mood and on this question.

'I want my dollar back,' said Mrs. Rouse, 'and if I do not get it I am going to the police.'

She went inside and started to dress.

Haynes had a hasty conference with Miss Atwell. She told him that Mrs. Rouse needed the money badly – had borrowed it late Saturday night after being refused by two or three friends and walking many miles. There was no time for too much talk. Would Mrs. Rouse take the dollar back and let the matter end there and then? Miss A., acting as intermediary, found little difficulty in persuading her. She needed the dollar too urgently. In less than ten minutes the episode was closed.

'I's all right, Mr. Haynes. And Mrs. Rouse promise not to say one word again about it.'

Haynes went back into the room and not knowing what to say to Maisie quietly began to read. She sat motionless for nearly an hour, then with a faint: 'Excuse me, Mr. Haynes,' she left, dressed and went out.

'I am sorry I cause you all this trouble, Mr. Haynes,' were her last words.

'It's quite all right, Maisie,' said Haynes, but meaning much more than he said. The Sunday morning was ruined. No long talk with Maisie, no gramophone playing, no jokes and gossip, nothing. She was not even there to give him his lunch, which was the meal of the week. Long after lunch she returned and came straight into his room, dusty and hot.

'Here is your dollar, Mr. Haynes.'

She was smiling faintly, but held out the money until he took it and was very subdued for the next twenty-four hours. But soon she was her old self, and a living torment to her aunt.

On the Sunday night following the outburst Mrs. Rouse happened to be away. Maisie, as usual, was in Haynes's room and he decided to talk to her seriously.

'Maisie, have a cigarette . . . Now, Maisie, no beating about the bush. Have you ever thought of getting some work to do?'

'If you tired of my coming in here so much, tell me, Mr. Haynes.'

But Haynes was prepared for these herrings.

'That is not going to work today. You can't go on as you are going. You must get some work to do.'

She suddenly became listless.

'I don't want to work, Mr. Haynes.'

She relaxed entirely in the chair and looked at him out of half-closed eyes.

'No. But you and Mrs. Rouse can't go on like this. Something is going to happen some day.'

'Let it happen. She can't beat me. You think I am afraid of that noisy blow-hard?'

'Suppose the police had come last Sunday, searched and found the dollar.'

'They couldn't find it.'

'You don't know what a police search is like.'

'Well, if they had found it they would have taken me down. I wouldn't have been the first woman to go to gaol.'

He looked at her non-plussed. She looked back at him, and then her face broke into a smile – slow, amused almost derisive.

'What next, teacher?'

'You want smacking,' said Haynes.

'Ha . . . You are getting on, Mr. Haynes. When you first came here you couldn't say boo to a goose.'

'Come, tell me something, Maisie. Leave this going to work alone for the minute. Have you any plans for your future, any sort of plans at all?'

'Plans for my future? I don't know what you are talking about, Mr. Haynes.'

Gradually, however, she spoke, more in jest than in earnest, but with an element of seriousness in what she said. For staying at home she had no plans. But she wanted to go to America to work for good money. In America you worked hard but you got good food and pay and had a fine time. Why the hell should she starve and slave to get a few shillings a week from some employer in the town?

Miss Atwell appeared at the door, the climax to a series of subdued mutterings and ejaculations with which she had accompanied the later stages of the conversation.

'Mr. Haynes, excuse me. But I can't hear this child talkin' to you as she is doin'. Mr. Haynes, she is headin' for perdition.'

'Now what the—'

'Very well, Maisie.' Haynes put his hand up. Maisie, who had half risen, sat down again.

'Miss Atwell is speaking for your good. Keep quiet, please. You will do as you like, of course, but just listen.'

'All right, Mr. Haynes.' But she turned her head away and looked out of the window.

Miss Atwell had nothing particularly new to say. She wished to harp on the fact that Mrs. Rouse had intended to lock up Maisie for the dollar note, and Haynes had difficulty in restraining her from following that line of argument. But she was fluent and effective on the necessity of Maisie's either making up her mind to behave better, 'to turn over a new leaf,' or getting some work to do out of the house. Maisie took little notice – only once or twice, when she displayed signs of irritation, Haynes motioned to her and made her keep still.

Miss Atwell paused for breath. But not for long.

'And the child has a lot of good in her, Mr. Haynes; she is a child with nice ways and—'

'I'm not going to stay here to listen to all this damned nonsense,' said Maisie, and in one stride and a jump she was in the yard.

'Mr. Haynes,' continued Miss Atwell, 'if Mrs. Rouse lose anything again she is not going to make a noise. She is going to send for a detective quietly. She says that she will have peace in her own house. You and me has to do something for that child, Mr. Haynes. She will listen to you. That girl is a mystery to me. She picks up six cents, car tickets, shillings, in your clothes or on the table. And I sit down here and hear her first thing as you come in, give you. And Mrs. Rouse can't leave a penny lyin' about Maisie snatch it up. As long as is Mr. Haynes she will behave, but anybody else—'

Maisie came back in.

'Mr. Haynes is people. All of you, like you and Mrs. Rouse, what all you are? All you not people to behave for. Old lady, go out of the gentleman's house and leave him in his privacy.'

But Maisie made a good-natured grimace at Miss Atwell which gave the words almost a friendliness.

'I'll see you a little later, Miss Atwell,' Haynes told her. 'I have something in mind. I'll speak to you about it another time.'

Maisie sat down, took a book and read for five minutes. Then she put the book aside.

'You want me to play some nice records for you, Mr. Haynes?'

'No, thank you, Maisie.'

'You see how you treating me? I just want to play for you.'

She put a record on, a piece of dance music, and started to beat time with her foot, humming. Haynes would not watch her.

She reached his pipe and tobacco pouch.

'Here is your pipe, Mr. Haynes . . . and the matches, filled, and not too tight . . . Now, Mr. Haynes, I have been thinking it over and I want to behave well and to stop troubling Mrs. Rouse.'

'I am glad to hear it.'

Came a pause.

'Tell me, Mr. Haynes, you have anything in mind which you think can help me?'

'What a little imp it is,' said Miss Atwell.

Mrs. Rouse came back just in time to hear Maisie, Miss Atwell and Haynes laughing 'as merry as fleas,' to quote Miss Atwell. She didn't seem too pleased.

But though Haynes would not yield to Maisie's blandishments

that evening he really did have an idea. He thought it over carefully and put it to Miss Atwell, who told him it was excellent, and
they approached Mrs. Rouse together. Mrs. Rouse, he knew,
would not consider the proposition at all if it did not come from
him. But he put it to her and after some demur she agreed to try
it. Maisie might tease Haynes in small things, but whatever he
wanted her to do she always agreed in the end and consented to
do her best.

The great arrangement was this. Maisie would be given some
specified work – keeping the books, washing, starching and iron-
ing, and a few other tasks. She would do them for Mrs. Rouse, who
in turn would pay her a fixed salary and give her food. Mrs. Rouse
would not be concerned with Maisie as long as the work was properly done and in time. Haynes was to pay Maisie out of the monthly
sum he gave to Mrs. Rouse. This particular concession had been a
delicate corner, but Haynes got round it with colours flying. The
whole idea was novel, but simple, and on the whole it worked well.
When Maisie wanted to be idle during the day, she used to rise
early, work like mad for some hours, and then stretch about the
place for the whole day, happy because Mrs. Rouse could not call
her. Whenever she was inclined to be slack, Miss Atwell or Haynes
gave her a reminder and did not find her refractory. Now she was
able to arrange her work so that she could spend as much time as
possible with Haynes. The pair grew closer and closer. Through
her, Haynes knew immediately every single thing that was going
on in the house – what Mrs. Rouse was praying for when her High
Priest visited her, the love affairs of the boarders, the mysteries of
Miss Atwell's wardrobe, *causes célèbres* in the town.

'Mr. Haynes, jokes,' or 'Mr. Haynes, news,' was a well-known cry, and whatever Haynes was doing he put it aside to hear. Sometimes she would tell him, 'Jokes. But not now, after supper.' Often she pushed chairs and the table to the side of the room to give herself gesticulatory scope.

Her range was wide, but Miss Atwell, on the whole, was her chief subject. Maisie had Miss A.'s vocabulary, diction and style to perfection. To hear her say: 'That is too-too excellent,' was to hear the very voice of Miss A., and Maisie was not one of the dry humorists. When she came into Haynes's room and said: 'Mr. Haynes, you is busy, but excuse me,' her face at the time would be all squeezed-up like Miss Atwell's, but immediately after she would relax and laugh her brilliant whole-hearted laugh.

Weeks used to pass before she and Haynes would have any serious misunderstanding. Sometimes she rebuked him for impatience and said that since he had come to No. 2 he had changed very much for the worse. But however good the cause with which she might speak sharply to him and bounce out of the room, not ten minutes after she would return, coming in quietly and asking him if he had called her, or if he wanted matches, or if she could play the gramophone, or if he was going out and wanted his shoes cleaned, or something of that kind, always in a very quiet and penitent voice, looking at him out of the corner of her eyes to see if he was still displeased. And she did things which he remembered for days and made Haynes feel that there was nothing he could not do for her.

One morning she brought in two pieces of cloth for his opinion on them. One was red, a bright vermilion, the other pale green.

That she sought his opinion was nothing unusual. All No. 2 used to do it.

'Which to choose, Mr. Haynes?'

'The green. Only Spaniards from South America wear red dresses.'

'But I like the red, Mr. Haynes.'

'Why did you ask me, then? You have to wear the dress, not I.'

'I didn't expect that you would wear the dress. I don't see why you should tell me that.'

'Don't lose your temper. Make your red dress. Only, when you are wearing it and I meet you in the street, please don't think anything if you see me looking the other way.'

'It's my dress,' said Maisie, and swept up the two of them. 'If you don't want to speak to me in the street, Mr. Haynes, don't speak to me. Don't speak to me in here either. I'll wear red, white and blue if I like.'

'I could get an old Union Jack for you if you . . .'

She stamped out.

Saturday morning there was a commotion. The dress had come to be tried on. Formerly Haynes's opinion would outweigh that of all the others in the house, but today—

'Mr. Haynes.'

Maisie was outside.

'Yes.'

'I can come in?'

'Yes.'

'I want you to tell me how the dress look.'

'I see. Well, if you think my opinion worth anything.'

'You will tell me as long ago? You not vexed?'

'Not at all. Come along. Let me see you.'

And when she came in, it was the green dress after all.

But this was merely the decoration to her unwearied personal attendance on him week in and week out. Her own shoes might go uncleaned for days, never were his so bright as under her skilful hands. She made and remade his bed five times a day. She spent hours looking for papers he had carelessly mislaid. Now and then his carelessness or untidiness (habits which Ella had encouraged) might cause her to say: 'But, Mr. Haynes, you are a troublesome man. People have no peace with you.' But she would look at him and smile while she spoke, or immediately after, to soften the sting of truth in her words.

Rarely did she ask for money. To pay a rampageous creditor, to buy medicine if she felt ill – once a month or perhaps less. Haynes gave her presents on occasion, but few things irritated her more than the suggestion that he should pay her specifically for anything she did for him. 'God! Mr. Haynes, you have a bad mind. I didn't do it for money.'

And yet another day when he asked her why her behaviour to him and her behaviour to the others were such miles apart, she said:

'Them! Who will bother to behave for them.'

Her regard for him extended beyond the borders of his personal comfort and well-being. Nobody could say anything against Haynes. She was at once a flame of protest. She guarded his property jealously, keeping track of books and records borrowed overlong by careless friends. She would rush into the room.

'Mr. Haynes, Mr. — is coming, don't forget to ask him for the records.'

When she saw him calculating his income and expenditure, she warned him not to forget to buy shoes or new socks as the case might be. When he came back from paying she would enquire and if he had neglected to settle one or two accounts which he had promised her to pay, she would show her annoyance and wash her hands of him for the time being. She enquired solicitously when he was likely to finish paying off the mortgage. She said she wanted to see him out of debt and free of worry. She sometimes even undertook useful bits of his education.

'No, Mr. Haynes, I am not going to fix those books again. Not till – till – next Saturday. I fix them yesterday morning and look what you have done with them. No, no, no. I have to teach you order.'

'Well, well, well, well, well,' said Miss Atwell one day. 'You speaks to the man as if you is his wife.'

'Tst, tst, tst, tst, tst,' said Maisie. 'What is that to you? Is you his mother?'

But Miss Atwell's words stuck in Haynes's mind. He wondered if the girl of his dreams, the divine, the inexpressible she whom he was going to marry one day, he wondered if in some things she would be to him what Maisie was in all.

Chapter Thirty

In August, Haynes, doing what he liked with old Carritt, claimed and got a month's holiday and made arrangements to spend it by the seaside. The last night he spent with Maisie and had a long talk with her, in which he begged her hard not to get into any trouble while he was away. Philomen's departure had steadied Mrs. Rouse. The tension had eased and Haynes decided to take the risk and go.

He made Maisie promise to do her work carefully and to keep away from Mrs. Rouse at all costs. He left his gramophone and some records at No. 2 so that she might have them to amuse herself with. The key of his room he gave to her. She was to sleep there, so that she might go and come as she pleased. If anything happened she was to send for him at once. He did not tell Maisie this, but he had already had a long talk with Mrs. Rouse, and she had very graciously promised to be as patient with Maisie as she could be. She deprecated the idea of spoiling Haynes's holiday; but finally promised to send for him if need be.

'You like Maisie a lot, Mr. Haynes,' she said and smiled

indulgently. 'If I didn't know that, she would have gone from here long ago. You'll find her here when you come back.'

'Hell,' thought Haynes. 'She knows. Anyway, I don't care.' And he didn't.

Peace endured during the whole month and no message came to Haynes except replies from Maisie whenever he dropped her a card. He sent a card to Mrs. Rouse also. In a letter from Maisie she stated that Mrs. Rouse had 'asked her to send kind regards,' a very good sign.

The holiday was uneventful except that Haynes tried Benoit's dictum on one of his seaside acquaintances and was sharply rebuked, but nothing daunted, tried again and added to his experience.

On the last day of August he returned to town to resume his regular life at No. 2. August 31st was a Sunday and it rained the whole day. The yard at No. 2 was a little morass of mud and water and for him to get to his room he had to walk carefully along two boards which Maisie always placed for him whenever it was wet, and had fixed since the early morning. After he had shaken hands all round in the kitchen, he stepped carefully across and remained alone with Maisie in his room. It was early, about half-past four. Mrs. Rouse had been cooking in the kitchen, but after greeting Haynes she had gone into Miss Atwell's room.

Despite the long absence there was just one brief moment between them.

'Glad to see me back?' asked Haynes. And she did not reply, but held his arm and squeezed it, a thing she had never done before. A second after she was unpacking his bag and chattering gaily. She gave him little bits of news – who had come to see him, how long they had stayed, what they had said, who borrowed books and records, how when she saw Mr. — coming, she had rushed and locked the door and said that Haynes had taken the key with him to the country 'cause he borrows the books and keeps them too long, Mr. Haynes.'

'And what about you, Maisie? What has been happening to you?'

'Me – I am O.K., Mr. Haynes.' She gave him a knowing smile. 'Nothing new. Just the same old story.' Then she leant forward and said in a low voice:

'But, Mr. Haynes, I have a piece of news for you. Such a piece of news. But I can't tell you that now. Later.'

Whenever she had anything exceptionally exciting to tell him (Haynes by now made no secret with her of his curiosity about all who lived in No. 2) she always made merry by dangling scraps of it before him and making a great mystery before she would say what it was.

'Oh, you and your special news,' he said. 'Some nonsense or other.'

She put her finger quickly before her mouth and whispered: 'Hush, not so loud!'

But he had spoken too loudly. For the rest of his life he would regret that piece of carelessness. There was a peremptory knock at the door. Mrs. Rouse. One glimpse of her face was enough for Haynes to be instantaneously aware that something was up. He knew that expression too well.

'Mr. Haynes,' she said, a thin surface of politeness above the volcano beneath. 'I want to speak to Maisie. Ask her to come to me, please.'

This to Haynes, and not looking at Maisie, who was standing not three feet away.

Having spoken she walked a few paces away to the centre of the yard and stood waiting.

'What is it, Mrs. Rouse?'

'Just a little matter between me and Maisie, Mr. Haynes. It can be settled in a moment.'

'What she wants to speak to me for? I don't want to speak to her, Mr. Haynes. I haven't addressed a word to her for a month.'

'That doesn't matter. Go on. Hear what she has to say and come back. Now, don't spoil it.'

'I am waiting for her, Mr. Haynes,' said Mrs. Rouse in such a cold and menacing voice that he wondered what Maisie had done. Under present circumstances especially Maisie was not the one to enquire from, so Haynes went to the door.

'Mrs. Rouse, I hope nothing is wrong.'

'No, Mr. Haynes.' Not a smile on her face. 'I only have a few words that I want to tell Maisie.'

Miss Atwell was in the kitchen and came to the door. Susan, the cook, came to the other. A lodger and her daughter peeped over their blind.

He turned to Maisie.

'Well, Maisie. Come on. Go out, hear what it is and come back. I am waiting for you.'

A black frown was on her face and she stood irresolute. Then—

'O Christ,' she burst out. 'I am not afraid of any damn body, man. She can't frighten me. Let me pass there, Mr. Haynes.'

She strode out and stood at the bottom of the step.

'Well, what is it you want to say?' and she eyed Mrs. Rouse dangerously.

'You know well,' said Mrs. Rouse, slowly and solemnly. 'I have warned you. As if you have not do me enough, you want to spread slander on me now. But beware! I am going to have peace in my own house. I work hard to build it. And I am going to have peace in it. Now I have warned you. This is the second time. I will not do it a third.'

No Cassandra could have prophesied tragic doom with more impressive dignity. But Maisie was quite unmoved. 'You hear me say anything?' she asked abruptly, and giving a quick and contemptuous shrug she walked off to lean against her old friend, the mango tree.

Mrs. Rouse went back into the kitchen.

Haynes beckoned to Maisie through the window to come back in. 'No, Mr. Haynes,' she said aloud. 'I am not coming back in there. I's an offence to speak to you. That is what it come to now. I have no right in there.'

'No, you have no right in there,' said Mrs. Rouse, coming again to the kitchen door. 'I don't know how a gentleman like Mr. Haynes can stand to have a thing like you about him. Look at you this Sunday afternoon.' Maisie was working and had not changed.

'Good God, woman, look at yourself before you look at me. If you can't see yourself go and look in a glass. You nastier than me. Ask anybody.' Which was an obvious truth.

'Now, you mind your stops, or I will put you out this afternoon.'

'Who you could have you putting out, but who you want you can't have.'

Mrs. Rouse was fast losing her carefully controlled temper.

'Why don't you ask one of those boys you always talking to in the front to put you in a house and keep you?'

'I'd only be following the example you set me.'

Mrs. Rouse advanced a step into the yard, shaking her finger at Maisie.

'When I ready for you, young woman, I am going to see after you.'

'Why don't see after the nurse and Mr. Benoit? They do you worse than me. And to besides, woman,' said Maisie, changing from her calm and speaking without passion, but with a deliberately assumed pretence of mere irritation, 'the days of slavery past. My tongue is my own to say what I like.' She walked from the mango tree towards the centre of the yard. 'I not going to let an old blow-hard like you frighten me. You always to put me out. After all, people is not dog. Let me see you put me out. I, Maisie—' (She was in the centre of the yard now, ankle deep in muddy water.) 'I, Maisie, stand up here and say that after all that talk you talk, Mr. Benoit come up here and make a fool of you again. He live with you and fool you and he gone again. I know you will deny it. But I see. With these eyes I see.'

Mrs. Rouse sped from the kitchen and seized her by the shoulders. But Maisie was awaiting the charge. She held on also and the two of them swayed in the slippery yard. Indignation lent strength to Mrs. Rouse and making a sudden heave she threw Maisie forcibly from her so that Maisie fell full length in the mire. Mrs. Rouse staggered a little with the effort but retained her feet.

There had not been time to do anything. But as Maisie, quite unhurt, scrambled to her feet and made for Mrs. Rouse, Haynes ran down the steps and gripped her by the arm, while Miss Atwell rushed to Mrs. Rouse's side.

'Come, Maisie, enough of this,' he said. 'Come in here with me,' and he tried to pull her away.

'Come on,' said Mrs. Rouse, standing immovable, her chin raised, her arms by her side and her fists clenched. 'Come on! You think because I am old I am feeble. But come on! I have given you one tumble. If you want another I am here to give it to you. Let her come, Mr. Haynes.'

'No, no, Mrs. Rouse,' said Haynes. 'Miss Atwell, take Mrs. Rouse inside. You come with me, Maisie'; and holding her by the arms, he pushed her by main force up the steps and into the room.

From outside came Mrs. Rouse's voice.

'You dirty little whore. Mr. Haynes give you his key and you had his own friend, Boyce, in there while he was away.'

Maisie screamed and leapt towards the door, but Haynes was just in time to pull her away.

'It is not true. He came but he got nothing from me. Mr. Haynes, let me go. You are not my friend. You see that old bitch insulting me and lying on me and you keep me here.'

Mrs. Rouse had won the first round, but if they held on again Maisie was going to beat her badly.

'O God, Mr. Haynes,' said Maisie, holding the top of the bed

and shaking it as if she were shaking someone, 'why you interfere? The woman is going to say that she beat me and put me out.'

'You sit down there,' said Haynes. 'No,' as she made another
attempt to go out. 'No, I am not going to see you do anything stupid. You are not going out there. You will have to knock me over
to pass. I don't believe anything against you, Maisie.' He closed one
half of the door and stood in the other half. Then he heard
Mrs. Rouse's voice and looked out to see her standing at the door
of Miss Atwell's room.

'You don't come back in here again. Here are your things. I
gave them to you and I am not going to keep them. Here,' and she
flung a dress out into the muck of the yard.

'Here!' Another dress.

'Here!' Another dress.

'Here!' A petticoat.

Maisie behind Haynes was shaking with rage. 'O God, Mr.
Haynes. Let me go out. You letting that woman triumph over me.'

Haynes thought she would assault him.

'Don't mind all that. I am not going to let you pass. Let her do
what she likes. We'll fix things after. But for the time being be
quiet.'

A little crowd had gathered and people were peering through
the hedge. 'Don't tell me anything, Miss Atwell,' said Mrs. Rouse.
'I don't want to hear.'

'Merciful Father!' said Miss Atwell, returning to the kitchen
door. 'This quiet Sunday afternoon,' and could say no more.
Meanwhile Mrs. Rouse continued to throw until dresses, under-
wear, stockings, shoes, hats, Maisie's sorry wardrobe, covered

the centre of the muddy yard. Then with a dramatic gesture she came out and locked the door, and put the key in her pocket.

'That is the end of you,' she said, and coming down the steps walked across the yard into the kitchen with her head high in the air, trampling Maisie's clothing into the mud as if she did not know that they were there.

Haynes had said nothing, not a word, nor made any attempt at interference, but for the first time since he had lived in No. 2 he was in a ferocious temper with Mrs. Rouse. It had come at last and he was on Maisie's side. He stood fuming for a minute and then went to Maisie who was sitting crouched in a chair, her eyes fixed on the ground, clutching at her hair with both hands. He put an arm around her and didn't care who saw.

'Now listen to me,' he said. 'I am going out for those clothes.'

'You needn't waste your time. I don't want them.'

'But you must have them. What are you going to wear?'

She burst into a rush of furious tears.

'Now, promise me to sit here and wait until I come back in. Please, Maisie.'

She didn't answer.

'Please. Promise.'

'All right.'

'Now, you are not coming out to begin to fight again?'

'No, Mr. Haynes,' and she gave him a reassuring squeeze.

'Good.'

Pushing open the door, he went out and began to pick up the clothes. That, he knew, would annoy and wound Mrs. Rouse. Miss Atwell came from the kitchen to help him.

'Leave them, Mr. Haynes,' she said. 'That don't suit you. Look at the lodgers watching. What will they think? Look at you' shoes and you' trousers in the mud, Mr. Haynes,' and then she whispered to him. 'I's better she go, Mr. Haynes. I's better she go. If she stay it will mean sessions for one o' them.'

'I suppose she will have to go now,' Haynes said. 'I don't see how she can stay after this.' And checked himself in time from saying: 'And I am going too.' But he picked up the things in a way that showed Mrs. Rouse and all who were looking what he thought.

And then Maisie appeared, astonishingly, at the window of the room Mrs. Rouse had just locked with such finality.

'Come on, everybody. Here,' she screamed and she pitched one of Mrs. Rouse's dresses through the window into the mud.

'Here!' she said and threw two others.

Mrs. Rouse came to the door of the kitchen to see Maisie holding up a dirty chemise.

'Here!' she said, but she did not throw it. She caught sight of Mrs. Rouse and paused to speak to her. 'You are a bit old-fashioned, Mrs. Benoit. And the chemise nasty. Humph.' She put it to her nose. 'Christ, but it stink. No wonder, although the man come back he had to leave again.'

She let it float to the ground.

Mrs. Rouse rushed from the kitchen and in a second was on the steps.

'Just let me put my hands on you,' she panted and fumbled in her pocket for the key.

'Oh, you coming to open, eh?' said Maisie. 'Come on,' and continued with her catalogue.

'Here!' she said, and Mrs. Rouse's buttoned boots plunged into the mud. 'Old stuff. The days for button boots over, old woman.'

Mrs. Rouse turned the key and wrenched violently at the door knob. It came away in her hand and she nearly fell backward. Maisie had bolted the door on the inside.

'Here!' continued Maisie, remorselessly. She held up, as if gingerly, between finger and thumb, an intimate garment, a capacious intimate garment. She held it before the infuriated Mrs. Rouse and dangled it so that the people watching shook with sniggering laughter.

'Ah,' said Maisie, as if a long-concealed light had broken in on her. 'I see now. This is why the man wouldn't stop. I see now. All you look at this thing. Old lady, people don't wear these balloons today. They make them out of celanese now. You didn't see those the nurse used to wear?'

Mrs. Rouse, talking distractedly to herself like a mad woman, had rushed up the steps into Haynes's room to find that the careful Maisie had pulled the bed away, and after passing through the connecting door had locked it behind her.

'O God, show me a way, show me a way,' she screamed at last. She turned her face to the sky and raised her clutched hands and shook them at Heaven in agonized supplication.

'Here!' said Maisie, and she threw a rolled pair of stockings so that they hit Mrs. Rouse on her chest. 'And here is your hair dye.' She poured it out. 'You lose the man. He ain't coming back a third time. So what you want with hair dye? Show your dirty, grey hair to the world and stop thinking of men.' She lifted the bottle high as if she would hit Mrs. Rouse with it, but she threw it hard into the mud instead.

Haynes neither could nor wished to interfere with Maisie breaking up his life at No. 2. For the moment he pushed aside all thoughts of the future and stood lost in a fearful admiration at her winning her last great victory.

'But, Father in Heaven, what is this here today?' said Miss Atwell.

'What is it? I's murder,' replied Mrs. Rouse. She ran into the kitchen, took up the hatchet, and going to the door began to break it open. But by this time Maisie was finished.

'Stop breaking down your door, old woman,' she said. 'Stop or I'll break this bottle on your head.'

'For God's sake, Maisie,' said Haynes, 'that's enough.'

'All right, Mr. Haynes. I'll spare her for your sake.' She left the window.

'Let me just put my hands on you,' said Mrs. Rouse over and over again and made powerful strokes on the door with the hatchet.

Maisie had disappeared, but suddenly there was a shout from a few of the people who had crept into the yard to witness the disturbance. She had slipped through the window at the back. By the time Haynes reached round he could just catch a glimpse of her walking up Victoria Street, bareheaded, in an old pair of soft slippers, no stockings, her head and neck and half her dress still plastered with mud from Mrs. Rouse's tumble, and a small crowd walking behind her. Gone. And gone for good.

Mrs. Rouse in the back had collapsed in a welter of tears and mud and Miss Atwell was trying to console her.

Chapter Thirty-One

The whole of the next day passed and he did not hear from her. In the night he went to the room where they usually met. She did not come. Who were her friends? He did not know one of them, had no idea where to begin to look for her. Two days passed. At No. 2 he came in and went out and had nothing to say to anybody, nor had anybody anything to say to him. The cook brought his meals and he kept his door closed. At last on the fourth day, at about five in the afternoon, a woman's voice on the telephone told him that Maisie wanted to see him that night and would meet him at ten o'clock in the park – he knew where. She was punctual as always when meeting him and his heart beat when he saw her. Never before had he felt so much like taking her in his arms and holding her tight to him. They held hands.

'Well, Maisie,' he said. 'So you have gone.'

'Yes, Mr. Haynes. I couldn't put up with her any more. And I had to give her something to remember me by. Mr. Haynes, you enjoyed it?'

And then the two of them stood up in the park and laughed and laughed as if they were never going to stop. When they recovered they walked along together and Maisie told Haynes what he had guessed in the interim, but rather vaguely.

During Haynes's absence Benoit had been coming regularly up to No. 2 and used to talk to Mrs. Rouse, she in the kitchen, he in the alley. At first Mrs. Rouse didn't want to have anything to do with him, or, as Maisie said, 'pretended' that she didn't. But later, they had made it up (Maisie had always been a shameless and adroit eavesdropper) and they used to meet and make love. But the reconciliation had not lasted long. Benoit had promised to make a definite break with the nurse, but had not done so. He asked Mrs. Rouse for some money to pay some debt or other before he came back. How exactly it went Maisie did not know. At any rate he had had his time with her and gone off again. 'I am not lying, Mr. Haynes, I am telling you the God's truth. She was waiting for him. That day when Parkes came she was going to take him, but as soon as Benoit came she tell Parkes no. And not only I know. Other people in the alley know. A thing like that can't hide for long. But one day I was alone in the kitchen and I hear her say how people slandering her and saying she living with Benoit again, but she warning everybody that the day she hear anybody with her own ears she going to take the law in her hands. Was me she meant. Because nobody else was in the kitchen. But I didn't bother with her. Anyway, Mr. Haynes, that is over.'

'Yes, Maisie, but there is something else. What about us? When shall I see you again?'

She did not answer at once. Then, 'I'll ring you up tomorrow,' she said.

'Where are you sleeping?'

'Don't ask me that, Mr. Haynes.'

'As you wish, Maisie.'

She turned and faced him.

'That is over, Mr. Haynes.'

'Over? What do you mean?'

'You and me, Mr. Haynes. I's you that made me stay at No. 2. If it wasn't for you I would have gone long ago. I didn't want to leave you. But now it's happened, I am going to America. I have been to my uncle. That's why you didn't hear from me. I told him that he had never given me a damned cent in his life and I wanted some money now.' She laughed.

'He gave it to you?'

'He had to. I said I was going to stay there until I got it, and he borrowed it and gave it to me.'

'How much money?'

'Thirty dollars.'

'That can't pay your passage to America.'

'No, Mr. Haynes. But the stewardess on the — line has an assistant and sometimes two. And if you pay her twenty dollars you get the job. She has been after me a long time.'

'Why after you?'

'She likes to get young coloured girls who are nice. The white officers like them.'

'So you mean, Maisie—'

'Mr. Haynes. I want a job and I am going to get it. The captain and the whole crew can't get anything from me unless I want to give them. The boat is in and if I get the job I am going. You have papers to sign that you are coming back. But when that boat hit New York and I put my foot on shore, if it wait for me before it leave, it's going to wait a damned long time.'

'So everything's fixed, Maisie.'

'Everything, Mr. Haynes.'

There was a harshness and determination behind the casual air with which she spoke that stunned him into acceptance.

'When are you going?'

'I don't know, but soon.'

Something in his voice seemed to move her. For the second and last time she held him of her own accord.

'You sorry I am going, Mr. Haynes?'

Haynes was choking and could only nod.

The cathedral clock boomed out eleven, and Maisie rose slowly.

'I have to go now, Mr. Haynes,' she said.

They stood up, but made no move. At last she held out her hand and he took it.

'Goodbye, Mr. Haynes,' she said faintly. He kept her hand in his, but said nothing.

'You'll remember me sometimes, Mr. Haynes?'

'Write to me, Maisie. I shall be waiting anxiously to hear from you.'

'I'll write, Mr. Haynes. Goodbye.'

And with a last pressure of her hand she pulled it away and went.

Chapter Thirty-Two

She did not ring, and he never saw her again. Two days after the night in the park a boat left for America and he could only suppose that she had gone with it. Well, that was that. It was no use crying over it. The next thing was to get out of No. 2. He owed Mrs. Rouse for August. He wasn't going to bother himself about that. She would do without. He would pay her on the fifteenth and give her a fortnight's notice. The thing to do was to find Ella. He went to her old home. She had left there and they didn't know where she was. So he wrote to her people in the country and asked them to let Ella know that he wanted to see her at the office as soon as possible.

At No. 2 work went on as usual, but the household was undergoing one of its recurrent periods of gloom. Haynes met Mrs. Rouse face to face one morning and they greeted each other, Mrs. Rouse timid and appealing, Haynes polite but firm. His resentment was almost gone, but he knew that without Maisie No. 2 was no place for him. If he were leaving it was best to leave while this discord lasted. To soften the blow he would tell her that the money she still owed him she could pay at her convenience.

On evenings he could not stay in No. 2 at all. Memories of Maisie seemed to haunt the place. To eat without her moving round the table, bringing in dishes and talking to him, giving him the news of all that had happened during the day; after dinner her constant coming in to see if he had finished any work he was doing or wanted anything, filling his pipe (better than he ever filled it), giving him a gay *'Au revoir'* and going out to see the boys if Haynes was busy; the long, lazy evenings when they sat and talked, or she played the gramophone, the thousand ways in which she filled in all his hours, they were suddenly torn up by the roots out of his life and he could not fill the gap. His old loneliness descended on him again; but now he couldn't endure it as he used to in the old days. To sit in the room alone was like being in a prison. So he ate his meals hurriedly and went out again, to the cinemas, to see acquaintances long neglected, or merely riding on his bicycle. The only thing was to find Ella, clear out of No. 2, and then think over things. He would sometime or other find another girl friend. But another Maisie, never. Why had he let her go? But how could he have kept her?

Mrs. Rouse and Co. he kept at a distance. 'Good morning' and 'Good afternoon'. For a week that was all that passed between them. He kept his face wooden when chance brought Miss Atwell across his path. She almost fled from his presence.

On the second Saturday after the upheaval he bolted his food as usual and went to the pictures. But the show bored him; long before it was over he left, and not knowing what to do with himself he came back slowly home, put his bicycle under the house – Maisie always used to do that – and mounted the steps into his room. As usual nowadays, he closed the door, then threw himself on the bed. Saturday night had always been a gay time. 'Jokes, Mr. Haynes,' 'Mr. Haynes, news.' Maisie was always at her most brilliant on Saturday nights. Then Sunday morning, lots of time and no work to do, the long drawn out lunch – he would miss Mrs. Rouse's meals. Maisie would be nearing New York by now. He wondered if she were sleeping with the captain. There was a firm and decided knock at the door. Who the hell— He did not want to talk to anybody.

'Who is it?' he asked without encouragement.

'It is me, Mr. Haynes, Mrs. Rouse. I want to speak to you.'

The long avoided explanation. Well, he would tell her tonight exactly what he was going to tell her on Monday. It was all ready. He opened the door.

'Come in, Mrs. Rouse,' he said, but his manner softened in spite of himself.

'I can't come in, Mr. Haynes,' she said. Something was up. But something was always up in this wretched place, and he was jolly well tired of it. She had a shawl around her shoulders and didn't take it off. 'Mr. Haynes, I am in sore distress, and I don't know where to turn. You will help me?'

'I shall do all I can, Mrs. Rouse.'

His conscience pricked him that he had not paid her the money. Under the urgency of her voice and manner the last traces of his resentment vanished, and he felt a return of all his old regard and consideration for her.

'Mr. Haynes,' she continued, 'Mr. Benoit is in trouble.' (Always that Benoit.) 'He got a stroke a few days ago and the nurse has left him. He has been in a room two days by himself. I only hear this afternoon. I don't know what is happening to him. I want to know and I am going. But I don't want to go alone. Will you go with me?'

Haynes blew out his lamp immediately.

'Certainly, Mrs. Rouse. Where is it?'

'George Street.'

It was at the other end of the town.

'I tell you what I shall do. I shall walk on ahead up Victoria Street. You follow. I am sure to meet a taxi and then I'll come along and pick you up.'

'All right, Mr. Haynes. Thank you.'

As Haynes hurried up the road and hailed a taxi he thought of Maisie and what a glorious piece of news this would have been.

During the drive down Mrs. Rouse did not speak. She had her beads and told them with a tense concentration which seemed to be unaware of him sitting at her side. Benoit. So that good-for-nothing had been stricken and the woman had left him. Served him right. Poor devil. Maisie, perhaps in New York now, was missing it all.

The taxi drew up and Mrs. Rouse jumped out. 'Wait for me, Mr. Haynes,' she said. He waited, but only a few seconds, and when she returned it was not to call him but to come back into the taxi.

'He not there, Mr. Haynes. The ambulance come for him about six o'clock and they carry him to the Government Hospital. Chauffeur, drive to the hospital.'

'But they wouldn't let us in tonight.'

'I know. But I am just going to make sure.'

When they reached, Haynes told her that they might as well dismiss the taxi, and they did so. Together they made enquiries at the porter's lodge. Yes, Benoit had passed in that afternoon. No use going to ask anything about him now. Come in the morning, and if visitors were allowed they could get a ticket from the matron.

'I'll have to come in the morning, Mr. Haynes,' she said to him, all the life gone out of her voice.

'So it seems, Mrs. Rouse,' and they stood irresolute for a while. Then they walked up the street together.

'Now, what exactly has happened, Mrs. Rouse?'

'I don't know much, Mr. Haynes. They were in Pendleton up to a week or two ago. Then I lost track of them. But things were bad with her and they moved to a little room in George Street – she, the man and the child. I didn't know that till suddenly my friends tell me he got a second stroke. The nurse couldn't turn it this time. I didn't bother myself too much about it, Mr. Haynes. I have troubles enough of my own. And they are man and wife, lawfully married. But this afternoon I hear the woman leave him.'

'Just walked out and left him lying on the bed?'

'Walked out, give the neighbour the key to hold and say she coming back, and gone. Lucky for Benoit he was nice with the woman. So I heard this afternoon. He used to be there the whole day and the woman's husband out to work and sometimes the nurse out too. He is a man like that, Mr. Haynes. I's his nature, he can't help it. And, anyway, she mind him for a day or two. At least he had someone to hand him a cup of water when he was thirsty. But I don't know what happen. Perhaps he get worse or she get weary. Anyway, he is in the hospital.'

They were passing the Church of the Immaculate Conception. It was late, but the choir was practising and the door was open.

'Mr. Haynes!'

Mrs. Rouse stopped.

'You wouldn't mind excusing me. I want to go in.'

'I'll go home and wait, Mrs. Rouse.'

'I wouldn't be long, Mr. Haynes. You are displeased with me, Mr. Haynes, over Maisie. I know you have cause. I was waiting until you had cooled down a little before I talked to you about it.'

'Don't bother about that now, Mrs. Rouse. Let us do what we can for Benoit first.'

As he walked home he looked up at the myriads of stars, shining in the moonlight. Did people live there? And if they did, what sort of life did they live?

Chapter Thirty-Three

He found Miss Atwell in their drawing-room sewing, on her nose her glasses (a late acquisition).

'You back alone, Mr. Haynes! Where is Mrs. Rouse?'

'She went into the Immaculate Conception to pray.'

'Poor soul. Come in, Mr. Haynes.'

Haynes told her briefly of their ill-success. 'But you ever see anything like that, Mr. Haynes. Who would believe that she was goin' to go lookin' for that man after all he do her? Two nights she in bed next to me and she ain't sleep. Every time I open my eye, she up or she prayin'. She say she certain something happen to Benoit. So when she tell me she hear that he sufferin' and she want to go and see 'im, I tell 'er to go.'

Haynes said nothing.

'What you think, Mr. Haynes? You don't think I was right?'

'I should think so, Miss Atwell.'

'Well, well, well. Look at life, Mr. Haynes! When I first come here—'

'How long ago was that?'

'Three years, month after next. The man was in his pride and glory, 'e used to scorn me. When they ask me why I was so thin and I say is my nature, 'e used to laugh – 'e used to say: "Nature what! You don't eat." But I am still erect on my hind legs, Mr. Haynes, and look where he is.'

'I am sorry for him,' Haynes said. 'Benoit is a very pleasant fellow. But it is his own fault.'

'I am sorry for him too, Mr. Haynes. I wouldn't be a Christian if I was not. But 'e goin' to suffer. My father had a stroke and where 'e lie down 'e wasn't the man to move for three years and nine months. And we had to do everything for 'im.'

'But what is to become of him?'

'God knows. 'E in hospital. They will keep 'im there I suppose.'

'He made a terrible mistake when he left here to marry the nurse.'

'I's that marriage that kill Mrs. Rouse. If 'e did leave her and only live with the nurse, they would have been able to patch up that. But i's the marriage.'

'But didn't he come back here the other day for a time, Miss Atwell? Maisie told me so.'

'Mr. Haynes, Maisie tell so much lies, I don't know what to say. Mrs. Rouse tell me that 'e used to come around here and used to talk to 'er from the alley about how 'e sorry, how 'e treat 'er and so on. She tell me so herself. She say that she doin' her work in the kitchen and 'e come in the lane and talk. Well, she talk. But I hear Maisie say this thing, and I hear other people in the alley say that 'e was livin' with her again. But Mrs. Rouse swear no, and since that afternoon when she nearly kill Maisie I don't meddle. What's happened to Maisie, Mr. Haynes?'

'I really don't know, Miss A.,' said Haynes. He called her Miss A. to soften the rebuke.

She took off her glasses, put her work aside and remained silent. Then she spoke again. 'Eh, Mr. Haynes, look at life. Here today and don't know where tomorrow. I remember the day you come here. I was inside and I only hear your voice talkin' to Ella. And I say, "Well, I ain't see 'im. But 'is speech like a nice young man." I don't know how you stand all this, Mr. Haynes. If I was you I would 'ave gone long ago.'

Haynes made a non-committal gesture with his hands.

'Poor Mr. Benoit,' continued Miss Atwell. 'Yes, Mr. Haynes, as you say, I sorry for 'im. "Man that is born of woman has but a short time to live and is full of misery." The words of the Scripture, Mr. Haynes, is true words . . . And not only man, but woman. Look at the misery and torment that man put poor Mrs. Rouse in. And where she should be sitting down, restin' in her house, 'e have her trapezin' all over the road lookin' for 'im. She comin' now.' Miss Atwell leant forward to listen.

Footsteps were approaching.

'Yes, i's she,' said Miss Atwell, and Mrs. Rouse crossed the yard quickly and came into the room.

'Mr. Haynes, you here with Miss Atwell? I was hoping you wouldn't go.'

'I was waiting for you,' said Haynes.

'I stayed in church a long time and then when I leave I sit down on a bench on the promenade and then I come home.'

'So, my dear, 'e gone to hospital.'

Mrs. Rouse shook her head, took off her hat and shawl and sat down.

'But I not going to leave him there,' she said calmly. 'I am going for him tomorrow.'

It was a bombshell.

'You goin' for him tomorrow!' broke from the astounded Miss Atwell at last. 'What for?'

'To bring him home. I can't leave him there to suffer.'

Mrs. Rouse spoke as one whose mind was irrevocably fixed. Miss Atwell lifted her bird-like head and stared at Mrs. Rouse, turned to stare at Haynes and then stared at Mrs. Rouse again.

'But,' she began, and stopped.

'Mr. Haynes.' Mrs. Rouse addressed herself directly to him. 'I couldn't leave him there. I couldn't do it. All my mind is to bring him back here. So what you say? You don't think I better do what my mind give me to do?'

'If you want to bring him here, Mrs. Rouse, I don't see why you shouldn't.'

'I glad to hear you say so, Mr. Haynes.'

Miss Atwell had grasped each arm of her chair and was looking from one to the other of them as if they were a pair of lunatics.

'Miss Atwell,' said Mrs. Rouse, 'as if you not pleased.'

In her voice was an immense patience. 'Don't think it will make any difference to you here.'

Speech came to Miss Atwell at last.

'God forbid, Mrs. Rouse! It isn't that I am thinkin' of, Mr. Haynes, it isn't that. As there is a God above me it isn't that.

But you has me surprised, Mrs. Rouse. When you leave here you tell me you was only goin' to see 'im, and find out if 'e want anything and come back.'

'Yes, so I say. But I didn't see him. And I went in the Immaculate Conception and when I come out I sit down on the promenade and ask God what to do and He show me.'

'Mr. Benoit has nobody else?' Haynes asked.

'He and his family fall out from the time he take up with me. They find he was too good for me. I's only me he have.'

'You are going for him, Mrs. Rouse, but he is a very ill man, and perhaps you had better leave him for a few days.'

'That is what I was thinkin', too, Mr. Haynes,' interposed Miss Atwell. ''E goin' to want a lot of mindin'. Who goin' to mind him, Mrs. Rouse? You can barely struggle with the cakes. Look at the work you have to do. Leave 'im till 'e a little better.'

'If the hospital give him to me, I'll take him. I will manage, Miss Atwell . . . I will manage . . . God will help me.'

'You will need His help,' said Miss Atwell. 'You have enough on you already and now to take 'im. Eh, Mr. Haynes?'

'Mrs. Rouse will do her best,' said Haynes. It was no use arguing with her, so the only thing was to make it as easy as possible.

The three of them sat and looked at one another and were silent. All the turmoil and passion which had raged and stormed in No. 2 during the past year seemed to have come to a final conclusion, leaving them as if stranded on a high beach.

Mrs. Rouse sat in an upright chair, her fingers clasped in her lap, her shoulders bent and leaning forward, very tired, but no sign of mental conflict in her face, only a calm determination. Miss Atwell sat in a rocking chair, but upright and sharp as a terrier on watch. Haynes sat in another little wooden chair by the door. An old kerosene lamp flickered on a small table in the centre. The room contained nothing else. All the neat furniture Haynes had seen on the first day had long ago been sold or pawned.

Mrs. Rouse began to speak.

'Mr. Haynes,' she said. 'I know you wouldn't laugh at me. But plenty people going to laugh at me. They going to have a lot to say. But I can't think of them. Eighteen years we have been together, Mr. Haynes, he and me, and eighteen years isn't eighteen days. He do me enough. Only I know how much he do me. But I leave God to punish him for that. We hope to be forgiven so we must forgive.'

She sat unmoving, her eyes fixed vacantly on a patch of shadow at the foot of Haynes's chair. Now and then she raised her eyes to his, but seemed too tired to keep them there for long. But she spoke on and on with few pauses. Haynes did not interrupt nor did Miss Atwell, who maintained her upright position, her eyes fixed on Mrs. Rouse's face, only glancing at Haynes occasionally to see the effect of any observation which was more than usually astonishing. But Haynes had little time for her. He sat watching and listening to the weary woman who was trying to make them see the reasons which had led to her decision. Perhaps she was explaining them to herself as well.

'Mr. Haynes, he and me build the house. We sweat and we strain to build it, and while it standing there I can't see him want a shelter.'

And later.

'Mr. Haynes, you remember the man and how he used to be here. Where he is in the hospital now he is like a pauper. In the blue nightgown the paupers wear. I ain't see him, but I know. With all sorts of people round him. I can't leave him there, Mr. Haynes. Not while these walls standing.'

The lamp which had been burning lower and lower gave a sudden flicker and went out. She started up, her hands crossed on her heart. 'Oh God! I hope nothing happen to him.'

'No, no, Alice,' said Miss Atwell, jumping up and holding Mrs. Rouse by the arm, 'the lamp has no pitch oil. It was goin' down all the time.'

'You don't think—'

'No, no, no. Look at it. It's dry. You forgot to put oil in it tonight. I went out to the stove to get some, but that dry, too. Calm yourself, darling. Nothin' goin' to happen to him. My father lie down on his bed for three years and nine months before anything happen to him. She doin' the best thing, eh, Mr. Haynes? I's the two of them build the house. And for she to be here and know he sufferin' there, it must wring her.'

Mrs. Rouse sat down again.

'Ah, Miss A., you understand. Mr. Haynes, in the night I can't sleep. Every time I doze off I see the man lying on the bed in torment, stretching out his arms to me and calling for help. "Alice, Alice, don't leave me to perish. Come to my rescue. Come to my assistance." Mr. Haynes, when he call I must reply.'

Haynes had no answer to give, nor did she seem to want any. In the darkness he could hardly see her face, could only hear with the distinctness which darkness gives the tones of her voice charged with fatigue, and with settled determination.

'God put this fiery love in my heart for Mr. Benoit, Mr. Haynes. I try to root it out, but it wouldn't come out. God plant it there for His own wise purpose. I going to show Mr. Benoit that though he press me down to the ground I am the one who will lift him up from it.'

Another long silence.

'But, Mr. Haynes, you not saying anything? You don't think what I am doing is right.'

Haynes pushed away the interminable vision of the worry and expense of the overburdened Mrs. Rouse attending to the stricken Benoit and said wholeheartedly:

'You are doing the best possible thing, Mrs. Rouse. Don't you think so, Miss Atwell?'

'God is love,' said Miss Atwell. 'We'll go for 'im in the mornin'.'

Eleven o'clock struck. Haynes rose to leave and they came to the door with him. He stood on the last step, the two women on the threshhold above.

'Well, then, until tomorrow morning,' he said.

'Until tomorrow,' said Mrs. Rouse brightly.

She was glad that those who lived at No. 2 had sided with her so heartily.

'Ah, Mr. Haynes,' she continued, 'if only Philomen was here now! I miss her before, but i's now I am going to miss her.'

Haynes was going, but he stopped.

'Mrs. Rouse,' he said, 'I hope you wouldn't mind my asking something.' He saw an opportunity to solve one of the few events in No. 2 which he and Maisie had often discussed without being able to come to any sort of conclusion.

'No, Mr. Haynes, what is it?' But she sounded apprehensive.

'It's not about Maisie. I don't wish to talk about Maisie any more. It's about Philomen. Why was it that she had to leave here? I have always thought that there was something strange about it. I never cared to enquire, but hearing you say that you need Philomen I thought I would ask.'

'We have no secrets from you, Mr. Haynes,' she replied, but she hesitated.

Miss Atwell came to the rescue.

'Come, Ma Rouse, tell Mr. Haynes. He is an intelligent man. He knows all about these things.'

Thus encouraged, Mrs. Rouse explained.

'You see, Mr. Haynes, I have someone who guides me in my life. He is a man who can do things and I can tell you he has helped me a lot. And when I went to him once he told me that my blood and coolie blood don't take. He say that's why Mr. Benoit treat me as he did. He say I have nothing to expect from coolie blood but treachery. I ask him how me and Mr. Benoit keep together so long. He say is because Mr. Benoit was only halfcoolie. And he warn me against having any coolies around me. He say so long as I have, things bound to go bad. I tell him all that Philomen was to me and all she do for me, and if I send her away that would be ingratitude. He stop a little bit and he say, "Well, God wouldn't like you to show ingratitude." (He works by God you know, Mr. Haynes. Some work by the Devil, but some by God, and he work by God.) He tell me that not to tell her to go, but to treat her

255

in a way that she would have to leave. So that is why you see Philomen not with me today . . . You see how it is, Mr. Haynes?' she added anxiously.

'Quite,' said Haynes. 'You see, I didn't know all this.'

Said Miss Atwell, filling an awkward pause: 'God lets us know His will through His chosen, you know, Mr. Haynes. And where they shows us the way, we has to follow.'

'Quite so, Miss Atwell,' said Haynes.

What was the use of arguing? Philomen was gone. Nothing he said could bring her back. Better to leave it there. But acting on a sudden impulse he changed his mind.

'But, Mrs. Rouse, tell me, do you really believe that Philomen would harm you?'

'Mr. Haynes,' she replied at once, 'I don't know what to say. At the time I believe him, until poor Philomen leave. But sometimes I feel sorry and wish I hadn't sent her away. But then again, the man told me so many things that come out true. I am confused. You don't believe in people like those, Mr. Haynes?'

'Not at all. In fact, Mrs. Rouse, to tell you the truth, I believe they are a set of imposters. You had to pay him a lot of money, I suppose.'

'Five dollars every visit.'

'You shouldn't throw that money away, Mrs. Rouse, you want it. You believe in God, you pray to God, well, trust in God. But these fellows are after your money and nothing else.'

'I believes you are right, Mr. Haynes,' said Miss Atwell. 'Mrs. Rouse, if I was you, I'd send to call her first thing tomorrow. Five dollars! But you know is only now I think of it, Mr. Haynes. I has to work two whole weeks for five dollars. And that man give you a lot of bad advice and make that money so easy!'

'Speak to Philomen in the morning, Mrs. Rouse,' said Haynes, 'and keep your five dollars. You will want it to help Mr. Benoit get better. Good night.'

'Good night, Mr. Haynes,' they said almost together.

'God will bless you, Mr. Haynes,' said Mrs. Rouse.

'That He will,' said Miss Atwell.

As Haynes searched in his pockets for matches he realized that he would have to postpone indefinitely his plans for leaving No. 2. 'I am going to die in this damned house,' he said resignedly and threw himself into bed.

It was a long time before he dropped off to sleep. So the prophecies had been fulfilled and Mrs. Rouse was taking Benoit back. Maisie! Poor Maisie! How she would have raged and sneered. The things she would have said. Never since she had gone had he missed her so much. What a day the following Sunday would have been. But she was gone and gone for good.

Next morning he rose early (he had not slept well) and went and stood in the yard near the corner of Victoria Street and the alley. A woman who lived in the alley said good morning and passed him. Then she turned back.

'I suppose you know about Mr. Benoit, Mr. Haynes?'

'Yes,' said Haynes, 'he is in the hospital.'

'No,' she said, 'I don't mean that. He died this morning about half-past three. I met a wardsman from the hospital and he tell me. That one in there,' she pointed to No. 2, 'wouldn't be sorry for him, eh? He do that poor woman enough.'

Chapter Thirty-Four

As Benoit's spirit had dominated the life at No. 2 even when he was not actually present, so with his death, the life at No. 2 came to an end.

Mrs. Rouse got the corpse from the hospital and it was buried from home. And then a day or two after the funeral she told Haynes she had decided to sell out. She had neither the courage nor the strength to continue, she said. Mr. Rojas was arranging her business. She would take a smaller place. Gomes would continue taking cakes from her. 'I will manage, Mr. Haynes,' she concluded.

There was little for him to say.

'And what you going to do, Mr. Haynes? I tried to get a place with a room for you, but I couldn't get at the price.'

'I shall look for rooms, Mrs. Rouse.'

'You must send for Ella, Mr. Haynes.'

'Yes, I know.'

'She will come?'

'Wherever she is working she will come if I go for her,' said Haynes.

Ella came at the first call, got rooms for him and he moved into them on the first of October, leaving Mrs. Rouse and Miss Atwell still at No. 2. The two of them would continue to live together and there were legal formalities still to be gone through before No. 2 could be sold.

After they moved Haynes went to see them fairly regularly, but after a time became rather remiss.

Maisie he got one letter from saying that she had safely jumped the boat and was with friends. She promised to write again and send an address, but nothing more ever came. After the desertion of Benoit, public opinion turned against the nurse. Her defence was that Benoit was living with the woman next door and she left him to her. But her clients dwindled, and with her child, Sonny, she went to America too. Haynes never saw her from the day she was sentenced in the court. Philomen he sees often. Gomes's house is near to his rooms and she pays him visits through the front door, to the unfailing annoyance of Ella, who cannot stand the sight of anyone who lived in or had had anything to do with what she continues to call 'that cursed house'. But Philomen does not take any offence, grows fatter than ever and is happy because she is high in the good graces of Sugdeo. She and Haynes are good friends, and she never fails to let him know when she has passed by No. 2. Whenever Haynes passed there in the tramcar he used to make it a point of duty to look. But of late forgets more often than not.

One night, however, he was walking along Victoria Street and almost instinctively came to a halt when he reached Minty Alley. The front door and windows were open, and from the street he could see into the drawing-room. Husband and wife and three children lived there and one of the children was sitting at the piano playing a familiar tune from Hemy's music-book. Over and over she played it, while he stood outside, looking in at the window and thinking of old times.